TANGLED INNOCENCE

A DANTE'S CIRCLE NOVEL

CARRIE ANN RYAN

Tangled Innocence
A Dante's Circle Novel
By: Carrie Ann Ryan
© 2014 Carrie Ann Ryan
ISBN: 978-1-947007-68-0

DEDICATION

To my two Charitys. One holds my sanity; the other holds the reason I get to do this every day. Thank you both.

ACKNOWLEDGMENTS

Thank you Lillie for saying "bear shifter body shots" and telling me to do it. No questions asked.

This bear shifter is for you.

Thank you readers for wanting Dante's story so much that he's the #1 requested character of all my series.

Love you guys!

TANGLED INNOCENCE

As one of the seven lightning-struck women, Nadie Morgan knew that her fate would be forever changed and revolve around a certain dragon.

From the first time Dante Bell saw Nadie, he knew that she was the one for him. There's just one problem: there's another in his life Dante's waiting on, as well.

When Jace Goodwin, a bear shifter and Mediator, finally comes back to the human realm after years away, his first stop is Dante's Circle, where he not only finds his dragon but also the woman they've *both* been waiting for.

Once secrets are told, and the sparks fly, Nadie's new life becomes something she never thought possible. However, there's another realm at play, and Jace and Nadie's dragon will have to fight against the realms themselves to keep the two mates he's wanted and waited eons for.

DANTE'S CIRCLE CHARACTERS

With an ever growing list of characters in each book, I know that it might seem like there are too many to remember. Well don't worry; here is a list for you so you don't forget. Not all are seen in this exact book, but here are the ones you've met so far. As the series progresses, the list will as well. A special thanks goes to my FAN CLUB (https://www.facebook.com/groups/CarrieAnnRyanFan-Club/) for helping with this list.

Happy reading!

Agda—Brownie council leader.

Agnes—Sole female on the Angelic council.

Alec—Nocturne Pack council member. Friends to Hunter and Becca.

Amara Young—One of the seven lightning struck women. Works at an inn. Has a past that is very secretive.

Ambrose Griffin—Warrior angel, Shade's mentor. Father to Laura (deceased) and Nathan (deceased), husband to Ilianya (deceased). Mate to Balin and Jamie, story told in *Her Warriors' Three Wishes*.

Azel—Black-winged angel. Striker's third in command.

Balin Drake—Non-soul devouring demon, son of Pyro. Mate to Jamie and Ambrose, story told in *Her Warriors' Three Wishes*.

Becca Quinn—One of the seven lightning struck women. Works as a bartender at Dante's Circle. Mate to Hunter Brooks, story told in *An Unlucky Moon*.

Bryce—Lily's ex-fiancee.

Caine—Angelic council leader.

Cora—Shade's ex-fiancé (deceased).

Dante Bell—Dragon shifter. Owner of Dante's Circle. Story told in *Tangled Innocence*.

Eli—Bakery Owner.

Eliana Sawyer—One of the seven lightning struck women. Works as a welder.

Faith Sanders—One of the seven lightning struck women. Works as a photographer.

Fawkes—Demon, son of Lucifer, friend of Balin. Mate of Leslie. Story told in *His Choice* (Found in the Anthology *Ever After*).

Fury—Leader of the demon council.

Glenn—Lily's sleazy ex-boss.

Hunter Brooks—Wolf and Beta of the Nocturne Pack. Met Ambrose, Jamie, and Balin in hell during the demon games. Mate to Becca, story told in *An Unlucky Moon*.

Ilianya—*(deceased)* Sister to Shade, wife to Ambrose.

Jace Goodwin—bear shifter and Mediator for all realms. Story told in *Tangled Innocence.*

Jamie Bennett—One of the seven lightning struck women. Bookstore owner and lover of romance. Mate to Ambrose and Balin, story told in *Her Warriors' Three Wishes.*

Kobal—Old djinn council member, ally to Pyro.

Laura—*(deceased)* Daughter of Ambrose .

Law—Gray-winged angel, Striker's second in command.

Leslie—Pack member of the Nocturne Pack. Mate of Fawkes. Story told in *His Choice* (Found in the Anthology *Ever After).*

Liam—Nocturne Pack council member. Friends to Hunter and Becca.

Lily Banner—One of the seven lightning struck women. Worked as a lab chemist in solid-state NMR. OCD and quirky. Mate to Shade, story told in *Dust of My Wings.*

Lucifer—Infamous demon from hell and Fawkes' father.

Nadie Morgan—One of the seven lightning struck woman. Works as a school teacher. Story told in *Tangled Innocence.*

Nathan—*(deceased)* Son of Amborse.

Pyro—Demon from hell, father to Balin.

Shade Griffin—Warrior angel, ex-fiance to Cora, brother to Illianya, mate to Lily Banner, story told in *Dust of My Wings.*

Striker—Angelic council member, leader of the rebels.

Temperance—New Djinn council leader.

Thad—Co-worker of Lily's. Had a crush on her.

Timmy—10 year old brownie.

CHAPTER 1

"I'm done with men."

Nadie Morgan barely resisted the urge to roll her eyes at her friend Faith's proclamation. She was pretty sure the woman had said something similar before in the exact same exasperated tone. Faith usually said things like that, considering she was trying to find a man to match who she was and who she wanted to be.

Not an easy thing when Nadie wasn't sure Faith knew who she wanted to be in the first place. Well, Nadie probably shouldn't be casting stones, considering she stood in an eerily parallel place.

Faith ran a hand through her blunt black bangs, leaving them in their perpetual disorder, then curled her lip up in a snarl.

"Don't you roll your eyes at me, Nadie Morgan. If you'd ever get off your virgin ass and actually tell him you want him, maybe you wouldn't be in the same predicament as me."

Nadie froze, the sounds of the bar slowly faded away so she couldn't hear her friends' reactions—if there *were* reactions. An odd numbness settled in, tunneling her vision so all she saw was Faith and her wide eyes set in a pale face.

Out of the corner of her eye, she saw the rest of their friends stiffen as well, then turn toward Faith, their mouths opening, most likely to defend Nadie where they thought she would never be able to defend herself.

In most cases, they'd have been right.

"Well, that was blunt," Nadie finally said, her throat dry. What else was she supposed to say? She was surprised she could speak at all. It wasn't as if Faith was saying anything untrue or far from Nadie's mind. It just hurt to hear it in the first place.

She'd rather have buried it forever and not looked back, but she knew that would have been weak.

Weaker than she'd been acting already.

"Oh crap, I'm so sorry, honey." Tears filled the normally strong-willed woman's eyes, and Nadie immediately forgave her. There hadn't been any true damage, and all Faith had done was tell the truth.

"It's okay." She raised her hands at her friends, and they quieted whatever words they were about to say. "No, really. You just got dumped. It sucks, so you lashed out, and I'm a pretty good target at the moment."

Faith shook her head then got up and walked around the circular table where they always sat when they came to

Dante's Circle. Normally, it was a place that had become a sort of home to them, and right then, it was nice to have that familiarity. Faith wrapped her arms around Nadie and Nadie hugged her back. Hard. "No, it's not freaking okay. I'm hurt and in a pissy mood, but that doesn't give me the right to act like a cruel bitch."

"Just a normal bitch then," Becca, deadpanned, then flipped her fiery red curls over her shoulders.

"Hey, don't call Faith a bitch," Lily added in then came up to wrap her arms around Nadie's other side. "Well, she might be one, but we're trying to change that. And Nadie honey, I love you. Don't listen to what Faith said."

Soon, Amara, Eliana, Jamie, and eventually, Becca moved to join the group hug. Nadie could feel Faith's tears seep into her shirt and knew that her friends weren't there to comfort Nadie, but Faith. The woman wouldn't accept the comfort otherwise, and everyone knew it.

Sometimes she and her friends just had to be sneaky about things like hugs and showing Faith they loved her just as much as they loved the rest of the girls.

"Okay, break it up. I can't breathe under all of you," Faith snapped.

Nadie just shook her head as Faith wiped her tears, straightened her shoulders, and then sat back in her seat on the other side of the circle.

"So, we hate Chadwick," Amara said as she pulled her auburn hair into a ponytail. She smiled prettily at Faith who rolled her eyes.

"His name was Chad, not Chadwick," Faith answered.

"Stop making him sound like some dweeb who loves his mom and the country club."

Nadie tilted her head then took a sip of her lemon drop. "Um, but he *did* love his mom and his country club. Wasn't that the whole point? That he wanted to be with mommy and her money rather than stand up for something more? I thought you said something about the snooty mommy and her leech of a son."

Faith narrowed her eyes. "You're not supposed to throw my words back in my face."

"On the contrary," Amara put in. "We're you're friends. If he's a right bastard with mommy issues, that's our job. You're the one who told us that dear Chadwick was a limp neck—and probably had limp other things too—mommy's boy. Or should we call him *mother's* boy. He seemed like the guy who would raise his eyebrows all haughtily and call for his *mother*." Amara tried and failed to use a British accent—which Chad, not Chadwick, did not possess, and the girls fell over in giggles.

"Oh sweet baby Jesus, stop making me laugh like that. I think I'll start leaking," Lily said as she pressed her hands to her breasts. The new mom had control issues sometimes. Lily. A mom. So weird yet perfect at the same time.

"Oh God, you leak when you laugh?" Becca asked, her eyes wide before she turned to Jamie. "That'll be us in a few months."

Nadie just smiled and took another drink of her lemon drop as her now-mated friends talked about babies, leaking, and growly mates. She didn't want to feel jealous, but the little green monster wrapped its spindly arms around her, and she winced. It wasn't Becca's, Jamie's, or Lily's fault that they had met their true halves and something like a perfect life had actually stuck.

So much had changed in the short time since the world had grown around them that sometimes Nadie couldn't run fast enough to catch up.

She frowned and thought about the date then sat straight up. "Well, hell." The other girls stopped what they were doing and looked at her.

"Did you just curse?" Jamie asked, her hand on her baby bump. "You never curse."

Nadie snorted. "I curse, you just never listen. That isn't the point though. Think about what day it is and where we are."

Amara's eyes widened. "Well, hell," she repeated. "It's been two years, hasn't it?"

Nadie nodded then sat back as she watched the reactions wash over her friends' faces. It had been two years since the seven of them walked into Dante's Circle like they normally did, but they'd left with something much more.

Something most of them *still* didn't have a handle on.

Lightning had hit the building, or at least *inside* the building, on that day. Nadie, her six friends, and the owner of the bar...Dante, were struck by that same bolt of lightning. She could still remember the screams, the feel of her body rising from her chair then slamming down to the ground, and the heated sensation of something...else...

5

flowing through her in an arc. It still haunted her nightmares sometimes.

After all of that, none of them had been the worse for wear, just a few cuts and bruises and, of course, Amara's broken arm, but that was it. Amara had healed quickly, as had the rest of them. Too quickly, in Nadie's opinion.

They had been forever changed though.

Lily had been the first to notice—though they all had in a way considering it was weird that eight of them had been struck by lightning and hadn't been killed or injured beyond falling to the ground.

They'd discovered that their human world wasn't quite human.

Every human who called themselves human, Nadie included, were diluted versions of supernaturals, and most weren't in the know about the fact that hundreds of realms existed near and entwined with their own realm.

"I can't believe it's been two years since I met Shade," Lily whispered then gave a little smile.

Shade was a warrior angel and Lily's true half. Apparently supernaturals had another part of their souls out in the world, and they were lucky when they found it. Or at least they were lucky when they found it, and the other half actually *wanted* it, but that was another story altogether.

"And I met Ambrose around that time, though it took another year to meet Balin," Jamie put in.

Jamie had not just one mate, but two. Nadie held back a blush at that thought. What on earth would she do with two men? She hadn't even been with one let alone two. Oh no way, too much for her. That didn't mean she couldn't have her own fantasies though.

"That means it's almost been a year since I met Hunter," Becca said as she frowned. "It seems like so much longer, you know? I mean, Jamie and I are pregnant, and Lily just had Kelly. We're bonded with our mates and have seen so...much."

Nadie nodded, knowing what she meant—at least when it came to what they'd seen. That was the other part of being struck by that particular bolt of lightning.

Each of them had a new energy within themselves. It was as if the lightning had altered their DNA, which the scientist Lily said was possible, considering the paranormal worlds were so much different than the human one. Now, apparently, once one of them met their true half—or the other two-thirds in Jamie's case—they started to grow weak, as if their body was rejecting itself. Then once they made love with their true half, they turned into a paranormal creature.

It was as if she were now in some sci-fi movie that she couldn't quite wake up from. Lily had turned into a brownie; Jamie, a djinn; Becca, a leprechaun. Each of them had met with others of their realm and, in some cases, fell right in step with that part of their lives while others had fought for their right to live—at peace and in general. Not everyone in the realms was happy about the turn of events.

Frankly, Nadie wasn't sure she was either.

The others were talking about how much had changed and how the rest of them still needed to find their true halves. Nadie, though, knew she was in a different place than the rest of them. While the others had hope for a future or were on the bliss side of happiness, Nadie knew she had nothing like that. No, she had nothing. She had a feeling she'd known her true half longer than the rest of them, longer than they'd even known what true halves were, yet he'd done nothing about it.

She closed her eyes, a sudden rush of something more powerful than herself seeming to wrench whatever energy she had left from her bones. Pain arced across her body, bile filling her throat as something clawed at her, her body growing weak. Her hand shook as she set down her lemon drop, but she didn't think anyone noticed. Life was moving on for the rest of them, yet Nadie didn't think she'd move on with her friends.

She swallowed hard, the truth slapping her in the face.

Again.

Her dragon didn't want her.

Well, not *her* dragon, as he never would be hers. He'd seen to that. The tattooed, sexy bar owner, Dante, had known her for years and yet hadn't taken one step toward her beyond being her friend. And he'd started to move away from even that since the lightning. They weren't the friends they'd once been and the loss was almost too much to bear. She'd had a crush on him ever since she could remember and *she'd* never done anything about it, either.

He was a freaking dragon, meaning that even when she'd been human and ignorant of all that went beneath the surface of the human realm, he would have been able to feel her as his true half, would have been able to feel that pull, that deep desire not only to have the other person in his life for eternity, but to have them in all ways possible.

Yet he'd done nothing about it.

Well, that was just fine then. She didn't need him anyway.

Another wave of pain drenched in power washed over her, and she closed her eyes, willing it away. Damn that dragon. No, damn her as well. If she'd had the courage to actually speak her mind, maybe she'd have been able to see what he wanted from her or, rather, what he didn't want from her.

Now she was alone and too scared to do anything about it.

Honestly, she had only herself to blame for it.

She wasn't weak, but she sure as heck was acting like it. Her fingers slid over the smooth wood on the table as she tried to regain some semblance of control. She didn't want this to be the last time she came with her six girlfriends into the bar that had become their getaway, but it was looking more and more like that was what would have to happen.

She couldn't come into the place that called to them and not think about the dragon who filled her dreams. Not that she'd ever seen him in his dragon form, but his human form was exactly what she wanted.

"Hello, ladies," Dante said as he walked up to them. His piercing blue—not that blue was a good enough word for the pools of color she saw—eyes met hers for a moment before moving on to the rest of the girls at the table.

9

His attention elsewhere, she could do what she loved best—study her dragon. While she was the plain Jane with straight blonde hair and a way-too-innocent face, according to Faith, Dante was the exact opposite.

He'd tied his long black hair in a ponytail so the blue streaks stood out even more. She wasn't sure if he dyed it that way or if black and blue just came naturally. Since he was a dragon, it could just be who he was. He'd chopped off a lot of it recently, something she wasn't sure about, but she thought he was sexy no matter what. So it settled in the middle of his back. She knew that if he didn't keep on it, though, it would grow so long that it touched the floor again.

God, she envied his hair.

He was built, but not too bulky, and wicked tall. At five foot three herself, everyone seemed a bit tall to her, but Dante was a couple inches over six and a half feet. She felt like a tiny fairy next to him, but she liked it.

If she ever wanted to kiss him, though, she might need to stand on a chair to accomplish it.

She blinked away those thoughts, knowing it was a lost cause.

There would be no kissing when it came to the dragon. He couldn't even stand to look at her for too long.

Her eyes went to the tribal dragon-like tattoos running down his arms and the small black hoops in his ears and brow. When he spoke, she could sometimes catch a glimpse of the tongue ring he wore, but he'd never flat out shown it to anyone. Becca thought that Dante might have a few more piercings...lower on his body, but Nadie and the rest of them had never been brave enough to ask.

"Nadie, are you okay?" The deep voice broke her out of her thoughts and sent decadent shivers down her spine.

Nadie look up at Dante and swallowed hard. "I'm fine," she croaked out.

He tilted his head, his penetrating gaze not leaving hers. She needed to stop looking at him because once she left the bar she wouldn't be coming back. Yes, she'd come to that conclusion. She couldn't force herself to live in the shadow of what she'd once been and think she wasn't good enough for him anymore. It would make it only that much harder to leave him if she didn't stop staring at him.

"If you're sure," he said, his voice telling her he didn't believe her.

Well, it was his fault anyway she was feeling like this. He'd ignored her for years, so apparently she wasn't good enough to be his true half. The thought that she wasn't good enough in his eyes burned, but she'd get over it. She had to. Leaving might kill her, but she'd walk out of the bar with her head held high.

She might be rejected, but she wouldn't be kicked while she was down.

"I'm sure. Thank you for asking." She held back a wince. No matter how hard she tried to act cool and unmoved, those stupid manners her parents had droned into her never quite went away.

Dante frowned at her, his eyebrow ring moving delicately as he did so. She didn't like to see him frown, even though she'd noticed him doing it more than usual since the lightning strike.

Not that she'd been watching him or anything.

Much.

Wow, she needed to stop this. Before she knew it, she'd be following him home, climbing through his bedroom window, and watching him sleep.

Stalker much?

She looked up at the man she'd been trying to forget and gave him a small smile. Damn her, she just couldn't stop doing that. His eyes brightened—or maybe that's just what she hoped had happened—and he smiled back.

"Okay then. Well, ladies, you all are closing down the house tonight as the rest of my customers have decided to call it in early. And since I'm closing at ten anyway. Do you want another round, or are you done for the evening?"

The others talked, mumbling their words to each other, but Nadie couldn't keep her eyes from Dante. Something was up with him, but she couldn't put her finger on it. The strain in the corner of his eyes and the firm set of his mouth that he thought he hid so well didn't escape her notice. Before the lightning strike, she might have gotten the courage to ask him as he'd always been a friend and had never made her feel insignificant. Now though? Now she was afraid, too afraid to do anything about it.

And *that* made her feel insignificant.

Something she'd have to change by leaving and never coming back.

She was better than this, better than the empty shell she

was becoming.

However, right then, with the slight tension she saw creeping over Dante's shoulders, it wasn't about her but about the dragon who seemed to literally be carrying the weight of the world on his shoulders. She didn't know how to help, or even if she could.

Another flash of weakness—the one that came with meeting her true half but not completing the bond—wrenched at her, and she gasped. Her friends turned toward her, but before she could lie and say she was okay, something odd happened.

It was as if someone siphoned the pain from her, inch by inch, and suddenly, she was fine. Well, not fine, but at least better than she'd been. It made no sense. It shouldn't have been happening like that. Oh, she'd thought it had happened once or twice before, but never to this degree. The pain slid away, and Nadie swallowed hard, able to breathe again.

Dante let out a grunt beside her, and she blinked up at him through clear eyes.

"Dante? You're pale. What's wrong?" she asked as she stood up, worried. She put her hand on his upper arm then froze at her action.

He looked down at her hand then wiped the sweat that hadn't been there before from his brow. "Just a little dizzy, my sprite. I'll be fine." He placed his hand over hers, squeezing, and gave a strained smile. "Thank you."

She swallowed hard at his touch and smiled back.

He slowly slid his hand away and she moved back as well.

He'd called her *my sprite*. Well, that was different. Darn it, she had no idea what was going on with this man, but it was something. Something he was hiding. She needed to gain the courage to ask him. It didn't matter that she was leaving for good. He was her friend, and it looked as though he needed one right then.

But if past experiences were anything, she knew *she* couldn't be the friend he needed.

Not anymore, not with the fact he'd ignored what she was to him for so long.

"If everyone is fine then, I'm off to go to Shade and Kelly," Lily said, and then she said her goodbyes. Faith got up and walked to Dante, whispering something in his ear, but Nadie wasn't sure what it was. Soon the rest of the women left, either not noticing the tension or ignoring it altogether. That was exactly what she needed right then, and she was grateful that her friends seemed to know it.

She followed her friends out the door, letting herself take one last look over her shoulder at the man she wanted but could never have and then went to her car. The others left the parking lot as she got in and tried to start her car.

Try being the operative word.

The car made this annoying chugging sound then ticked before refusing to turn over. She slammed her hand on the steering wheel then cursed when she hurt herself.

"You've got to be kidding me." Everyone had left her probably thinking she'd be right behind them, and honestly, she didn't want to call them back just to leave her car there. She searched for her cell phone and cursed. Damn it. Where had it gone? Nothing was working right. She fought back tears of frustration, annoyed with herself more than anything. They'd all gotten in their cars together, not knowing hers wouldn't start. It wasn't her friends' fault she was stranded, but she still felt alone.

She'd have to go back into the bar and call a tow truck or something. Maybe she'd left her phone at the table. This was not the night of eating chocolate while having a good cry she'd had in mind.

The knock on her half-open window startled her, and the scream that ripped from her throat at seeing the man outside would have made any horror movie heroine proud.

The blond man, his hair falling to his shoulders, held up his hands, his green eyes wide. "I'm sorry, honey. Didn't mean to scare the crap out of you. I was just going to see if you needed help with your car."

The man had to be taller and wider than even Dante, and that didn't make her feel any less freaked out. The barrier of the car door would be nothing to a man like that, and all she could think about, despite his soft words, was an image of him ripping the door off, throwing her over his shoulder, and taking her away.

Damn it. Why didn't she have a weapon of some kind in her car?

And why didn't she know how to use said weapon?

"I'm a friend of Dante's. I won't hurt you. I promise." Hands held out in a surrender position, he slowly backed up. "Why don't I get Dante and get you some help? Okay? I'm Jace by the way."

She blinked up at the man named Jace, unsure of what to do. He might have said he was a friend of Dante, but considering the bar's name was in his line of sight, that could have been a wild guess and a pretty damn good lie.

Nope, she wasn't getting out. She'd just call the bar from her car and have Dante—or the cops—come to her. She reached in her purse and cursed because she'd forgotten she didn't have her phone to begin with. As she had just started to really panic, she let out a breath when she saw Dante himself walking toward them.

"Nadie? Jace? What's going on?" He didn't sound alarmed, more like curious.

"Nadie?" Jace rasped. This time there was something like awe in his tone, and she had no idea what he meant.

Had Dante told him about her? No, that would be stupid. There was no reason for Dante to do so. She was nothing to the dragon.

Dante walked up to Jace, cupped his cheek, and then gave a nod. Nadie felt as if she'd been slapped—she hadn't known Dante had someone...let alone a man. No wonder Dante didn't want her. He already had his mate. Oh Jesus. Fate really was that cruel to her.

Yet something important clicked inside her at the same time at the intimate sight.

"What's going on?" she asked, her throat dry.

Dante moved, pushing Jace a step back then stood by her car door. "Come on into the bar, Nadie. We have a lot to talk about."

She shook her head. "Tell me here. What's going on?"

There was something off about this, something she didn't understand. It wasn't fear running through her right then—no, it was something much warmer, something filled with undeniable promise. She needed to put a stop to it before it went anywhere...especially since it seemed Dante and Jace were an item—or something much more.

And once again, Nadie had been left on the outside looking in.

"Nadie, please," Dante begged. "Come inside. For me?"

At that last word, she nodded. She'd never seen her dragon beg, and she didn't want to see it again. He wasn't the type to do so, and that meant something far greater than she could imagine was going on here.

"Fine, but you need to tell me what's going on when we get in there."

Dante nodded. "Yes, I'll tell you everything. Finally."

She got out of the car and swallowed hard. She looked at Jace and blinked. The feeling of being by his side was strangely just as intimate and heated as being by Dante's. That didn't make any sense, and yet she wasn't sure she wanted it to. For some reason she wanted to move closer to them both, hold them and never let them go. The warmth in her belly wasn't a mere attraction, no, it was something far greater.

Something tugged at her heart, her breath, her...everything.

She had a feeling she'd just taken a step toward a future she hadn't thought possible, but this time, she wasn't turning back.

CHAPTER 2

D ante Bell had to take a deep breath and get a grip, or he'd lose it. As it was, he could practically feel his talons scraping his fingertips, so he fisted his hands and fought for the control he'd had for thousands of years. It wouldn't be good to go dragon in the middle of his bar in front of the woman—and man—he was trying to soothe.

Not good at all.

He'd let Nadie walk out to the parking lot herself, despite the fact he'd told Faith he'd go out with her to make sure she was okay, because he'd known Jace was out there getting off his bike. The man had texted and let Dante know he was there, and Dante had wanted Jace to meet Nadie, or at least see her and keep her safe. Dante had told Jace who Nadie was, what she looked like. Even if it took a moment for the bear to understand, deep down, Jace would have felt that pull, would have known that

Nadie was important to them. He hadn't known her car would break down, and he'd end up in his bar alone with them.

Not that it was a bad thing.

Oh, not at all.

He stepped into his bar, Nadie and Jace right behind him, and inhaled. He loved his bar. He'd built it from the ground up and had changed it over the years to make it blend in with society. With his magic, the humans had never caught on that he never aged and was still the same black-and-blue-haired man he'd been for decades. He'd only added his adornments—the piercings and the like—in the past ten years or so when they came back in style, and he quite liked them.

He knew Nadie liked them too.

Not that he'd done anything about it.

Not that he *could* have done anything about it.

He'd watched Nadie from the first time she'd walked into the bar and had never stopped. Just seeing those wide eyes and plump lips had sent his dragon into overdrive. He'd known from the start who she was, what she could be, and would be with him and Jace, and subsequently had known that he could do nothing about it until the time was right.

Considering his age, he hated not being able to do as he wanted. Those actions had left both of them in pain, and now Dante was ready to face the brunt of her anger at what he was about to tell her. He would deserve it, as would Jace, but damn, he was so fucking happy they were both here.

This moment, this time, was theirs, and it had been an eon in coming.

Dante, Jace, and Nadie didn't speak when the three of them were finally in the bar, and now he found himself at a loss for words. No matter how many times he'd envisioned this in his head, he still hadn't quite found the way to get it all out there.

He'd fight the world for the two in front of him, and yet he couldn't stop fighting himself.

How could he say what he'd been feeling for years, decades in Jace's case, and not sound like an idiot? It wasn't as though he wouldn't deserve any anger directed his way, but getting started was another matter.

"Dante, why don't we sit down? You're looking a little pale under all those piercings." Jace laughed, but Dante and Nadie didn't join in. The tension in the room was too thick at the moment to even think about doing something as simple as laughing.

He cleared his throat, knowing they probably needed a drink to get through this. Yes, he could get the three of them drinks. That would help keep his hands busy and might help Nadie calm down so she wouldn't beat or kill him right away.

Not that he'd blame her if she tried.

"Um, I'm going to get us drinks." He sounded as scattered as he felt. He *never* sounded scattered. "Take a seat. Oh, and I only have one piercing on my face," he said absently, and Jace let out a small laugh, the tension in the room lowering just a little bit.

Thank the gods for his bear.

He risked a glance at Nadie. Hopefully Jace would soon be *their* bear.

"I don't know if I need a drink, Dante," Nadie said, her voice soft and just as sexy as it had ever been. "I've already had one with the girls."

"You might need another now, my sprite." Damn it. He'd called her the pet name he'd always had for her in his mind twice now without thinking, and both times her eyes had widened. He'd been so careful keeping his endearments to himself, but he couldn't anymore apparently.

Hopefully, he wouldn't have to for much longer.

Nadie tilted her head and frowned. "You're scaring me. Actually you both are, and I don't even know Jace or why he's here. Not scared in that I'm worried for my safety because, for some reason, I feel like neither of you would hurt me physically, but scared in another sense. Why won't you just tell me?"

He went back behind the bar, ignoring the thick envelope with his name written in calligraphy on the front. He had other things to worry about now rather than the summons that seemed to have come out of nowhere. That would still be there later, and he'd deal with it then. Right now, he had a bear and the woman that could be theirs in his bar.

He got the drinks with a deftness only years of bartending could bring, set down the beers and her lemon drop, wiped his hands so they wouldn't be too cold, and cupped her face. Her eyes widened again, and she froze.

"I will tell you everything. I will, my sprite."

He watched her throat work as she swallowed, felt the pulse at her neck flutter and the heat of her skin against his fingers as she flushed. Gods, he wanted this woman for his own. He kept his eyes on hers but thought of Jace. Yes, he wanted this woman for them both.

"Why do you keep calling me your sprite?"

His thumb traced her cheekbone, the soft skin smooth and inviting. His dragon practically rumbled at this closeness—the kind he'd been avoiding for as long as he'd known her because, once he touched her, he wouldn't want to let her go.

There was only so much control a dragon could possess.

"That's what you are," he whispered. "Mine." She narrowed her eyes before pulling away. He let her, knowing that, with his strength, he could have held her forever, but that was another matter altogether.

"No, no. I'm not. I'm not yours, and I haven't been anywhere near that label. Ever." She ran a hand through her hair then took a gulp of her lemon drop. Her face scrunched as she swallowed the sour and sweet, but he didn't go to her, just stayed away as he had all this time.

"Why don't we just sit down and talk this over?" Jace said as he stood between the two, worry lining his face.

"Why don't we just talk about what Dante wanted to talk about, huh? And why I should be in here with the two of you when I don't even know you, and when Dante hasn't even given me any indication he's ever wanted to be alone with me. No, he's always been part of the crew but with a clear line drawn."

She faced him then, the pain on her face lancing through him like a hot blade. "I don't even know what's going on right now."

"Then sit down and let me get it out," he said, wincing at his lack of tact. He'd had thousands of years to learn how to speak to women, and apparently he'd thrown it all out the window with the one woman and man who mattered.

"Good one," Jace mumbled then turned to Nadie, effectively cutting Dante off.

He needed to breathe, to understand what the hell was going on with him. Gods, he'd been walking on eggshells and killing himself over what was happening for far too long, yet he had no idea how to use a little finesse to say what needed to be said, needed to be done.

This wasn't like him, and he didn't want to become whoever this man was.

"I'm Jace Goodwin, Nadie."

Her eyes sharpened, and she snapped her fingers. "I know that name. You're the man who helped Hunter and Becca."

Dante let out a sigh. Yes, this would be a good place to start. Get her to know who Jace was then slide into the fact that she was the key to their future and happiness.

Yes, no pressure at all.

He ran a hand over his face then clicked his tongue ring against his teeth. He had to calm down. It wasn't every day he had a chance to reveal she was not only mate to one but two people.

Jace sat down at the table next to Nadie, and Dante pulled a chair so they sat in a triangle, able to see each other fully. "Yes, I'm the one who helped Hunter and Becca with their Pack. Though, in reality, they did most of the work themselves. I was just there in case they needed me."

"That's not exactly how Becca put it." Nadie shook her head. "She said you were a mediator or something?"

Jace grinned, and Dante relaxed. The bear's smile always soothed the beast within, and Dante knew, at least in their case, it had more to do with who the man was than his position as a Mediator of the realms.

"I'm a Mediator. Capital M if you care about those sorts of things. My role is to go to warring, or about-to-war, Packs, dens, and other realms, and try to find a way to peace. If that doesn't happen, then it's my job to take out those who break their oaths or find new treaties and other ways of keeping the realms safe."

Nadie tilted her head, her gaze never leaving Jace. Dante could tell she felt the pull toward the other man, the same pull he himself felt for Jace and Nadie, the type of pull he knew she felt for him.

"Becca said you're a...bear, right?"

Jace grinned even harder, and Dante had to grin, too. Jace was always in a good mood and tried to make others feel the same unless something or someone he loved was threatened, then Jace was the bear inside him in all ways that mattered.

You didn't fuck with Jace Goodwin.

"Yes, a grizzly as a matter of fact. Not as big as the dragon over there, but one of the larger paranormals."

Nadie's gaze shifted between the two of them, and she frowned. "It's good to meet you, but I'm still confused as to why Dante wanted me to meet you and talk with both of you."

Dante swallowed hard. "I think you know, Nadie. At least some of it."

She shook her head. "No, you need to say it because whatever is going on in my head makes no sense and is so far out of the realm of what has ever happened to me that I'm not even going to say it."

Dante had a feeling whatever she was thinking was perfectly on the right track, or at least he hoped so, but he let her keep those thoughts to herself.

For now.

"When the lightning hit," he began and hoped he was going in the best direction, "you and the others started your transformations."

Nadie nodded as her eyes slid to Jace.

"He knows about what happened, Nadie. There aren't many secrets between me and Jace."

Her eyes widened, and she let out an "oh."

Jace's gaze met his, and Dante let out a breath. "I'm getting ahead of myself here."

"And yet you're not getting anywhere," Nadie mumbled, and Dante choked off a laugh. He loved it when Nadie spoke her mind and actually used the attitude she was born with rather than the quiet one she tried to pull off.

It hadn't helped that he'd had to put distance between them after the lightning struck. It had taken all of his control not to claim her as his right then.

If he had, though, it would have been for naught.

If he had, he'd have left Jace behind, not completing the mating in truth and only hurting the three of them more.

Only Nadie hadn't known that.

"No, I guess I'm not. Well, shit, okay. So when the lightning hit, you were able to start to feel what it was like to be a paranormal."

She shook her head. "No, I haven't. I still have no idea what I would turn into if I...uh"—she blushed—"completed the mating with my true half."

He nodded, knowing this was where it got tricky. "You've been feeling a pull though. Right? And even a little weak." The last part was a partial lie. He knew she'd been feeling a hell of a lot more than *weak* when it came to their proximity to one another.

He'd stayed away from her for a reason, and yet no matter what he'd done, it hadn't been enough.

She narrowed her eyes, and the dragon within him rumbled, ready to take the brunt of what would come next.

"You're my true half, my mate, Nadie."

Her face didn't change. She didn't even bat an eyelash. He watched the rise and fall of her chest but didn't breathe with her.

"Nadie? Are you okay?" Jace asked.

She blinked at him then stood, forcing Jace and Dante to stand with her. The two of them towered over her small stature, yet she didn't look scared.

No, she looked fucking pissed.

"You've *got* to be kidding me. You just now tell me I'm your mate, and yet you've known for how long? No, don't bother. I've known since the lightning hit my body who you were. I knew then that we could have something more, something worth the pain, weakness, and unknown. I could have loved you more than anything and anyone in the world. Can't you understand that? It might have taken Lily and Shade's courtship for everyone to make complete sense of all this, but I knew that you were meant to be something to me. Or at least that's what I thought. You would have known from the start, Dante. You would have known since I walked in here with the others and had to wear that damn hand stamp because I wasn't even old enough to drink. Yet you've done nothing. Even when you must have figured out that I knew we'd be something together, you didn't step up."

He opened his mouth to speak, but her look forced him to stop.

"Shut it. I want my say. I had to stand by and watch three of my friends fall in love with mates who fought for them. Yeah, Ambrose took his sweet time, but that's because he didn't think he was good enough for her. Don't lie to me and tell me you're thinking the same thing because we both know that's not true. You're the one who stood on Jamie's side when Ambrose needed to grovel, so that couldn't be it.

"No, all of this means that, no matter what fate wanted,

you didn't want me. Fine. I get it. Whatever. I'll deal. I've been dealing since I walked in here and saw you."

Her body shuddered, but Dante couldn't speak. The pain radiating off her wasn't the physical kind he could heal—had been healing since the lightning strike. No, it was from deep within, and he didn't know what words to use to fix what was going on between them...if there were even any words to begin with.

"I'm not a dreamy-eyed girl, Dante. I might have been when I first met you, or at least a dreamy-eyed woman, but I'm not one now. You stayed away and left me in pain for *years*. What am I supposed to say to that?"

"I had to, Nadie."

She narrowed her eyes. "Excuse me?"

He looked at Jace, who had the same achingly painful expression on his face that Dante knew he had on his own face.

"It's my fault, Nadie," Jace said, his voice that low growl that Dante had missed for all those years they'd been forced apart. Before Nadie could speak, Jace held out his hands. "You see, you're not just supposed to be with Dante, but me too."

She backed away, shaking her head. "Oh no. No. What are the two of you talking about? I've been alone all my life and now the two of you are standing before me and telling me this? No."

"Think about Jamie, Ambrose, and Balin. Within the paranormals, triads are commonplace. It's how we're wired," Dante explained. "Sometimes we just want, no, *need*, two different people to feel whole."

"And we're not just a triad, or at least not just a possibility of one," Jace said, his gaze never leaving Nadie's face, and Dante was glad for it. "The three of us are mates. Three parts of a whole. I know you can feel that spark because I sure as hell did when I saw you in your car tonight. Now, we need to sit down and hash out the particulars as to why Dante had to keep things from you, and then we get on to the part that is actually important. Us."

Dante held back a grin at Jace's words. The man had a point. No matter what happened, the future they *could* have together was a hell of a lot more important than his own hurt feelings. Fuck, he'd been waiting for ten thousand years for them. He couldn't screw it up now.

At least not any more than he already had.

Nadie let out a sigh that ended on a sob. Tears formed in her eyes, and Dante let go of whatever was holding him back and pulled her into his arms. "I'm sorry, my sprite. I'm so, so sorry."

She clutched at him, wrapping her arms around his waist, and he tightened his hold. He felt Jace's hand on his back, and from the way the bear was standing, he had a feeling Jace's other hand was on Nadie's back.

Dante's dragon took the attention as though it was his due.

Fucking dragon.

He needed to get everything out in the open, and then

they could start from there. Keeping secrets and hiding behind hurts was only making this harder.

"I met Jace over eighty years ago, Nadie, and I knew from the moment I met him that he was one of my mates. But while we were blessed to find each other, we both knew that there was another one out there for us. While others could have dealt with that and continued on with just each other, both of our animals are far too predatory for that. They needed, no, *we* needed the three to complete the bond. It wouldn't have been the same otherwise."

He met Jace's eyes and cursed at himself. He wasn't saying this right.

Jace gave a small smile. "I know what you meant, Dante. It's not that we weren't good enough for each other and that we couldn't love each other and be enough, but we needed our third to make ourselves whole. It was agony not to be near and yet even worse when we were near, knowing we were missing something."

Nadie pulled away, her gaze shifting between them. "So you stayed away from each other all this time."

Dante swallowed hard then nodded. "Yes. We had to."

"And with my role as a Mediator, I had to leave for long periods of time anyway, and I couldn't contact him. We were both on the lookout for you though."

"I've been here for a while now though," she said, hurt still in her tone. "If you've known all this time, why didn't you say anything?"

"That's why I said it was my fault," Jace answered. "I was off on a job, my duty, and was trapped there. I couldn't get back, and by the time I did, I needed to make sure I could cut ties if I needed to. I still don't know if that is possible, but I couldn't wait anymore. Dante thought he had to hold back and wait for me because he couldn't find me. I'm so sorry."

Nadie sucked in a breath then shook her head again. "You could have said something, Dante. You've had all this time. You could have told me *why* you were waiting. I…I was left in the dark, and I feel like a fool. I don't like feeling like a fool."

Dante cupped her face and licked his lips. "You aren't a fool. I am. I had to keep us apart because if I had broken my promise and told you everything, I wouldn't have been able to hold back. With the way you were weakening, I didn't think I'd be enough for you alone while we waited for Jace. It could have killed you."

He didn't tell her that while he used his powers to push energy back into her body, it wouldn't have been enough. He'd only been able to keep her as healthy as he could because he was a dragon. If he had been any weaker, any younger, he might not have been able to do it at all. He didn't know why Nadie's paranormal reacted the way it did considering he didn't even know *what* she was, but he had a feeling it was one strong creature. He'd taken her pain into his body, not letting her know because he had been too afraid of what she'd do if she knew. Without their third, and the full bond, he'd never have enough energy to keep her alive…and she'd have eventually faded away, pulling him with her if he'd let her.

And he'd have let her.

She pulled away again. "No. You should have told me. It was my choice to make. Not yours. You treated me like a child, and yes, I understand you're a few hundred years older than me, but that doesn't give you the right."

"A few more years than that," Jace mumbled, and Nadie shot him a glare.

"I need time to think," she continued. "I had planned on walking out of here for the last time. Did you know that? I was going to throw in the towel because whatever fate wanted with us hurt too much to deal with it here. I was going to find a way to live my life without you, and yet you changed it all. Again."

The thought that she'd walk out of his life made the dragon want to rage, but he didn't let it show. He would have found her. A dragon always found its treasure.

"Being a dragon doesn't excuse you, Dante. And you, Jace? I don't even know you." She ran a hand through her hair. "I'm human. Or at least mostly. Don't you see this is weird? That everything we've talked about today makes no sense, or at least wouldn't have in truth a couple of years ago. I need time to think, and I can't do it if I'm in the same room with either of you."

He nodded, knowing this was far better than her saying she would leave forever.

"I'll drive you home," Jace said, shooting Dante a look. It seemed Dante had said enough that night and now it was Jace's turn to pave the way. He would never be jealous of the man. After all he felt the same way about Jace as he did about Nadie.

"I don't know you," Nadie whispered, but it wasn't fear in her tone; it was sparked interest.

Good.

"Then get to know me. We're starting from scratch, you and I. We both might have history with Dante, and that will come into play, but you need to know all the facts and we need to start with open eyes. What do you say?"

Nadie looked at both of them before nodding. "I...I'll take the ride home, but I need to think. I wasn't expecting this tonight," she said on a dry laugh.

Dante went to her then and cupped her face one last time. "Neither was I." He let his lips brush against hers, a promise of a kiss rather than one. His dragon perked up, ready for her, for their life, but he held back, knowing it was important to go slow—even slower than they already had been going. "We'll figure it out."

They would, he promised himself. Because he needed his mates by his side if what he thought was happening around them was evidence of what was to come.

He watched them walk out of his bar, Nadie so much smaller than Jace but almost at ease with his size. As soon as they left, he sucked in a breath, a primal fear washing over him. He was a dragon, he shouldn't be scared...yet he was.

He went back to the envelope on the bar and sighed. Could he ignore it for a few more moments? Would they notice?

The building shook around him, its walls quaking as if

the whole place were the epicenter of an earthquake. Dante gripped the sides of the bar, knowing this was only a warning and would pass soon. This was not of his power, but that of something that haunted the dreams of those around him. The room gave a few more shakes before settling down as if nothing had happened. Oh yes, they were pissed.

Dante's time had run out.

Something was happening—something far greater than he, Jace, and Nadie, and Dante was afraid he and the lightning-struck were in the center of it.

CHAPTER 3

T here had to be a precedent for this situation, but if it existed, Jace Goodwin had no idea what it was. He'd purposely left Dante back in the bar while Jace and the woman both men wanted stood outside, knowing Nadie not only needed her space but time with him as well.

Well, he might have been adding on that last bit, but *he* needed to spend time with *her*, so that had to count for something.

Now he stood right outside the front door to Dante's Circle looking down at Nadie, who seemed to be at a loss for words. That made two of them. He stuck his hands in his pockets and rocked to his heels.

His bear growled and slid across his skin, wanting Jace to make a move—or at least reach out and cup Nadie's face. Each time Dante had touched her so carefully, so sweetly, Jace had forced himself to step back and let the dragon take control. It wasn't that he was jealous—okay, maybe a little bit—but he didn't hate Dante for it. It just sucked that he hadn't known her for as long as Dante had. In retrospect, though, that might not have been such a bad thing considering the anger burning off her at the moment, aimed at a specific black-and-blue-haired man.

"Thank you for taking me home," Nadie whispered, her voice slightly hollow. The woman had been through so much that night her entire world had been rocked to its core. And from what he'd heard from Dante, this hadn't been the first time everything shifted for her. He didn't blame her for sounding as if she had no idea where she was going or where she wanted to be.

Jace shrugged, unsure if he should take her hand or just walk beside her. Damn. He was over a hundred years old and a grizzly bear for fuck's sake, and he was acting like a high school boy near a girl he had a crush on.

He had to get back that semblance of control he was so famous for.

"I haven't gotten you there yet," he said, his voice gruff. "I should have mentioned that I don't actually have my truck with me."

She backed up a step so she could see him. Considering he was over a foot taller than she was, it only made sense.

"Then how are you taking me home? My car is out of commission, which reminds me that I need to take care of that. Crap." She ran a hand over her face. "I think I need a nap. Or to go to bed. Or a lot of tequila."

He snorted then took a chance and rubbed her temples

with his thumbs. She stiffened then let out a little moan that shot straight to his cock. She tilted her head to the side, her cheek resting against his wrist. She was so tiny compared to him, and his bear loved it.

"I can look at your car in the morning. I'm not a professional mechanic, but I can tinker with the best of them. If I can't fix it, I know my brother, Red, can. He's an actual mechanic with way more experience. So don't worry about that part of it. I'm sure it's something small like the battery since it got you here. And, no, I don't have my truck, but I did come on my bike. It's not that cold out, and you have long pants on at least." He pulled away slightly to look down at her soft gray pants and pink top. "I don't know how far it is to your house, but you should be fine on the back of my bike."

He lowered his hands so she could speak since he figured it had to be awkward talking between his two large paws. She was such a tiny thing compared to him and Dante, but that just made his bear want to protect and shelter her all the more.

Yes, fate had gotten it right.

He wanted Nadie Morgan.

"I've never ridden on a motorcycle before," she whispered then smiled. "Unless, by bike, you mean a pedaled one, then I don't know if I could sit on the handlebars for as long as it would take for us to get home."

He threw his head back and laughed, the tension between them easing just enough that he knew they'd be okay as long as he got her to her place. Once they were past the introductions and, then, after she had her arms wrapped around him as they rode his bike, it would be better. After that, well, then it would be time for him to find a way to make what they could be work. It wasn't going to be easy, not at all. He'd just met her, but from Dante, he knew more about her than she of him. Way more. He felt as though he'd known her for years just by being by her side and knew that came with their connection through fate. That might make it easier for him, but it wouldn't be the same for her. If she gave in to what could happen, rather than what had happened, then maybe they could find that future a little faster.

It was all up in the air, and a planner like Jace didn't like that.

It was still jarring to him that she was here in front of him when he'd been waiting a lifetime to find her—when Dante and he had been waiting a lifetime apart. Gods, he'd missed Dante. He loved him, though he'd never said as such. Not yet. They'd both had an unspoken rule that they were waiting for their third, whether it was a man or a woman. They were both bisexual and had experience with men as well as women, but being with each other was different. They'd held back from touching beyond a soft graze and had only kissed a few times when they'd found each other.

He was not only starting anew with the woman in front of him, but also with the dragon in his heart.

He couldn't wait.

"No, not a pedal bike." He gestured and looked down at his six-eleven frame. It seemed to radiate the idea of the bear within to most folks. "I think I'd break a damn bicycle just sitting on it."

Nadie's gaze raked over him, and he grinned, liking the heat in her eyes. She might have been confused as to why he was there at that moment and what she should do, but she wanted him. She felt that pull—the same as he did. And from what Dante had told him about her, Jace liked who she was as well—not just how she looked.

Because, damn, he liked the way she looked, all innocent heat. And she could just fit right there in his pocket.

"You *are* kind of big. Even bigger than Dante. I think I'm going to get a crick in my neck if I keep staring up at you two for long."

He shrugged then got to his knees. She was taller than him now, but not by much. "Better?"

She snorted then shook her head. "So you're just going to walk around on your knees when you come near me?"

He didn't think she noticed that she was talking about him as part of her future, but he'd take it. "I'd find a way." He reached out with his senses and made sure they were alone. "Just to warn you, though, I'm even bigger in my bear form. Oh, and Dante is a beast as his dragon."

"You know, I've never seen him as a dragon. I don't think any of us have."

He grinned and stood, taking her hand. "He's careful about it. If you asked, though, I have a feeling he'd show you in a heartbeat."

"I might have to do that." She stopped and closed her

eyes. Her knees buckled before she fell, and he lifted her in his arms, cradling her to his chest.

"Nadie? What's wrong?" His bear clawed at him, nudging him to take her to his den and keep her safe.

She took a deep breath, and she shook her head. "I'm fine. I can usually handle the pain that comes with not being able to find my paranormal side, but I think since you *and* Dante are near, it's a little too much for me."

Jace held back a curse at the thought it was *him* causing her hurt. Damn it. There was only one way for Nadie to find her paranormal, thereby relieving her pain, and that was to create a bond through mating.

None of them were ready for that, despite how much he might want to.

"I don't know if we should take my bike if you're feeling like this, Nadie." He looked around for Dante's SUV and debated what to do. He could just take Dante's vehicle, and the dragon wouldn't mind considering what was going on with Nadie, but it already felt odd that Dante wouldn't be going with them tonight. He knew Nadie needed space, and taking Dante's SUV might not be the best way to get it.

"I'm fine, Jace. I can hold on to you, and I won't be standing, so it's not that big a deal. Let's just get home. Okay?"

He looked into her eyes, trying to see the pain that had flared so quickly and hot he could almost taste it, but he saw only the resignation that came with her knowing this wasn't the first, nor the last, time she'd be in this situation.

"I'll keep you safe," he promised, hoping she understood he didn't just mean for right then.

They made their way to his bike, a new Harley Road King that he'd had custom built for his frame. It wasn't easy finding anything big enough for him, but this one did the job nicely. Plus, it had the back seat that Nadie would be able to use, though she'd have to cuddle real close.

Not that Jace minded.

She looked at him closely, and he stood still. "I think you will."

The man and bear let out a relieved sigh, and he set her on her feet. He kept his hands on her shoulders, making sure she was steady then stepped back.

"I'm going to get on first. Then I want you to hold my shoulder with your right hand, put your right foot on the bar, and then swing your left leg over. I'm sturdy enough that you won't rock me, but don't go crazy." He grinned as she rolled her eyes then secured her purse in his saddle bag and put his extra helmet over her head.

He sat down on the bike, and she did exactly what he'd told her to do. She might have been scared a bit at first, but she dove right in.

That boded well for their future.

"Where do you live by the way?"

She chuckled against his back, and his bear nuzzled closer. Damn bear. She gave him directions, and soon they were flying down the road, Nadie's gasps and laughs sliding right through him and making him want to go faster. He'd do it next time for sure. Every dip and valley, she'd tighten her arms around his chest and snuggle closer. His bear preened, loving the attention. He swore the grizzly was more of a teddy bear sometimes rather than one that killed with one swipe.

When they pulled up in front of her place—a cute little house with pale blue shutters that seemed to fit the Nadie he'd heard about and was just getting to know—Nadie got off the bike like a pro…until she fell flat on her ass.

"Shit," he cursed and got off the bike in a flash.

She looked up at him from the ground and burst into giggles. "I can't believe I did that."

"Are you okay?" He knelt in front of her and ran his hands up and down her body, checking for broken bones.

"I'm fine, just a little embarrassed. You might want to keep your hands to yourself now since I'm pretty sure my neighbors are staring through little slits in their curtains to see the man I brought home. Groping me is probably not the best way to introduce you to the neighborhood." She grinned as she said it, and he felt heat creeping up his neck. Sure, he'd felt the curves under his palms, but he'd been a gentleman. At least for now anyway.

He stood up quickly and held out a hand. She slid her hand into his, and he pulled her to her feet. She squeaked and slammed into his chest.

"Crap, sorry. I'm stronger than I thought." Or she was smaller, but since it got her hands on his chest, he'd take it.

Okay, now he was sounding like that teenager with his crush again.

They parted, and she went to her front door. He

followed, not wanting to leave and since she hadn't said goodbye, he'd take it as a good sign. After all, she might need time, but she also needed to get to know him in order to make her decisions...or at least breathe again.

He stepped inside and took in the delicate décor. Oh yeah, this was a place for a small woman who lived alone. He looked down at his big hands and even bigger feet. He didn't quite fit in.

"Uh, should I take off my shoes?"

Nadie turned to him and frowned. "No, I'm not a neat freak like Lily." She looked around at her house and bit her lip. "I guess it's a little girly and small for you in here, huh?"

He shrugged and went to her. "I don't care that your couch is too small for me, Nadie. I just want to get to know you."

Her teeth nibbled on her lip then she sighed. "This is weird, isn't it? Normal people don't go home with a guy they don't know. Wait, yeah, they do, but *I* don't. And the only reason you're here, other than to give me a ride home, which thank you for that by the way, is the fact that you think that I'm not only your mate but Dante's as well. That's so far out of my realm of experience that I have no idea what I'm doing. You know?"

He ran a hand over his chest, not sure what she wanted him to say. "I'm a bear, Nadie. I'm not used to how humans would see true halves and mating." That was as honest as he could be. If she'd been an angel or bear or something else paranormal, they'd be in a different situation. But then she wouldn't have been Nadie.

She just shook her head and walked to the kitchen. He followed her, wanting her sweet scent lingering over him for as long as possible. She smelled of honey and fire, a delicate and strong combination that was perfect for him and Dante.

She got out two glasses and filled them with lemonade from a pitcher in her fridge. From the scent he knew it was fresh and homemade. His bear perked up, wanting anything she'd made, anything that had to do with the woman in front of him.

Hell, his bear was even more twitterpated than he was.

Not that he was twitterpated.

No, he was alpha and male and not so far gone he had stars and hearts in his eyes.

Maybe.

He choked on his first big gulp, knowing he was lying to himself.

"Are you okay, Jace? Too sweet?"

"No, it's just fine." He licked his lips, and thanked the gods he hadn't spilled any down his chin and on his shirt.

Not the best first impression on a night of shitty first impressions.

She gave him an odd look then sat on one of the bar stools. Her legs dangled, but his reached the ground perfectly.

Seriously, she was just too cute.

"Are you really that mad at Dante for what he did?" he asked, unable to hold that question back. He might be there for her to get to know him, but Dante was part of this no matter what.

"He lied to me." She scrunched up her face. "No, that's not exactly right. He kept something from me. He kept all these secrets—secrets about you and what I could be—and didn't even hint at it. How am I supposed to trust him and follow that tug on my heart when he did that?"

Jace reached over and covered her free hand. "I don't know if I'd have done it differently." He held back a curse at her wince. "I was trapped in that other realm dealing with another people's upcoming war, and he couldn't reach out to me. What use would it have been to tell you what you meant to him? No matter what he'd done, he'd still have had to hold back because, without me, the bond wouldn't be complete."

"That still didn't give him the right. It might have hurt to hold back, but I don't like being kept in the dark because he didn't think I was strong enough to deal with it."

Jace was up in an instant. He stood between her legs and slid his hand through her silky, smooth hair. His bear closed his eyes and growled, loving the way they were so close to Nadie. "Never think for a moment that he thought you weren't strong enough. Never. You wouldn't be connected to a dragon and a bear if you weren't strong enough. You might be small, but you are mighty."

Nadie snorted a laugh—the exact reaction he'd intended. "Mighty? Cute, Jace."

He gave her his best grin. "I try."

"I don't know if I believe you, but thanks anyway."

"Hey, everything Dante does is for others. He might be a dragon, a kind known for keeping to themselves and never helping another unless it's for their own good, but that's not him. He likes humans and other supernaturals."

Her eyes brightened a bit. "I don't know much about Dante beyond what he's shown us. Meaning his human half. I don't know anything about dragons, and the others like Shade and Hunter don't know much either."

"Then you can ask him. I only know because I've done the same. I can even tell you about bears if you'd like."

"I'd like that," she whispered. "It's all so surreal, you know? One minute I'm ready to leave the bar forever, the next I have a dragon and a freaking bear laying claim."

"It's just the way of the supernaturals. We find a mate and we want to get started. Or at least want to when all the players are in place. We have time to find who we are and how we'll mesh. I'm not saying we should bond right this minute and call it a day."

She blushed hard and ducked her head. If what Dante thought was true, then their Nadie had never been with a man, period, let alone two at once. That would be an experience.

For all of them.

Time to change the subject. "How are you feeling? Still weak?"

She shook her head. "It comes and goes. I'd rather it go away forever but as we've learned from the others, there's only one way to do that."

His bear nudged at him, knowing *exactly* what that way was.

Clearly he hadn't changed the subject far enough.

"If you feel something coming, let me know and I can get Dante over here to help."

She narrowed her eyes, even as her cheeks went flame red. "I thought we said we weren't ready for that."

He chuckled then. "No, not the bond, but how he siphons off your pain. I know he takes it into himself and that just about kills me, but he can help alleviate some of yours so you can function."

"What the heck are you talking about?" Flecks of anger scattered over her eyes and Jace cursed.

"I take it Dante held back that piece of information as well?" Dear gods that dragon was in for a world of hurt when Nadie got back to him.

"I'm going to kill him! Who does he think he is to take my pain?" Tears filled her eyes and she wiped them in angry strokes. "Is he hurting? Why would he do that? I don't want him to hurt because of me."

He cupped her face and wiped away another tear. "He does that because he cares for you. Because Dante and I aren't lightning-struck we don't feel the same pain and weakness you do when we find our mates. Yes, our beasts are a little more aggressive since we haven't completed the bond, but it's not the same. He does it because he cares."

"He had no right," she whispered. "I'm going to beat him up for that. Or something that I can actually do since I'm the size of your leg."

"Hey, I like your size."

She rolled her eyes. "No wonder Dante calls me a sprite. I can't even reach you on my tip toes."

"Then it's a good thing you're on this stool. You're at perfect height."

She tilted her head, her cheek on his palm. "For what?"

"For this." He lowered his head and brushed his lips along hers. She let out a little gasp then pressed closer. He took that as an invitation and licked the seam of her lips. She opened for him, and he groaned. Their tongues touched briefly, but he kept himself back, not wanting to take it too far.

His bear growled, wanting more, wanting it all, but Jace was in control.

He pulled away, the sweet taste of honey mixed with the tartness of lemons from her drink on his tongue.

"Wow," she whispered, and he laughed softly.

"Wow indeed." He tucked a lock of hair behind her ear and studied her face. Her cheeks were flushed, and he loved the glint in her eyes. "I'm going to go now. I'd like to come back tomorrow and pick you up to take you to Dante's home. I think the three of us should spend some time together."

She took a deep breath then nodded. "I agree. If I'm going to find out how to move on, how to be who I have the possibility of becoming, I need to get over my anger, but it won't be easy."

He had a feeling she was more than halfway there, but he wasn't going to point that out. From what he'd heard from

Dante, Nadie was a forgiving person. He and the dragon would have to grovel though.

"I'll take a look at your car and see if I can help. If not, I'll call my brother. Good night, Nadie."

"Thank you for helping. Good night, Jace." She touched her fingertips to her lips then smiled. "It...it was nice to meet you."

He snorted then shook his head. "Hell yeah, Nadie. But it won't be the last. Not by far."

He wanted this woman, no matter what she turned into when the bond was set and the time came. His bear had laid claim, and the dragon, in his heart, had as well.

Nadie would be theirs.

Soon.

CHAPTER 4

"He's found his mates. We'll have to act fast so he understands his responsibilities."

Rock seethed at Alexander's words but did as he'd always done and didn't say anything. He merely nodded like the good little dragon they thought he was. He was the man's man or, in essence, the dragon's dragon. He never stepped out of place and never let the others know his true thoughts.

He was the perfect candidate, yet he wasn't the one they wanted.

Fucking Dante.

"What's your plan then?" he asked, knowing Alexander would have a plan. The older dragon *always* had a plan. Rock had done well to learn from him or, at least, had tried to listen when the other man went on his insanely tedious tangents.

"He has the summons. He will come. If he doesn't..." The man shrugged, the action slow, uncaring. "He knows the consequences of not answering a summons from us. He, like you, is one of the few who have been allowed such knowledge to pass his ears. If he decides to ignore us for the more...carnal pursuits with that bear and the abomination, he will be taken care of. There is no other way. If the dragon ignores us, we take away his distractions. That's how it's been done. How it will ever be. No one refuses us. We are gods."

Rock nodded, making sure his face showed the right level of respect for the man in front of him and contempt for a dragon not following the guidelines and practices of such ancient matters. He made sure the older dragon had no clue that, while Alexander might want Dante to answer his summons, Rock wanted the black and blue dragon to fail.

Failure would mean Dante's death and Rock's eventual exaltedness.

That was what Rock desired, what he'd *earned*.

There would be no other outcome.

DANTE'S HOUSE SURE DIDN'T LOOK LIKE A DRAGON'S CAVE. The thought brought a reluctant smile to Nadie's face. For some reason, when she found out what Dante actually was, she'd always had the little thought in the back of her mind that he'd hoard his jewels and gold in a vast cave with stones and jagged cliffs to protect it from marauders. In Dante's case, the dragon had a large two-story home off a residential area, but it was tucked deep within the trees. The effect was that it looked as tough he was all alone out there but close enough to the city that he could be near his bar and other people so he wasn't so isolated.

She liked it.

"Ready to go in?" Jace asked her from her side, and she nodded, though she wasn't quite sure that was the truth. Oh, she knew she *should* go in, but she wasn't sure she was exactly ready. She'd ridden there on the back of his bike, wrapped around him like she had been the night before. Was it wrong she really loved that? Jace said her car might have more issues than just a battery, so he was having his brother tow it to their den to fix.

Their den.

Her car was going to a bear den that she hadn't yet seen.

Talk about crazy.

The blond Viking of a man towered over her, but though he looked as if he'd smash anyone that came near them, she felt safe. For some reason, she knew he'd never hurt her.

She'd gone to sleep soon after Jace had left the night before, dreaming of dragons and bears and frolicking down a yellow brick road. Apparently her subconscious was a little illogical. Today they were going to sit down with Dante and just…be. She'd never really been alone with Dante for longer than twenty minutes before considering she was usually at the bar with her friends. She did her best to ignore the fact she'd only been alone with him because she'd purposely come early or stayed late in order to do so.

For the past year, though, she'd been snippy and rude to him. She knew it had to do with her own unresolved feelings and the pain riding her, and she was ashamed of how she'd acted. He'd kept his feelings and his own pain from her, believing he was protecting her. She'd tell him just what she thought of that today though. He couldn't go around treating her like she was less than him. He also wouldn't be allowed to hurt himself for her. He might have held key things from her, but that didn't mean she had to act as though she hated him.

Maybe if she hadn't been so mean, lashing out when she could, he'd have confided in her. Not that she thought that was a real possibility considering he and Jace were way too alpha for that. She'd just have to show them that she was strong enough to take it.

During her dreams and after she'd woken up, she'd come to the conclusion she would take this one step at a time and not look back. She had to. She couldn't force herself to run away from something that could be amazing because of fear or hurt feelings.

Fate was giving her a gift, and she was going to take it.

Well, she'd take it after she got a few things off her chest.

Namely, making sure the dragon knew he couldn't keep sacrificing his health for her and keeping secrets.

No, that wouldn't work in the future.

In their future.

Jace walked right in without knocking, though that didn't surprise Nadie for some reason. The men had a history—one she would want to know about. For some reason, she felt a little thread of jealousy at that, but then it went away quickly. These two were *together* in a sense and weren't just bookends. She wouldn't be one either. Nadie had already decided to talk to Jamie about how she dealt with two men on a daily basis, though she hadn't talked to any of her friends about what had happened in the past twelve hours.

For some reason, she wanted it to be just between the three of them. She'd tell her friends about everything later—the same way the other three women who had been in this situation had done.

Dante came out from one of the back rooms and stopped in the hall, putting his hands in his pockets. It might have been wrong of her, but she was glad she wasn't the only one nervous. Jace stood with a smile, but she could also feel the tension radiating off him. They were there for something far different than anything she'd ever done or even thought about doing.

The man they'd come to see wore tattered jeans and a rock tee, his normal attire. She liked that he wore casual clothes and really seemed to fit in with the world around him rather than standing out like a sore thumb. After all, he'd said he was way over a few hundred years old, so he would have learned to blend in with the rest of them.

Well, as blended as Dante could get. His brow ring and tribal tattoos, which she'd studied over the years, formed an ancient dragon that didn't let him blend as easily as others. Then, of course, his long black and blue hair just screamed rebel.

She loved it.

He'd left his hair out of the band today, so a long piece hung over his shoulder while the rest went down his back. It might have looked feminine on anyone else, but not on Dante. She looked to her left at Jace and couldn't help the grin. He had that Thor blond hair going on. It helped that she totally had a crush on Chris Hemsworth, and Jace looked as though he could match him punch for punch— and swoony glare for swoony glare.

Nadie held back a groan and closed her eyes.

Okay, she really needed to get her mind on what she was supposed to be thinking about, not going off on random tangents because she was too nervous to do anything else.

"You two made it here okay, then," Dante said unnecessarily.

"We did," Jace rumbled beside her. "We gonna sit down, actually hash this out, and get comfortable or stand here like strangers? Since Nadie and I are the only two here who could possibly qualify as strangers, I don't think the latter works well."

She sank into the couch without another word, nervous, but oddly ready to just...be. Curious, she looked around the place and felt at ease. Everything might have been made for a man much larger than her, but she didn't feel uncomfortable. Even the colors and fabrics were soothing, as if it was for a man who had lived long enough to know what he liked. In Dante's case that was true many times over. "I've never seen your house before, you know. I like it. At least what I've seen."

Dante grinned, and her heart fluttered. Damn heart. "Only Jace and a few others from my past have seen my house. I can give you a tour later if you want."

"So not even Balin has seen it?" Balin was not only one of Jamie's mates, but a friend of Dante's that he'd known in hell before the dragon had been banished. She'd have to get the banished story out of him at some point too. It seemed her dragon held more secrets than any other man she'd known. It only made sense, though, with how he lived.

Alone.

Dante shook his head. "Before the lightning strike, when I hid who I was from you girls, I didn't want to show the girls the place only to have to use magic to wipe your memories of it when you started to notice I didn't really age. I do think Becca would have caught on eventually." She grinned and agreed with him. Becca was tenacious when it came to things she didn't know and wanted to figure out. "I didn't show you because I was waiting for Jace. And I didn't show Balin or any of you when things were brought out in the open because…" He shifted uncomfortably, and she would have sworn a blush darkened his cheeks. "Because I wanted you to see it first."

She swallowed hard. "Oh. Well…I'm glad you did." She ducked her head. Darn it, she hated acting like the innocent virgin who didn't know what she was doing. So what if that label happened to be true? That didn't mean she had to *act* like it.

"How long have you lived here again?" Jace asked, and soon they were talking about trivial things that didn't matter but at least made them relax. The man seemed to always know when they needed words that didn't mean much or time to breathe before they worked on other issues. It must have been because he was a Mediator.

Nadie pulled her feet up to tuck under her body and leaned against one of the large pillows on the couch. This was nice, sitting in a room with these two men and just talking about random things. She liked the way they were already friends but, because they'd spent so much time apart, were still learning about each other—the same as she was.

She didn't feel as though she was on unequal ground—just an uneven one since they still hadn't discussed the giant elephant in the room. She held back a grin. With the dragon, bear, and now the elephant in the room, it was getting a bit crowded.

Dante sat on the ottoman in front of the L-shaped couch where Jace sat and turned to her. "What's funny?" he asked.

She looked into those blue eyes of his and knew the time for casual conversation was over. "I was just thinking we're dancing quite nicely around the giant elephant in the room." She paused as the guys looked at each other before looking back at her. "Then I thought about how we already have a bear and a dragon, why not add the giant elephant?"

Dante's brows rose, and Jace snorted. "I'm quite a bit larger than an elephant in my dragon form."

She leaned closer, interested. "Really? Will you show me what you look like as a dragon?"

He gave a slow nod. "Yes, I can do that. I have a field a

little off from the house that's protected by wards where I shift and fly undetected in the human realm. I don't go to the dragon realm often to rejoin my people, so I've learned to make do with what I have."

Nadie reached out and traced her finger along his hand, the pull within her needing to touch him. He turned it so it faced palm up, and she followed the lines there. "Why is that?"

"That's a long story for another time. I will tell it all, I promise. There are things even Jace doesn't know. I'd rather talk about that elephant you mentioned first, and then we can talk of the dragons and their fire."

Jace scooted a bit closer on the couch and put his hand on her knee. The warmth seeped through her jeans, and she relaxed. Odd that a man she'd just met would do that to her, but right then, normal didn't make sense.

Normal wasn't part of her life anymore.

Hadn't been since the lightning.

"I was so angry with you, Dante. So freaking angry," she started, her voice oddly calm. She'd tried to think of what she'd say to him, what she'd say to Jace, yet it had all come out in rambles. "I don't like that you thought you could control me by keeping secrets."

His eyes widened, and he grasped the hand she'd placed on his harder. "What? I wasn't trying to control you."

She tilted her head. "Weren't you?"

Jace squeezed her knee then reached out and slid his hand over Dante's knee as well. She liked the connection that made; the three of them entwined as they might be if they could get past the oddness.

"That was not my intention," he said slowly, his blue eyes pained.

"But it happened nonetheless. By taking away my choices, by not letting me know what *could* be, you controlled that aspect of my life. Of *our* lives. I don't like that, Dante. Hell, I hate that."

He grinned at her cursing, but that slid off his face quickly. "Nadie...you have to believe that I didn't mean to do that. I only meant to keep you safe, or at least in less pain than you would have been if you'd have known."

She narrowed her eyes. "Yes, about that pain. We will discuss your intentions there in a minute."

Dante glanced at Jace, who grimaced.

"Don't blame him for telling me something you should have."

"Nadie—"

"No, let me get this off my chest first. Please." He nodded, and she took a deep breath. "Don't ever take away my choices again. If this is going to work, then you'll have to be honest with me." She looked at Jace, not knowing if Dante had held secrets from him as well. "No, *us*. I know you have your secrets, and I don't want them all at once. I know you have things that are close to your heart, and I hope one day that you'll trust me enough to share them, but when it comes to things that are important to us,"—she motioned between the three of them—"you need to tell me.

Tell us. You can't hold them back because you're afraid I'll be hurt."

She paused and licked her lips, but the others didn't say anything.

"I know I'm the little fish in the vast ocean of things that aren't human, but holding me back and thinking I'm not strong enough to take it won't help. I know I'm not a fighter or anything like that, not like what the others have had to become when they changed into their own paranormals. I know that. That doesn't mean I'll always be as weak as I am. No, weak isn't the word I want, but I can't think of another. I want to learn about who I can become." She sucked in a breath. "And I want to become that person with you and Jace along the way. I know it's crazy, and I should wait to see what happens and think of things like a human, but I'm not human. Right?" She shook her head, feeling lost yet determined at the same time.

She took a deep breath then continued. "I'm not human, not in the same sense that I was before the lightning hit. Treat me like someone who has the potential to be something far greater than I am, and then I can be by your side and take the future as it comes. Treat me like I'm less than you by hiding things, and we won't have a future at all."

Dante was on her in a flash, and she gasped as, suddenly, she was on his lap and he was sitting where she'd been just a moment before. Jace had moved as well, sliding so he was thigh to thigh with Dante. The dragon had his hands on her face; the bear, his hand on her hip.

"You are *not* less than me. You never have been, and you

never will be. I will tell you everything, Nadie, but you can't make me promise not to protect you." She opened her mouth, but he gave one sharp shake of his head, shutting her up. "You can't ask that. I will *always* protect you and Jace, just as Jace will do the same for us. That doesn't mean, though, that I'll keep secrets. From here on out, if something happens, I'll tell you. I promise."

Something flashed in his eyes, but she couldn't quite tell what it was.

Jace, however, seemed to have noticed it as well. "What are you still keeping secret, Dante?"

Dante closed his eyes then shook his head. "That is something we can discuss soon. I promise."

Something was wrong, but she couldn't tell what it was or how to help. But if he said he would talk about it, like he'd said he'd explain about the dragons, then she had to believe him. If she didn't, then that made her whole speech useless. There was no use in telling him that she'd trust him for their future if she couldn't trust the words out of his mouth right then.

"Okay then," she said. "I trust you. You were being logical before—or at least thought you were. I get that. But, damn, you should have spoken to me. I forgive you for that though." Surprise flecked his eyes, but he didn't say anything. "If I didn't forgive you, then I couldn't move forward. I'm trusting you in this."

He nodded, and she relaxed, only to realize she was sitting on his lap, straddling him with his very rigid cock pressed against her heat.

She froze, then blushed as she became aware of how close they were, how close they all were.

"Nadie," Dante groaned. "Don't give me that look. You're not ready."

Jace squeezed her hip and a wave of weakness hit her like a train. She gasped and swayed. The men kept her upright, and she tried to shake it off. The weakness came in waves, never responding the same way twice. Sometimes it would be worse when she was near Dante—and now Jace— other times she felt it at home when she was alone. She sucked in a breath as she felt her pain siphon off again.

Only this time she knew who was helping her pain.

She narrowed her eyes at the dragon who just blinked back at her, not caring that he was taking her pain.

This would have to stop.

"I can't help it, Nadie. I see you in pain, I have to help. It's my dragon."

Well then, she'd just have to make sure there wouldn't be any more pain for him to take.

"I…you know I've never done anything like this before, right?" she whispered, embarrassed as all heck, but if she wanted to have a mature adult relationship, she would just have to get over it.

Dante tucked a piece of her hair behind her ear. "I know, my sprite. I know. We're not going to do anything you're not ready for."

Jace slid his hand up her side. "We have time."

Something deep inside pushed her to say her next words, and she jumped on it. She shook her head at the men. "I don't want to wait. I know it's crazy, but I want to move forward, and I can't do that if we're all tiptoeing around the fact that I'm in pain because we don't have the bond." She hit Dante's chest and narrowed her eyes. "And you're killing yourself trying to keep me alive. I'm going to have words with you later on that."

"Nadie, honey, what are you saying?" Jace asked, heat in his tone, along with worry.

She glanced between them, meeting their gazes, and then raised her chin. She might not be a temptress, but she wanted these two men, and if she was going to jump off the deep end and find a future with them, she wasn't going to wait.

Not any longer.

She was tired of waiting.

She wasn't human. She wasn't the person she'd been before the lightning. She wanted to be the person she was meant to be, not the person she'd tried to be. She, Jace, and Dante were meant for something. She was sure of it.

Damn the conventions she'd learned growing up. It was time try something different.

Something more daring.

"I want to feel the bond that I'm missing. I want to move forward and find who I can be. I need the two of you to do that. I...want you both. I don't care what that makes me, but I'm not human. Not any longer. I'm not going to conform to those rules." Like she'd been doing her whole life. No, she was ready to grow. Ready to grow with them.

She blinked at the shock on their faces. "Well, uh, that is if you want me." She winced. "If not, well...hell."

Dante moved close, so close their noses touched, and she saw the fire in his eyes. For a moment, she thought it was real fire and not just the heat in his eyes that scorched her.

"Not want you? Not a chance in hell, my sprite. I want you. I've wanted you in my bed, my life, my future since I first saw you. Don't ever think I don't want you."

Jace cupped the back of her head and forced her gaze to his. The action left Dante's heated breath on her neck and behind her ear, sending delicious shivers down her spine.

"I want you, Nadie. I'm not gonna lie and say I've only been thinking pure thoughts where you're concerned. I've only known you in person for a short time, yet I can feel you here." His fist hit his chest, such a bear thing to do. "That's something that supersedes time. If you feel you're ready, then all you have to do is nod and let us take the reins." He cupped her face. "You've never done this before, love, so we'll show you what to do, and we'll make sure you feel everything and love it all."

She let out a shaky breath, knowing this was the moment she'd waited for yet hadn't had a clue what she'd feel when it finally came. She wasn't the Nadie who taught little children and wore the prim clothes her parents wanted her to wear. She might not live with them anymore, but their judgments and lectures still rang in her head. They'd never leave her memories, her actions, as long as she still feared who she could be. She wasn't the one who never stepped out of line for fear of what was to come. The punishments for stepping across the line were long gone. She had to remember that. She didn't want to be the scared Nadie.

She was the Nadie who would be bonded to a dragon and a bear.

This was the Nadie she wanted to be.

This was the Nadie they'd show her *how* to be.

"Love me," she whispered, and she was lost.

CHAPTER 5

Nadie watched the rise and fall of Jace's chest as he took in her words and felt the same from Dante beneath her. She could still feel her dragon's breath on her neck, the heat of his body, and the jean-clad erection between her legs telling her that at least his body wanted her. And from the heat in his eyes she knew he wanted her as well.

Without speaking, Dante stood, his hands cupping her bottom, taking her with him. She immediately wrapped her legs around his waist.

"You never have to ask us to be with you," he whispered as he carried her to the back hallway. His low rumble shot down her spine, and she shivered. He grinned down at her, that glint in his eyes telling her that he knew exactly how he made her feel.

She looked over Dante's shoulder at Jace. He prowled behind them, the grin wiped off his face. Instead, the hunger now there made her belly—and some place much lower —clench.

This was really happening.

She was about to make love with not only the man she'd crushed on for years, but the other man that, in her heart, she knew would be part of her future, *their* future.

Dante climbed the stairs, her weight seemingly nothing in his strong arms. Yeah, she would totally swoon at that later. They entered one of the bedrooms in the back of the house, and she looked around, taking in the dark, heavy furniture, the cream walls, and shades of blue.

He set her on her feet then pinched her chin, forcing her gaze upward. The stark need on his face made all thoughts of décor and colors beyond that of his eyes—and Jace's— disappear from her mind.

His tongue darted out, and he licked his lips, letting the metal of his tongue ring catch the light. She'd read enough and seen enough gifs online to have an idea of what that little ball and bar would feel like against her skin...and other places.

"I...I don't know what to do," she whispered then tried to duck her head. Dante's firm hold on her chin stopped the action, and she gulped.

"Then let Jace and I show you what to do," Dante said simply.

"Um, I've seen movies and things...so I'm not as innocent as you think." If she were to put her hands up to her cheeks, she was pretty sure they'd burn.

Jace let out a rough chuckle and came to her side. When she hadn't been looking, he'd taken off his shirt, leaving him bare chested with a light dusting of blond hair.

She just about swallowed her tongue.

"What kind of movies have you been watching, Nadie Morgan?" Jace asked, his voice teasing. "Dante and I here are pure and innocent, so I have no idea what you could be talking about."

Dante let out a snort, and Nadie rolled her eyes, finally pulling away from Dante a bit so she could get a better look at both of them.

Both of *her* men.

"Pure and innocent? Really?" She blinked up at him and tried to keep a smile off her face.

Jace pressed his lips together then put his fist over his heart and nodded. "Yep. Totally innocent."

Dante full out laughed, and Nadie joined in, the tension releasing from the room like air from a popped balloon—just like Jace must have intended.

"How about we take it from here and let you just feel?" Dante asked as his hand traced up her side, his fingers tugging up her shirt so his skin touched hers.

She gasped at that small contact then smiled.

Oh yes, this was so going to be amazing.

"We won't do anything that you don't want," Jace said as he came up from behind her.

She nodded then closed her eyes at his touch. She felt their hands on her sides, their lips on her neck. Jace's lips traced her collarbone over her shirt while his large, calloused palm slid up her stomach to cup her breast over her bra. A gasp escaped from her lips at the contact, his hand so much bigger than hers yet so caring. So utterly sexy.

She'd met Dante so young and had been hiding her desires for so long because of where she'd come from that she'd never had a man touch her. Damn, she'd been missing out on so much, but she also knew if she hadn't waited, she wouldn't have had the two men who would make every-thing mean so much more than a touch here with her now.

She'd waited for a reason.

She just hadn't known until right then what that reason was.

Dante's lips were on her neck while his hand was on her back, softly caressing. Finally, he moved so his lips brushed hers, and she opened for him. It was not lost on her that he'd never kissed her more than the whisper they'd shared the day before.

She wanted more.

She *needed* more.

His tongue lightly touched hers, and she moaned. He growled, the vibration going right to her core, and then deepened the kiss. His tongue ring slid along the roof of her mouth, the intrusion sexy as hell. He put his whole body into the kiss, the hard line of his cock pressing against her belly.

Too soon, he pulled back and smiled, his eyes glowing with the fire she'd seen before but had thought was just a catch of light.

"Your eyes..." she whispered, and he grinned.

"I'm a dragon, my sprite. I have fire in my blood, and right now that fire wants you on that bedspread beneath me while I take you for your first time."

"Don't forget me," Jace growled playfully behind them, and she turned to face him fully, her dragon's hands still on her.

He leaned in and nipped her lip, the sting causing her to moan before he devoured her mouth. Her men moved quickly then, stripping her shirt from her body, the only time they would allow her mouth to be free from one of them.

They took turns kissing her, their hands never leaving her unless they were taking the clothes from her body. While one would kiss her mouth, the other would trail his tongue along her skin. She could tell the difference between Jace's broad, flat tongue and Dante's, with the piercing on it, immediately and loved knowing who was who even with her eyes closed.

Dante moved away from her but kept his hand on her side. She opened her eyes to see the two men staring at not her, but each other. No matter how heated she got from their touches, the look just then scorched her even more— or at least the thought that it would be the *three* of them. Jace grinned, and Dante moved forward. Their mouths collided, their breaths panting. Nadie stood off to the side, but both men still held her slightly, keeping her part of their embrace. They kissed each other rougher than they did her, and she loved it. Loved the way their relationship was unto itself and just as sexy.

Possibly more so because she got to be the observer and enjoy it with them. Was this their first kiss? Or at least their first time together like this?

Dante pulled back, his chest heaving, then moved back to Nadie to kiss her again. She moaned, leaning closer, wanting his mouth on her for longer, but he moved away. She was only alone for a moment before Jace's mouth met hers, and she opened for him. Her mind whirled, her body ready for the next step as these two men took care of her.

"Did you like watching that, honey?" Jace asked, whispering in her ear. His warm breath slid across her neck, and she shivered.

"Yes. Oh yes. Can you do it again?"

Dante slapped her ass, and she started. She turned to him, and he grinned at her. It wasn't a funny grin, but one so full of promise and hunger that she about came on the spot.

Who knew a dragon's intensity could do that?

"We're going to do that and more, my sprite."

She soon found herself naked between them, her breasts bare, her nipples hard points against Jace as he kissed her. His hands were on her ass, molding, caressing, sliding between her cheeks as he teased her. He still wore his jeans but had undone the top button so she could see the crisp hair there. The long—*thick*—line of his cock bulged at the zipper. She swallowed hard at the sight of the crown of his cock peeking above his jeans, as if it were too big to be confined.

Her bear went commando.

Nice.

She slid her hands up his back, letting herself fall into the moment, ignoring whatever fears or insecurities she might have.

Jace lifted her up then turned so her back was to the large bed in the room. He laid her down slowly then stood up. His blond hair brushed his shoulders, and he ran a hand through it, pulling it back.

"Hell, look at you, Nadie. I don't think I've ever seen anyone so fucking perfect in my life. What do you think, Dante?"

She blushed hard, pressing her knees close together. Though she'd used a vibrator on herself and had given herself orgasms, she'd never been this far with a man before. Let alone two.

Talk about coming out of her shell.

Dante came and stood beside Jace and raked his gaze over her body. Unlike Jace, though, he'd taken off *all* his clothes.

Nadie swallowed hard and broke out in a sweat—the *oh-my-God-I-get-to-have-sex-with-both-of-them* kind.

Dante's tattoos weren't just on his arms but on his hips too. The same dragon tribal symbols that she couldn't wait to lick. Though Becca had thought otherwise, his nipples weren't pierced.

However, as Nadie's gaze lowered, she sucked in a breath because, though his nipples weren't pierced, his cock was.

Why hello, Prince Albert.

"You're fucking amazing, Nadie. I should have been telling you since the day I met you how much I want you. And I see your eyes on my cock. You want me to take out my piercing? It'll feel really fucking good when we're making love, but since this is your first time, I don't want to have that as an added pressure."

She shook her head then leaned up on her forearms so she could get a better look. Jace shucked off his pants as she did so, and she blinked.

"Jesus," she whispered, and Jace threw his head back and laughed.

When she'd first thought about the fact she was going to be mated with a bear and a dragon, who were also really freaking huge in real life, she'd been worried about only what she'd have to stand on to kiss them. She hadn't really thought about how, um, proportioned they were.

Jace was thicker, and Dante was longer, but either way, Nadie knew she was one lucky girl.

"Nadie?" Dante's voice broke her from thoughts of exactly what she'd be doing soon.

"You can keep it in," she said and blushed. Okay, she really needed to stop blushing when she talked about sex. She might be a virgin, but come on.

They didn't speak, but moved as one. Dante came between her legs, his hands on her knees. She let out a breath then let him spread her thighs. Jace came up to her side and kissed her softly, her tension melting away. Her dragon's tongue on her pussy forced a gasp out of her, which Jace swallowed as he kissed her harder. Her bear's hands came to her breasts, plucking her nipples before he moved to suck one gently into his mouth.

Her body bowed off the bed as Dante's lips brushed against her heat. He spread her with his fingers and latched onto her clit, his tongue ring applying an extra pressure and sensation that had her panting. Both men worked her, Jace playing and sucking on her nipples while Dante licked, sucked, and nibbled on her pussy, clit, and lower lips. She swallowed hard, unable to keep her mind straight on who was doing what other than she knew she had to come.

Now.

He speared her with his tongue as Jace bit down on her nipple, the dual sensation too much for her, and she came in a rush of pleasure and temptation. Her head fell back, and she didn't know how much time passed before she opened her eyes and found Dante above her, his face close to hers, his body between her legs.

He licked her lips then kissed her, the taste of herself on his tongue surprisingly erotic. He pulled back too soon, and she whimpered.

"We're going to complete the bond, my sprite," he whispered, his voice gruff. "In order to do that, it's not just me with you, then Jace with you. Do you understand that?"

She blinked, trying to clear the fog from her orgasm, then looked over Dante's shoulder at Jace, who stood at the end of the bed, the tension in his body straining from the look of corded muscle.

"You mean you and Jace as well."

Dante nodded. "Is that going to scare you?"

She cupped his jaw and shook her head. "Why would it? It's beautiful. The two of you with each other and then with me? I see nothing wrong with that. It might not be normal for others, but I know this will work for us. I uh...just don't know the order."

Dante snorted, his body shaking with laughter. "Oh, my Nadie. I'm going to make love with you, then Jace will. Then Jace and I will decide who gets to dominate first," he said then looked over his shoulder and growled. "We've yet to decide whose beast is on top."

Nadie giggled, surprised she could find anything funny while she was naked beneath the man she'd fallen for and in need of both men in the room to fill her.

"Who says you have to decide? Can't you just take turns?"

Jace barked out a laugh. "See, dragon? Nadie understands what you don't. There won't be submitting for any of us. Not even our sprite here. I can picture her leading us by our cocks and having her way with us." He raised a brow. "Doesn't that sound like a damn fine plan?"

Dante rolled his eyes, the brow ring moving as he did so. "Fine, I see I have no control here." He lowered his head and nipped her lip. "Ready, love?"

She licked her lips, soothing the sting where he bit. The laughter was gone now, just heady anticipation of what was to come.

"Ready, my dragon."

He smiled at her endearment then moved his hips. The tip of his cock breached her, and she stiffened under him, the sharp pain not as bad as she thought it would have been, but still stinging. Jace was on the bed in a flash, hands on her breasts, flicking and arousing. She melted, letting Dante go deeper.

Jace and Dante took turns kissing her as her dragon filled her, and soon he was inside to the hilt, his body straining above her. She knew he was holding back so as to not hurt her, and she was thankful.

He was big, and she'd never done this before, so of course it hurt, but she also had been horseback riding and using a vibrator long enough that it wasn't as painful as it could have been.

Thank. God.

When her inner walls finally relaxed around the girth of him, she moved her hips, wanting him to join her.

"Please, Dante. Please, my dragon."

He kissed her then, slowly, and pulled out of her. She winced at the feeling, almost telling him to stop, but then he slid back in, and she moaned at the sensation.

"Do that again," she panted.

"Anything you want, my sprite," he whispered, the soft growl in his voice going right to her pussy.

He pumped into her slowly while Jace rolled her nipples

between his fingers. They were both touching her, both showing her that she was the center for them. Jace's hand slid down her stomach to her clit, then he smiled.

"Come for me," he whispered, and she did. Hard.

She clamped around Dante's cock, and he shouted her name as he followed right behind her. She felt his seed fill her and a slow burn across her chest. A bond, yes, it had to be a bond, snapped into place, and she rejoiced in the feel of her dragon—the fire and warmth that came from Dante, a swirl of sensation that told her she was home.

Still panting, Dante pulled out, and Jace slid between her legs, entering her in one thrust. There was no pain this time, only intense need. She matched him, movement for movement, high on what she'd done with Dante and the connection she felt with her bear. She wanted it with Jace too, craved it.

The craving was something new…something that wasn't what she was used to, but she took it and everything her men gave her.

"I can't wait," Dante said from behind Jace, and she looked up at him and noticed how close to the other man he was. "Are you ready?"

Jace grinned at her then looked over his shoulder. "Always, dragon. Always."

Dante grinned right back, gripped Jace's hips, then thrust.

Jace moaned, and Nadie froze, and her bear did as well. "Thank God you used lube, Dante. You're fucking huge."

Apparently they'd been busy, and she hadn't noticed. She'd have to pay better attention next time. This was something she didn't want to miss again.

She was spent, but she wanted to be part of what Jace and Dante were sharing, as well as what she and Jace were sharing. Dante would move, then Jace would follow, thrusting into her. She wrapped her legs around as much of Dante and Jace as she could, then put on hand on each man, needing the connection.

They moved as one, and she lost herself to it. Her body rose, the wave of heat crashing into her as she came, yet again. Jace yelled her name then Dante's, coming with her. Dante must have done the same because as he screamed their names, the final bond slid into place.

The fire that came from Dante blended with the raw, earthy energy and spice of Jace. She felt the soft and light feel of her own energy mixing. The three threads wove together, the bond cementing, yet still fragile.

It tasted of home, of peace…of promise.

She closed her eyes, the intensity of what she was feeling too much.

"Open, open your eyes, love," Jace whispered. The warm glow of their bodies radiated within the room, their mating bond firmly in the place that would be the foundation of what was to come. It was as if she could see the future with them in that one moment, the essence of something much bigger than herself.

Tears slid down her cheeks at the beauty of it. She

opened her mouth to speak but couldn't catch her breath. Both men were moving then, one on each side of her as she let out a soundless scream. Her body glowed brighter, and she shook from side to side. In her mind, she knew that this was what happened when one of the lightning-struck became their supernatural, but that didn't make it any better.

It was like a thousand knives sliding over her, washing away the happiness and hope she'd felt when she'd bonded with her two mates.

A new hunger came from deep within her belly that she knew would never be sated.

She didn't pass out, not like the other women who had changed before her, but she looked down at herself, not knowing what she'd become, only that she had no idea if she'd ever be able to control it. Dark black leaves had been inked into her skin on her sides and hips. She felt the burn on her spine and shoulders and knew they were there too. Within the leaves were crimson-red roses, each dripping in blood, but not hers. It was only ink, but it had branded her like no other.

Jace's hand hovered over her hip, and she met his gaze. His face was awash in awe, but he didn't look scared. She turned to Dante, who licked his lips then cupped her jaw.

"What am I?" she asked, her voice hoarse from screaming.

Dante bent and kissed her softly. "You are our mate."

The bond flared between the three of them, and she

relaxed somewhat, remembering what they'd just done and how her future would be forever changed.

She nodded but wasn't satisfied. "What am I?" she asked again.

"You, Nadie, are a succubus."

CHAPTER 6

He'd put it off for far too long, and now Dante would have to follow the summons from the Conclave. Though he'd never been summoned before, he knew the outcome for ignoring the thick cream envelope and what it contained any longer.

Death.

With a sigh, he slipped from the bed after he untangled himself from Nadie's embrace. She'd slept between him and Jace throughout the night, exhausted not only from their lovemaking, but from the bond itself.

Not to mention she'd found her dominant paranormal gene.

A succubus.

Who would have thought Nadie Morgan would become a succubus?

In retrospect, it did make sense somewhat since she'd

been weaker than any of the other women when she'd found her true half. While Lily, Jamie, and Becca had all had some tremors and weakness as their bodies tried to find equilibrium, Nadie's was worse by far.

Her inner succubus had been draining her energy in order to feed since Nadie hadn't been able to feed it the normal way. Dante wasn't so sure that she would have made it without the energy of two mates, losing her virginity and finding her bond at the same time. Succubi needed the life force of their partner and would drain them to death if they needed it.

Since Nadie was now bonded to them, though, the feeding seemed to work like a conduit and flow back to him and Jace as well, much like Balin and his need for souls as a demon. Nadie would take in their energy to feed her beast and then, because of the bond they shared, would flow it back to them individually.

They would have to find a balance and teach her, like the others had been taught, what she needed to know about her new powers. Dante shook his head. Of all things she could have turned into, though, that one had not been on his list.

The benefits for him and Jace…well, he wouldn't be so lecherous to think about those right now. He'd just wait until he could talk them over with Nadie. He'd always known he'd have to teach her what lay in her future. In their core group, Ambrose, the warrior angel mated to Jamie, was eons old, but Dante was even older. It was their unspoken job to ensure the women and younger male paranormals knew what they were getting into. He'd seen and met every type of paranormal known to man, even the djinn before Jamie had turned into one herself, and succubi were some of the rarest.

He couldn't wait to see her come into her own, to see Jace do the same within their bond. He'd been alone so long...he didn't know how to be anything else other than who he was. That would change though, and he knew that he'd never be able to let them go now.

Their bonds would take time to form fully and strengthen the fragility they held now. When they were all ready, all at the point where they would be functioning as a unit at peace, he would be able to see Nadie bloom into a warrior far greater than he. It wouldn't be like what others thought when they thought of succubi. They weren't sexual leeches, but warriors who fed differently than others and were stronger fighters than many paranormals. She would have the ability to use the self-confidence she'd hidden for so long.

He'd seen too much in his time, yet he couldn't wait to see what would happen next.

He tended to live in the present; however, unlike some paranormals, he didn't try to think about how long he'd been alive and what he'd seen. He'd been there during the rise and fall of countless civilizations and watched the humans become who they were now almost at the beginning of the humans' existence. He'd seen them when they'd forgotten the other realms around them and thought themselves the only types of creatures in the world worth being. Though there were dragons far older than him, those tended to live within the dragon realm far away from the humans.

In fact, most dragons stayed in their own realm. They also preferred to be in their dragon forms while they worked, played, and did most things. They might be large and have claws, but they still had the dexterity to do what they wanted. Everything in their realm was also made to fit them so it worked out. Though sex was still something they did in their human forms. Some lines weren't meant to be crossed. Dragons even gave birth as humans, the same as all paranormals. If someone higher up in the dragon echelon actually thought hard about it, it had already been determined which side was more dominant between genetics and magic, and that would shake their elitist foundation to the core.

So they didn't think about it.

What was odd to Dante was other dragons' distaste for their human bodies. After all, humans were descendants of dragons and all other paranormals. Each shifter, fae, brownie, and other paranormal had always had the ability to shift to their human form.

They just hadn't always called it that.

It had once been so they could mask themselves from the others. Yes, they'd also needed magic to hide their signature scents that revealed who and what they were, but the human form was one that each had so they could blend easily within *the others*—the supernaturals themselves. It wasn't until the actual first humans had been born, without another form to shift into, that the supernaturals had to use their human forms to hide from other *humans.*

It was rare for a dragon to want to be in their far weaker human form for any longer than deemed necessary, but Dante wasn't like most dragons.

He liked the feeling of blending with the ones who might be weaker than him physically but contained within themselves the potential for something far greater.

They could change, adapt, and evolve.

Dragons were set in their ways. A fact that, to Dante, seemed detrimental to their very existence, though not many agreed. It was like that for many paranormals though. They were within their own realms and only a few types even mingled with humans on a daily basis. The shifters had their dens within the human realm since they technically didn't have realms of their own, but they were so hidden by magic, they were like realms of their own

Each realm had its own government, society, cities, rules, histories, and everything else that came with ruling over a civilization.

Including war, famine, and peace.

The humans were unaware of what lay around them, something that Dante didn't think would change anytime soon. The realms were hidden by magic and an age-old ability that there was no way humans would be able to find them.

The only way the humans would find out was if a supernatural flat-out told them.

Since that had almost happened with an angel on the

warpath only two years ago, maybe Dante should suppress his thoughts on that matter.

"Dante?"

The sound of Jace's voice jarred him out of his worries, and he turned to the bear who was shirtless but had put on a pair of Dante's sleep pants to walk into the kitchen. He held back a grin. He and Jace might have similar waist sizes, but the man was at least three inches taller and the bottom of the pants clearly showed some ankle.

It was kind of odd being the shorter one in a relationship considering he didn't find many people his height or taller outside of the dragon realm. Jace was one big fucking grizzly. His shoulders were broader, and Dante was pretty sure the man's arms and thighs were bigger too. Dante might have once thought himself huge, but then he'd met Jace.

He held back another grin at the thought of just what else was big on Jace. They would have time to explore each other in more detail later. Last night had been about Nadie, with her being the center. Dante could still remember the feeling of her tight pussy around his cock and, later, Jace's tight ass squeezing him as well.

He shifted slightly so his now-filling dick wouldn't tent his pajama bottoms any more than they probably already were. He'd had only a taste of both his mates the night before and hadn't had enough of Jace to sate even a fraction of his thirst. There would be time for more, and with so many people in bed, there would be many further tastes, positions, orientations, and just about anything else to enjoy before anyone was truly sated.

"I didn't mean to wake you," Dante finally said, his voice a little more gruff than he'd meant it to be. He couldn't help it, considering where his mind had wandered off to.

Jace just rolled his eyes and leaned in for a kiss. Dante sighed into him, savoring the light pressure and softness of his mate's lips. They weren't as soft as Nadie's—nothing he'd ever felt was—but they were perfect in his eyes.

He had to hold back a groan. He really needed to get his mind out of the unicorns and rainbows that was his love life and back into the darkness he was about to step foot into.

Not that he really wanted to tell Jace that, though the man, and the woman they'd left in bed, deserved to know.

Since he'd promised Nadie that he wouldn't keep secrets that affected them, he had no choice but to tell Jace why he was out of bed and why he wouldn't be there when Nadie woke up. He'd needed to leave about five minutes ago as it was. He was going to get in trouble.

Crap.

"You didn't wake me up," Jace finally said as he padded over to the coffee pot. Dante had one of those single cup coffee makers so he never had to choose what he wanted until he was thirsty. He'd lived long enough that he'd tried just about every form and way to make coffee. He didn't mind moving on to whatever was popular in the moment. Plus, it was easy as hell to have a cup of coffee when he wanted without having to waste a whole pot.

Now he knew he was ignoring the issue at hand if he was thinking about coffee and wasting pots of it.

"You have flavored creamer or just milk?" Jace asked, and before Dante could answer, the bear went to the fridge, got out the amaretto-flavored creamer he had on hand, and came back for his cup, which was now done.

It wasn't lost on him that, though Jace tried to act like a guest by asking the right questions, he was also right at home.

"I like you here, you know," Dante finally said.

Jace smiled over his cup, a knowing look in his eyes. "I like being here."

"You also act like you own the place. Something I like, too."

Jace rolled his eyes again and leaned against the counter. "I'm used to not living at my place in the den. I'm out more than in these days, so I can usually find my way around a kitchen if it's organized. Sometimes, though, people are idiots and put the plates near the trash can and the cups near the stove and the seasonings far away from the oven."

Dante tried to remember if he'd put his things in any form of order other than how he'd always had them then shrugged. "If something is in the wrong place for your delicate organizational sensibilities, feel free to change it. I might get lost, but change is good for me. Don't want to get set in my ways."

Jace took another sip of his coffee then set the cup down on the counter. He crossed his arms over his chest then leveled a look at Dante. The bear acted the cheerful man most times, but it was damn hard to hide things from such an astute being.

Namely Dante's thoughts.

"We wouldn't want that. Now you gonna tell me what you've been hiding from me? You're up way too early for a man who just spent the night prior wrapped around the sweetest and sexiest woman either of us has ever had—not to mention the fact you left me there too. You wouldn't have done that if something wasn't on your mind. Something that was heavy enough to leave a woman alone, one who just happened to have turned into a succubus of all things."

Dante let out a breath, knowing a small tendril of smoke escaped his nostrils. He knew that wouldn't surprise Jace. The man had seen him as a dragon before when they'd first met and were discovering each other and finding out if they could last as a couple before they found their third, but it didn't make him feel any better that he was worried enough to blow smoke.

Literally.

"I've been summoned."

"By who? Your council?" Gone was the lazy bear; the Mediator stood in his place. Jace had been through his own forms of war since he'd been born and had been god-touched as a Mediator.

It was also because of that role that Jace would know what the Conclave was and how they differed from the council that each realm held—another reason Dante wanted to hold back.

He couldn't though. "No, not by my council."

Jace frowned. "By another council? Can they really summon you? You're a dragon of the Azure House."

Dante held back an eye roll at the mention of his Royal House. Yes, he was a prince of the dragons. Technically. No one, however, had used that title in centuries around him since he didn't like it. Dragon society had tiers, named for the color of their scales. Most dragons were settled into their family Houses. In Dante's family, since they were all black dragons, they were from the Obsidian House. Dante was special in that he had been born with partially blue scales, hence why he was of a different house than his blood family.

One reason he didn't speak of them much.

Or ever.

The Azure House was one of two actual Royal Houses, and it was not based on blood, but by being god-touched. They ruled alongside the council within the realm.

At least that was what they said they did. Dante had never been part of it. He'd stayed away or at least far enough away that he didn't have to become responsible for a realm that didn't understand him or care about what he wanted or desired.

Dante tended to stay away from that, and again, he wasn't summoned by the dragons.

No, this was far worse.

"Jace, it wasn't a council that summoned me. It was the Conclave."

Jace's eyes went wide, and he paled, his body visibly shaking. "Oh shit. Oh *shit*, Dante."

Dante went straight to his mate and cupped his face, lowering him down so they were eye-to-eye. "Breathe. It'll be okay. It's just a summons." There was no such thing as *just a summons*, and both of them knew that. The lie, though, would calm them both down. "Not an execution order. I haven't done anything wrong."

Technically.

He'd helped each of his friends through their own battles with the other realms, something that was not forbidden, but it was frowned upon for a dragon. Dragons were supposed to be the supernaturals that stayed out of the business of others, as it was their way.

The Conclave, however, was something far worse than any council.

They were the council above all other councils, one that not even all supernaturals knew existed. Some would call them the gods that created the realms themselves since the masses didn't know the true breadth of the Conclave's powers, but Dante knew differently.

The Conclave was made up of two of each realm and only the councils, Mediators, and a select few, like him, were even privy to its existence. Its role, or so it claimed, was to provide a balance between the realms and ensure the species councils acted within their realms accordingly.

Considering what Dante had seen within some of the realms like the leprechauns, djinn, and even the hell realm with Lucifer himself, he wasn't quite sure what *accordingly* meant. Those who held a Conclave seat were far older than Dante and worked slow. They took each measure into consideration and decided something after each outcome was investigated and thought of to the point of death in most cases.

Dante had never cared for the Conclave—though he would never say that out loud. Each member gained new power as they rose into the ranks. The power was not only political within the realm's council, but something that was within their blood and would be an actual *power*. They'd become stronger, faster, and learned a new skill that Dante still couldn't figure out. It was something that happened within the Conclave once they were magically tied in.

He had no recourse for that.

He also had no idea why they would summon *him*. It might have been because he'd helped his friends, but he wasn't sure.

"Dante," Jace finally said, his voice ragged, the fear in the air so thick Dante could taste it. "Why would they summon you? It doesn't make any sense."

"I know. That's why I hope it's for something small." *Or maybe just to say hello. A dragon could dream.*

"You don't think it's about your parents, do you? Or your brother and sister?"

Dante gave a quick shake of his head then grimaced. "I haven't seen them in over a hundred years, and even then, it was by pure accident. I don't think they'd do anything to warrant the Conclave's attention."

Jace merely raised a brow, and Dante conceded the point.

"Fine. Knowing my mother, she *might* do something so

idiotic and barbaric it could warrant their attention, but I don't know why they'd summon *me* for it."

"You are the reasonable one of the family. And a royal. They might want your help."

They were reaching at straws, and they both knew it. "The only way we're going to find out is for me to go. Which I need to do now since I've held back long enough. I wanted to wait for you to get back to the human realm from your mission first."

Jace's eyes widened. "How long have you been sitting on that summons?"

"Not long," he lied.

"Dante."

"Three weeks."

Four, but who was counting?

"Dante. I can smell your lie and feel it in our bond. Stop protecting me."

Dante ran a hand through his hair then leaned into Jace's hold. "Fine. A month. Today actually. So it's good timing. I need to go now, and I'd rather not wake up Nadie."

Jace narrowed his eyes. "What did you *just* promise her?"

Dante growled, another tendril of smoke escaping his nostril. "I tried waking her to tell her and you an hour ago, but she's out cold. She expelled a lot of energy, and I don't want to tell her without her being at full strength. I'm not keeping it from her. I just need to go. Now."

"I'm going to tell her where you are then," Jace warned, and Dante relaxed. "Which is what you wanted all along."

Dante opened his mouth to speak then shook his head.

"No, that wasn't what I wanted. I'm strong enough to fight my own battles, but I don't want to worry her. I also promised her I wouldn't keep things from her."

Jace kissed him hard, leaving him breathless and surprising him. "Be safe. You got that? You need to come back here and be our third because we just found this, and I'm not about to let you go. I will tell her. We can at least use this as something positive." He gave a shaky smile. "This way we can talk about things and find a path that is just us."

"You both need that. Nadie and I need it as well. You and I too."

Jace grinned. "We will get all of that. We have time. Damn it. We better have time because the Conclave can't have you."

Dante closed his eyes. "I'll come back to you, Jace."

"And I'm telling Nadie *exactly* where you are and what the Conclave is. It's her right to know since I'm a Mediator."

Dante let out a breath then wrapped his arms around Jace. "Good. Be safe, my bear, and keep our mate safe as well."

Jace gripped the back of his head and brought him in for a kiss. "Come back to us."

CHAPTER 7

The sun beat down on Dante's face, and the wind brushed through his hair as he walked to the clearing he'd told Nadie and Jace about the day before. Had it really been only a day since he'd shown his mates his house and welcomed them into his life and home.

He paused. No, he hadn't shown Nadie his house.

Well, shit.

They'd made love, and then, their bodies spent, all three had passed out in a pile on his bed. Dante pinched the bridge of his nose, knowing he needed to be a better suitor if he was going to deserve Nadie's love and bond.

Yes, he might have the bond, and he thought he might have her love, though it was still too early to tell, but he surely didn't deserve it right now. Nadie was human, or at least had been raised as such. She deserved something more than what she was getting. He would just have to make sure she got it.

Hopefully, Jace would show her around or at least find his own way around the house. Dante had left the bear in the kitchen, declining his offer to accompany him to at least the clearing. Dante had wanted to ensure Nadie's safety and peace of mind by having Jace there. Though there might not be an actual reason for the safety concerns, Dante was old enough to have made enemies that might want to hurt his newly bonded mates, and he wasn't taking chances with their lives.

Jace would be able to take care of her, even though he didn't know what he would be protecting her from.

When he got back, he would see to courting the woman he should have been courting all along. He knew now Nadie was stronger than he'd given her credit for. The blood running through her veins was a testament to that. He should have told her why he was staying away instead of hurting her.

The dragon would have to grovel.

First, he'd have to meet with the Conclave. He and Jace hadn't said it, but they both knew that this meeting could take time that neither of them wanted to lose. The Conclave worked slow and could take him away from Nadie and Jace far longer than he wanted.

He should have woken Nadie or at least tried harder to when he could have. Yes, she had been drained and had passed out from her change, but he should have said goodbye.

He'd been too afraid of the words, and now it was too late.

For all the strength within his body, he still wasn't strong enough to do what was good for him and his life.

He ran a hand through his hair that he'd left flowing down his back. There was no use putting it up when he was about to shift to his dragon. The Conclave met as their respective species, meaning since he was a dragon he came as a dragon. Those that were dual natured and didn't have a dominant paranormal—like the children of two different paranormals—would come as the one the Conclave desired.

Though most of those who shifted had to take off their clothes in order to turn into their other form, dragons were different. They could bring their clothes with them during their shift because it was part of their magic. Anything that the dragon considered its personal realm would shift and disappear along with the human. Though they couldn't hide sentient beings so even if his dragon thought of his mates as its own, it couldn't hide them away. Once the dragon shifted back to human, they would magically bring back the clothes.

Elders still weren't exactly sure where the clothes went, other than it was a magic older than the idea of dragons themselves, so it was a common acceptance that it just...did. Also, unlike with some shifters, it didn't hurt Dante to shift.

Dante closed his eyes and thought of his dragon. Warmth and a sweet sensation danced over his skin. He knew if he opened his eyes he'd see a bright flash of light and others would see the human no more.

In its place stood a black and blue dragon larger than most houses. There were many variations of dragons, just like there were many variations of people. Some looked like the Far East versions depicted in human writings while he and his family looked more like the dragons in Western lore. He might have different color scales than his family, but the overall shape was similar. His scales glistened under the light, and he stretched out his talons, getting ready for the flight that was to come.

He swished his tail and bowed his head. He loved his dragon form, though his family thought differently. He just happened to love his human form with equal measure. That was not to be tolerated within his blood line.

Hence, why Dante, like always, was a little different.

He lowered his snout to the envelope he'd placed in the center of the clearing and blew a small tendril of smoke over it. The writing on the front swirled, and he let out a stream of fire, igniting the words. His name on the front burned, and then, in the blink of an eye, he found himself in the foyer of an immense building he'd never entered in all his life.

He had heard of the Conclave and knew what to do with the summons, but he'd never been there before.

He prayed he would be allowed to leave.

He prayed he'd never have to come again.

The building was a large ornate structure with intricate carvings that depicted various paranormals. If he were to look around the entire thing, he guessed that every paranormal in existence would be represented. The ceiling was a gold-painted dome that, oddly enough, didn't look ostentatious. It merely suited the grandness of the building.

Dante took a deep breath through his nose, trying to scent where he was but came up empty. He'd been to every realm there was and knew their scents. Even if the overall layers would change, the basic principles of each realm would remain the same, meaning Dante would be able to recognize it no matter what.

Since he couldn't distinguish the scent, that meant he was in a realm he'd never been in before.

Astonishing.

Not that he wanted to spend any more time here than necessary. Oh no, he wanted to go back to Nadie and Jace as soon as he could.

Preferably now.

He inhaled again and caught the barest of scents of the others in the building. He had a feeling once he was let through the large doors—large enough to let him and his entire wingspan through—he'd be able to scent the entirety of the Conclave. There must have been a type of dampening spell on the actual room where they met.

Dante wasn't even sure if the Conclave was made up of supernaturals who never left this realm or if they were actually supernaturals who lived within their own realms with their own hidden identities.

For all he thought he knew, he really didn't know much.

"Dante Bell, do enter." A disembodied voice echoed

through the foyer, and Dante steeled himself. He would not act like a new shifter and show any form of fear or even awe at what he saw.

After all, he was old enough that not much surprised him.

The large doors opened of their own accord, and Dante stepped through them with his head held high. They might have summoned him, but he'd be damned if he'd let them know he had something to lose.

That was the first step in protecting those you cared about—not letting others know they were your weakness.

"I see you've finally answered the summons," a djinn said from his chair.

The room was so immense that he wasn't sure he'd be able to see everyone without his keen eyesight. From what he knew, there were around five hundred different paranormals. At least. That meant there were over a thousand leaders in this room, sitting two by two, their chairs and seating areas looking more like opera boxes than anything else. The boxes, for lack of a better word, rose up to the ceiling where the others could look down at Dante standing in the center of the room.

As a dragon, he was the largest of paranormal creatures, yet right then, he'd never felt so insignificant. So small.

"I've come as requested," he said, his voice low, bland. He didn't want to show them any inkling of where his thoughts might lie. He knew they were powerful, but he didn't know *how* powerful they were.

He'd like to be able to live to see Nadie and Jace again.

"You could have been quicker," a merman said from his small pool within his box, his fin carelessly swishing water on the floor in front of Dante.

From the look on the merman's face, maybe it wasn't so careless as much as it was deliberate. He hated politics and mind games, and he'd just wandered into the Olympic version of lies and blind truths.

"I arrived as directed," Dante said, his tone as bland as he could make it. He could swallow that merman in one gulp and use his fin to pick the bones from his teeth, but he'd hold back.

For now.

"Do you know why you've been summoned?" One of the two dragon Conclave members asked him.

This one was older than the other if the slight dullness of his scales were any indication. Dragons were practically immortal they were so long-lived, but even the eldest of dragons changed over time. If this dragon had been spending most of its time indoors within the Conclave, it made sense the dragon would begin to fade, to dull.

Dragons needed the air on their scales and under their wings as much as angels like Shade and Ambrose.

Dante faced the older dragon, Alexander—yes, that was his name. It had been a millennium since he'd seen the old one, but he'd never forget the power that radiated from the dragon.

"I don't know the reason you've sent for me, only that I was to come. One doesn't ignore the Conclave."

Murmurs of agreement filled the room, but Dante

ignored most of them, trying to at least get a sense of who was there and if he needed to find a way to flee. There would be no fighting for him, not when he was this outnumbered. He would fight until his last breath, but he wouldn't win. Not here. Not now.

He still didn't know if the Conclave was friend or foe; however, Dante wasn't sure it mattered. They were far more powerful than he was, and even a friend in that position wouldn't sit comfortable with him.

Dante had been correct in assuming they had more power than he, but he'd been wrong in one clear sense. At least two of the members of the conclave were far, far younger than he. One of the wizards and a fae were less than a thousand years old. No, they weren't young men or as young as Jace even, but they weren't as old as the others in the Conclave. If he had to guess, he figured that some of the Conclave's ranks were beginning to shift.

A small tendril of fear slid up his spine.

This would not be good.

"You should be aware the Conclave has been following you for quite some time," Alexander said, his voice low and steady, as if he had all the time in the world to get to his point.

Dante frowned and lowered his snout. "Following?" He hadn't felt a presence following him, and he was damned good at spotting anyone looking for him.

The other dragon waved a claw and rolled his eyes. The younger dragon by his side snorted, an annoyed expression his face.

"We've known of you. You know of us because of your Royal House, yet you would have been on our radar regardless because of the sin you committed against the demon realm."

Dante held back a growl.

He'd made one mistake that he *still* didn't believe was a mistake, and it had haunted him for almost three hundred years.

He didn't say anything as there didn't seem to be any use. The other dragon would make his point eventually. Dante just hoped it would be before he rolled over and died.

"You killed the demon Conclave member to save a friend of yours, do you remember?"

The room silenced, and Dante raised his head high. It wasn't as if what he'd done was a secret to anyone in this room. He'd killed a member of their Conclave. Of course they would know. They'd been the ones who had given him his sentence—even if he'd never actually met them.

"Yes. He was killing a woman I considered to be under my protection." He wouldn't lie. There was no use. The kill had been justified. It didn't matter that the demon had held higher power than Dante in the grand scheme of things.

"You were banished from the entire hell realm because of it."

"I would do it again."

Again, no use in lying.

Murmurs filled the room again, this time some sounding on his side—including the two younger members.

Good.

"You saved the Goodwin bear and killed the demon," the wizard interrupted. "And now, by a twist of fate, that bear is the paternal grandmother of your new mate."

Dante clenched his jaw.

"Levi, you're ruining my fun by jumping in," Alexander.

"You would have taken too long to get there," the fae added.

"Tristan, don't help," Levi mumbled, and Dante held back a grin.

Under other circumstances he might have wanted to get to know Tristan and Levi. Right now, though, he wanted to leave and go back to Jace and Nadie. That didn't look like it would happen any time soon.

"You were banned from hell because you killed the demon conclave member," Alexander repeated. "You saved your mate's grandmother before your mate was even born. Such a twist of fate should not be ignored."

"Nor will it," one of the demons put it.

Dante wanted to ignore it. He wanted nothing to do with it. Jace's family knew what happened, and that's how he'd met Jace. He'd come back to the bear's den after being away for a long while and found his mate within the family that had taken him in. He'd save Jace's grandmother again and kill the demon just like he'd done before, but that didn't mean he wanted to be part of whatever plans the Conclave had for him.

"What is it you want?" he asked, fed up with their slow pace.

"I'm retiring," Alexander said, and Dante held his breath.

Fuck. That's exactly what he'd thought. He didn't want this and surely didn't want Alexander to complete whatever he wanted to say.

"You have been chosen as my replacement. You will begin your duties right away. To train, you must do as your brethren have done. All species have different time restraints, but as a dragon, you must stay within the Conclave realm for five hundred years before you will be allowed to leave. You will learn your new powers and learn how to rule. Only then will you be able to return to this home you have grown so fond of."

Dante blinked and held back a growl, a small tendril of smoke floating from his nostril. "Do I have no say in this?"

Five hundred years away from his mates? No, hell no. His body felt hollow, aching at just the thought of being without them. The Conclave couldn't take him from Nadie and Jace. They wouldn't be that cruel.

Dante, though, new *exactly* how cruel they could be.

Alexander looked perplexed. "Why would you say no?"

Dante tried to form his words carefully. He'd already been banned from one realm because of the Conclave. It wouldn't do to add another.

Or be killed for voicing his own desires.

"I've just found my mates and have newly formed the bond. I can't stay away from them for that long. They need me as I need them."

"Ah yes, the bear whose fate is entwined with yours and this human…who isn't so human, is she?"

There was something about the way the dragon said the

latter that had Dante's dragon standing on edge, but he put it to the side for now. He had to get out of there and get to his mates. Then he could worry about everything else and all the nuisances that came with this meeting.

"You don't say no to the Conclave," the merman said.

"I can't leave my mates." He wouldn't. Five hundred years might seem like nothing to a dragon, but a newly mated dragon needed their mates. Plus Nadie was still human in nature. She needed him. And Jace…

No, Dante wouldn't leave them behind.

"As he's newly mated, he should at least have time to… think about it," Levi put in while Tristan nodded.

Dante wanted to reach out and hug the two men, but held back. He'd give his thanks later…after he watched them for any hidden agenda for their help. One could never be too careful.

"Why would he say no?" the old dragon asked. "This is power, the most to be had in our realm. You'd be revered."

"I'd rather be with my mates," he said honestly.

"You dare defy me?" Alexander asked, and the room hushed.

He had to tread carefully here. "I need a choice. I need… time to consider," he lied. There would be no considering. No, he'd only spend the time to figure a way out of doing this. "I need to be with the two I have newly bonded with. True halves are something that are sacred. I can't break with that."

The dragon narrowed his eyes, and Dante knew he

hadn't fooled him. "You can go with your mates, but we will call for you again. Soon. You will give us your...answer then."

He forced himself not to react, only to keep his head raised. His gaze traveled to the two young members, who gave him nods. What that meant, he didn't know, but he had a feeling he would not be alone for long. These two seemed to be on his side. At least that's what he hoped.

"Don't disappoint us," Alexander said as a parting shot, and Dante held his breath.

The room disappeared, and he found himself in the clearing where he'd started earlier.

Holy gods, this was bad. This was worse than bad.

He didn't know how he would tell the others, but he had no choice. He'd promised Nadie no secrets.

How was he going to tell her that, though he'd finally had her in his arms, he'd now have to leave? For if he said no to the Conclave, Dante had a feeling he wouldn't live to tell the tale.

One, after all, didn't say no to the Conclave.

"HE SAID NO! DID YOU HEAR THAT?" ROCK SCREAMED AS HE paced the room in his human form. He'd just come back from Alexander's after the old bat of a dragon informed him that Dante had wanted time.

Time? Fuck that.

The fucking dragon prince, or whatever he liked to be called, should have gone down on his knees and thanked the Conclave's ass that he'd been sought after in the first place. Rock, on the other hand, had been looked over. What the fuck was up with that?

He was supposed to be the one who gained the power from their ranks. He'd been the one who had been by Alexander's side for so long, and how did the old fuck repay him?

By tossing him aside for the perfect Dante.

"Of course I heard, darling," the dragoness purred through lips that were overly plump on her skinny face.

He still thought she was fucking hot, and the way she rode his cock and sucked it through those fat lips of hers made everything worth it.

"Then what are we going to do about it, Stacia?"

She patted his cheek then laid on the bed, spreading herself for him. "We will find a way to fix this. My son, that bastard of a dragon, should not have said no. I raised him with the every care I could give, and yet he's betrayed all of us."

Rock slid into her, pumping his hips. He liked the feel of her around him and knew it would take off the edge. Her nails dug into his skin, making him bleed, and he growled. He spent himself then pulled out, throwing his body next to hers on the bed. She was always a quick fuck when he was angry, and considering her husband would probably be back any minute, he had to hurry anyway. He didn't care if she came or not since it took for-freaking-ever for her to do it. She usually just faked it for him if she didn't come right away.

"What are we going to do? I was going to have all the power and have you by my side." Well, maybe not that last part, but he needed Stacia, so he'd use her while he could.

The dragoness patted her breasts then sighed. "My darling, think. We can't have the power if he's part of the Conclave. Dante has long since ignored the family. Bastard," she spat. "What we can do though is...ensure that he won't be a problem and won't come back to be part of the Conclave at all."

Rock narrowed his eyes. "If he says no, the Conclave will kill him."

Stacia rolled her heavily made up eyes. "That's a chance we can't take. What if he were to say yes?"

"What are you saying?"

Stacia sighed then stroked his cock. He always seemed to think better with her hands on him. "If we kill him before he has a chance to say no, then he can't be in power, can he?"

Rock swallowed hard, her hand squeezing just right so he came again on his belly. "Kill him? Yes. We can do that."

Stacia giggled then patted his chest. "Good. Now do be a dear and clean up before Udell gets home. You know how fickle he gets when I smell like another man's seed. When you come back after he leaves, I do hope you have news of Dante's demise. That would really put a hop in my step."

The woman was clearly demented, but Rock loved the way she thought.

"Consider it done." He smacked her ass then walked out of the room, naked and annoyingly still hard.

With Dante dead, Alexander would finally see who should be the one in charge. Rock smiled and shifted to his dragon form. Yes, that sounded like a plan indeed.

CHAPTER 8

"Are you sure he's okay?" Nadie wrung her hands together, that prickly feeling on the back of her neck not going away no matter what Jace had said before.

She'd woken up alone in bed, the smell of coffee tickling her senses. She'd been in such a haze of needing caffeine that she hadn't thought about the fact she'd been alone, pleasantly sore, and in need of time to think about what she'd done.

What she'd become.

She's called her job right away, letting them know she needed to take a leave of absence. They had been relatively understanding about the whole thing considering she had given them warning. All of the women had put plans in place to take time away from their daily human lives in case they were thrust in a new change, a new world. In Nadie's case, she'd warned them she'd need to leave because of family reasons and had a replacement lined up. Her school was very private and very unique in that they actually cared about the teachers and their needs. She hated having to leave, but she couldn't do it all. Ever since Jamie had been taken to hell and had lost so much time, the girls had been smarter. Rather than scramble around, trying to fit their new lives into their old lives, they would step away and try to find a new balance.

That meant that someone else would be teaching her children from now on. At least until she got a handle on what it meant to be a succubus, have two mates, and have a new world to immerse herself into.

All of that, though, was on the back burner while she sat in the living room with Jace, needing to have him reassure her.

Again.

Her bear ran a hand through her hair, and the large calloused palm seemed as big as her face. She inhaled his scent, the earthy tone seemingly richer, more decadent that morning than it had been when she'd been fully human.

"He will be fine, Nadie."

She turned so she was facing him on the couch but still touching him. "I don't know if I believe you because I don't think you believe it yourself."

Jace sighed and pulled her into his lap. She leaned into him, surprising herself at the ache for him, the need for the bond to pulse and remind her she wasn't alone anymore.

"He told me he would come back, and he will. You know Dante enough to know that when he says something he means it." Jace squeezed her tighter. "He'll do whatever he has to in order to come back to us."

She let out a breath and closed her eyes. "And the Conclave? They won't hurt him?"

Jace had come to her as soon as she'd woken up, explaining about the Conclave and the summons Dante had received. He'd yet to explain *why* Dante had left without a word, and Nadie had a feeling even Jace didn't know.

That was another thing she and her dragon would have to discuss.

He couldn't keep treating her like fragile glass when it came to big decisions. Leaving her asleep while he went off to a group of paranormals that could hurt him classified as one of those things that he needed to at least mention to her.

Not just tell his messenger.

Apparently she was still a little peeved at that.

"Nadie, honey, I don't know." She winced at his honesty but didn't interrupt him. "I have no idea what the Conclave wanted with him, and, fuck, I was so scared when Dante told me where he was going. I'm one huge-ass grizzly, and I wanted to cower under the table and hide the two of you away forever."

She blinked at him. He needed to work on his whole don't-freak-out-Nadie thing.

He moved her so she was straddling him and they faced each other. "That doesn't mean the worst though, Nadie. All that means is that I know of the whispers and stories I was told when I found out I was god-touched and a Meditator.

117

Dante is stronger than anyone else I know, and he wouldn't have left if he hadn't had a way back."

She didn't know if he was lying to himself or trying to keep a good outlook, but either way, sitting there and fretting wasn't getting anything accomplished. She'd spent most of her life fretting over one thing or another, and she didn't want to spend the next part of her journey doing more of the same.

"There's nothing we can do right now about it other than worry some more, so let's try to think of something else," she said, surprised at how calm her voice sounded.

Inside she was a mess of contradictions, regrets, and fear, but right then, she wasn't sure Jace could tell. From the way his brows lowered, she was probably wrong about that.

"We can do that. Now, why don't you tell me what's on your mind that puts that little crease between your eyebrows, right here." He traced the spot with his finger, and she closed her eyes, unsure of what she was going to say...how she was going to say it.

"I feel like a slut. No, that's not it. I feel like I should *feel* like a slut. But I don't."

Okay, apparently she was going with the blurting-it-out method.

Jace growled, a low sound that vibrated along her bones and deep in her belly. She froze, her inner succubus—if that's what she wanted to call it—on alert at the danger in the room.

"You. Are. Not. A. Slut."

She shivered at the intensity of his words but didn't drop her gaze.

"Why would you even say that?" he asked, his look piercing.

Nadie swallowed hard, unbelieving he would even ask that question considering where she was sitting. "I slept with you and Dante last night. Together. Others might think that makes me slutty."

He narrowed his eyes. "We're your mates. Are you saying what we did was wrong? The bond we now share is somehow now abhorrent?"

Her heart hurt at his words, but she shook her head. "No, that's not what I meant. Stop twisting up my words."

Jace lowered his forehead to hers. "Then tell me precisely what you meant, Nadie."

She licked her lips, ignoring the way her bear followed the movement. No, this was *not* the time for those kinds of thoughts—even though they were yummy, warm, and oh so tempting.

"I met you less than two days ago, and now I'm sitting on your lap after mating with you. I was a *virgin* before last night, Jace. And now I've slept with two men and want to do it again. We didn't talk about anything other than the fact that we felt that spark and wanted to know more. What kind of person does that make me? And the thing is, I don't care. All I know is that it felt good and I shouldn't be feeling bad that I *don't* feel bad about it."

Jace growled again and nipped her lip. He licked the sting, and she shuddered at his taste. "You are a succubus,

Nadie Morgan. You've always had that dominant strain of DNA in your body. That's why you are the way you are. Having sex with your mates is *not* wrong. The hunger you felt for us was intensified because of the blood running through your veins. We are mates, Nadie. We might have come to this point backward and turned around, but that doesn't mean we weren't meant to be. So what if we have the bond already? So what if you crave the carnal side of our relationship as much as Dante and I do? All that means is that we're a match and we can give each other whatever the other needs. Also, even if you weren't a succubus? Who the fuck cares? Sex isn't a bad thing, and you don't feel bad about what we did. So don't harp on what others might think because they are too close-minded to think beyond what good girls do. Fuck them."

He made it all sound simple, but it wasn't. The whole idea of what she'd done and the changes in her life that came from it was almost too much to bear. She wouldn't, though, keep whining about it. Regrets and indecisiveness would not be part of the new Nadie Morgan.

"So you're telling me my overwhelming urge to ride you like a pony is because I'm a succubus?"

Jace blinked then threw his head back and laughed. "You can ride me any time you want. That image just then? Fucking amazing. I also want to point out that I think Dante and I had something to do with that urge." He raised a brow. "You don't want to ride anyone in general, just me and Dante, right?"

She scrunched up her nose. "Someone else? God no. I've

always only wanted Dante." She kissed his chin, at ease with his laughter. "And now you of course. That doesn't mean I'm ready to act all wanton and fall into bed every hour of every day."

"We don't have to *just* make love in a bed."

Jace's face was so serious that Nadie broke out into laughter and leaned on him again.

"Why were you feeling that way, Nadie?" Jace asked. "I have a feeling that this didn't come out of nowhere."

She sighed, not wanting to get into her past, but knowing it was inevitable and needed. "I don't want you to pity me for what I'm about to say."

Jace frowned but nodded. "I will never pity you. Tell me."

"I grew up knowing I had to be perfect, pure Nadie Morgan, or I would disappoint my parents. You see, my parents were far older when they had me than when they had my two sisters. My parents got married young and had Jessica and Heather, my sisters, right away. Jessica is only about fifteen months older than Heather while Heather is eighteen years older than me."

Jace's eyes widened. "Quite a gap for humans."

She snorted at that but kept going. "My parents wanted two perfect children and ended up with girls who wanted to prove to their parents they could get away with anything they wanted. Now, I'm not saying that Heather and Jessica are completely in the right on this because God no, that's not the case, but they had reasons for doing what they did."

"What did they do?"

"My parents were—*are*—very strict. None of us were

allowed to watch TV, eat sugar, have friends who were boys, or even go over to friends' houses if they had brothers. Our parents wanted perfect, pure little girls. What they got were Heather and Jessica. Instead of explaining to the girls when they were teens what it meant to be safe, protected, and responsible, they preached that girls shouldn't date boys and they should only have sex when they were married with the perfectly approved boy from a good family. So very puritanical but that is who my parents are."

"I take it that Heather and Jessica didn't respond well to that."

Nadie shook her head. "Oh hell no. They both drank, smoked pot and cigarettes, and lost their virginities at four-teen or so."

"Jesus." Jace's eyes widened, and she let out a breath.

"Heather got pregnant at sixteen and Jessica at seven-teen. So you see, I have two nephews who are older than me."

"I thought that only happened in paranormal realms where everyone is so long-lived that family trees get complicated."

Nadie shook her head. "No, it happened to us. Mom and Dad threw the girls out one by one. They ended up living with the fathers of their babies. I don't really know them. I was born in the aftermath."

Jace pulled her into a hug, and she sighed. "I've seen them before and have tried to form a relationship because, though they made bad choices as teens, it wasn't all their fault. They learned from their mistakes, at least somewhat.

They finished high school, got jobs, and at least are trying to be adults. My parents though wiped the slate. They started over with me and were even more restrictive. There wasn't an opportunity for me to even break free and rebel." She kissed his chin. "At least until now."

Jace growled. "Your parents put too much pressure on you. I'd like to meet them and talk some sense into them, but I think it would be a lost cause."

She smiled at his tone. "It's okay. I don't talk with them much even though they still try to control me. By the time I was ready to rebel and do what I want, I'd met Dante, and I didn't really want to find another man. Even though I didn't know that we were mates at the time, I think, somewhere deep down, my mind wouldn't let me think of another person while Dante was in my life. At least in my life in a sense that we were friends. Does that make sense?"

"Perfect, Nadie. You're talking to a man who stayed celibate for way too long waiting to find you."

Her eyes widened. "I didn't even think about that! Oh, you poor bear and dragon."

Jace grinned. "We can talk about how you can repay me later," he teased.

She let out a breath and thought about what else they needed to talk about. "Tell me what it means to be a succubus. I don't like being in the dark, and yet that's how I've felt for far too long."

He ran a hand up and down her back. "I will tell you what I know. As a Mediator, I know about many of the realms because I need to in order to avoid conflicts and wars. Each realm has its council and set of rules that makes everything very complicated. However, I've yet to be called to the succubus realm. They pretty much govern themselves and leave everyone else alone."

Though she wanted to ask him about his experiences with the other realms, that would have to come later. "What *do* you know?"

"The succubi and incubi—those are the males of your species—live in a realm that is completely separated from the human realm but for a few small passageways. It's much like the angelic or demonic realms where one must have an invitation or know of the existence of the passageway itself in order to gain entry."

She moved so she could settle next to him, rather than remain on his lap. There was only so much a girl could take when it came to that jean-clad cock beneath her.

"The women tend to rule and have higher positions in the council, but I'm not a hundred percent sure on that. I believe Dante would know more about that. As for how all of that affects you? A succubus, as you can see, is marked with the brand of their house. I don't know what house you are part of with your ink, but we can look it up. Each house is ranked accordingly, and they have an odd hierarchy that means there's a lot of politics within the realm. That and the fact that their powers are so different than others makes them tend to stay away from outsiders."

Her mind was roiling with all the information being thrown out at her, but she still hadn't heard how her newfound powers would affect her—or what they even were.

Jace continued. "Each house carries a different ability, and each person has a different strength using that ability. I don't know what yours is, but we can find it together once you get a good handle on what you need to survive."

"What do you mean by that?"

Jace let out a breath. "Not all stories the humans know are false. Succubi need sex in order to live. They take energy from their partners during intercourse."

She blinked and moved to stand. "I took your energy? Is that the power I felt? Oh God, are you okay?" None of the other women had hurt their mates, and yet Nadie's powers were to suck away energy?

Jace pulled her close and cupped her cheek. "Hey, stop it. It didn't hurt, Nadie. In fact, to others, it would have felt like one fucking amazing orgasm. To Dante and me, since we're your mates, yeah, it was one fucking amazing orgasm, an orgasm to end all orgasms, but then we got our energy back. With the bond, we end up like a circuit, constantly sharing our life energies so that no one ends up weak and your inner succubus is healthy and sated."

She swallowed hard. "Oh, thank God."

"You never would have hurt someone. The succubi who grow up with their powers learn how to sleep with their partners and never take too much. If they sleep with another of their kind, the process acts much the same way it did with us, but on a smaller scale than a mating bond.

Because you have *two* mates, you will be one healthy, sexy succubus, Nadie."

She grinned at the cat-in-cream look on his face. "And you get nothing out of that?"

Jace chuckled, his voice deep, rough. "We can talk about all the...perks when Dante gets home. He wouldn't want to miss out on any of that."

She warmed all over at the thought of both her men and the...perks it all entailed. Oh, she couldn't wait to figure them all out, and from the look on Jace's face, she wouldn't be waiting for long.

CHAPTER 9

J ace lowered his head, and Nadie cupped his face, the
bristles of his scruff ticking her palms. His lips
pressed against hers, and she moaned, loving the taste
of this new man in her life. He wrapped his arms around
her, his hands sliding down her back to cup her ass. She
rocked against him, wanting him closer.

Something inside her heated, almost clawing at her,
craving the man in front of her.

Nadie stepped back, gasping for breath. Jace moved
toward her, and she looked up at him, the concern on his
face making her want to hide under a table. She hated this
feeling, the inability to control what she desired, unable to
know if it was truly *her* who wanted this bear, this man,
rather than the succubus that lived beneath her skin.

Jace cupped her face. "Hey, hey, what is it?"

She shook her head.

His thumb brushed along her lip, and she arched, wanting more. "Tell me."

She swallowed hard. If she didn't tell him, he'd just keep asking. She had a feeling Jace was just like his bear half. Once a bear wanted something, it pestered—or roared—until it got it.

"I just *really* like kissing you."

Jace blinked and tilted his head. "And this is a bad thing because..."

Nadie grimaced. "Because I don't know if it's me who wants it or *her*."

Jace took her hand and led her to the bar area off the corner of Dante's living room. She found it funny the dragon who owned his own bar had a smaller version in his house, but that thought left her mind as Jace gripped her hips, lifting her so she sat in front of him on the bar.

"Is there a reason you just picked me up like a doll and set me where you wanted me?" she asked, teasing.

Jace moved so he crowded her, arms on either side of her hips, his face close to hers. "You're a succubus, Nadie. You're going to want to feed and be with us. That's okay. You already said you weren't ashamed of it." She opened her mouth to speak, and he kissed her. She moaned into him then drew back, blinking. "Let me finish. Now, your succubus might want all of that, but your human half, the half that you've been all your life, wants it too. I'm not telling you what your body wants. I'm telling you that you don't have to question it. You're part of your succubus too.

She's not some invader controlling your body every hour of every day. So when you kiss me and wrap your arms around my neck, go with it. If you don't want to kiss me and would rather hang out on the couch and watch movies, then we can do that. Just don't second-guess yourself because you think it's wrong to want what you want."

Nadie smiled at the man she was just learning about and knew in her heart she was doing the right thing. Her mind might be a little behind, but it would catch up eventually. She pulled at his shirt, and he leaned forward, kissing her softly. Since she was at the right height to make it work, she wrapped her legs around his waist and pulled him closer. He growled a bit, pulling back to nip at her lip.

"So tell me, Nadie Morgan, what is one thing that you've never done but truly want to do?" He licked his lips, and she had a feeling she knew *exactly* what topic his mind was on.

She thought to all the gifs, books, and other things that she'd seen and tried to come up with something perfect for just her and Jace and their first time alone. Her gaze went to the tequila beside her, and she grinned.

"How about body shots?"

Jace's eyebrows rose before he grinned at her. Oh no, it wasn't just a normal grin. It was one of those grins that made her heat up from the inside out and want to wiggle against him until they were both panting.

"You've never done body shots?" Jace asked.

She shook her head. "Never. There was this one time I almost went to a new bar with Faith to try it out, but we backed out at the last second since it was raining or something."

Jace narrowed his eyes. "Good. I'll be your first. And you'll enjoy our bear shifter body shots. I promise."

"Bear shifter body shots? Uh, I'm not going to actually have to lick up your body while you're shifted, right? Not that I think you'd look horrible as a bear, because I'm sure you're adorable, cuddly, and *manly*," she added when his gaze narrowed, "manly and fierce, but licking up all that hair doesn't sound tasty. Or hygienic."

Jace threw his head back and laughed. "No, I'll be in human form. *Shirtless* human form, my darling. I'll make sure you're just as naked as I am so we can lick up every drop of tequila. Every. Drop."

She just about swallowed her tongue at the promise in his gaze and nodded.

He slowly pulled his shirt over his head. Nadie's gaze latched to the thick, corded muscles of his arms and chest, swallowing hard. She wanted to trace each line with her tongue, learn every nuance of his body until she could close her eyes and *know* him.

When she lifted her head and saw the smile on his face, she had a feeling he knew where her thoughts had gone—not a bad thing at all.

"I love it when your eyes are on me...and when other parts are too," Jace drawled.

She grinned and went to lift up her own shirt when Jace stopped her.

"No, let me," he said before slowly, oh so slowly, stripping her of her shirt. He threw it over his head, his gaze never breaking from hers. His thumb brushed over her nipple through her bra, and she shuddered.

His mouth quirked in a grin before he undid the clasp of her bra, sliding it off her. "Lie back," he said, his voice low.

She did, the coolness of the wooden bar top shocking against the heat of her skin. Without speaking, he twisted off the cap of the tequila—very top shelf knowing Dante—and took a swig.

She raised a brow. "Is that how you're going to do shots, then?"

He grinned then kissed her, the liquid burn of the tequila mixing with his heady taste. She swallowed as he pulled away, the sting going down her throat, but she didn't care. She was already heated up from the inside out and wanted Jace. Now.

Her bear licked her breasts, and she arched for him, pushing more of herself into his mouth. He bit down gently, and she moaned before he pulled away.

"Like raspberries, so red and juicy," Jace whispered before sprinkling salt on her nipples. She laughed at the sensation, but didn't move, loving the way he spoke to her, cared for her. "Now don't move, darling."

He poured a small amount of tequila in her belly button and she gasped at the cool sensation dancing on her skin but forced her back to the wood of the bar, not wanting to spill. A small drop of liquid trailed down her side, and Jace moved quickly, lapping it up with his tongue.

"Don't want to make a mess," he growled softly.

He put a slice of lime between her teeth after kissing her softly then grinned. She about came just then at the promise in that grin alone. Jace moved to her breasts, licking up the salt on each nipple, biting and sucking along the way. Her body craved him, begged her to move into him, but she forced herself to stay still so she wouldn't spill any tequila. His tongue trailed down her stomach, and her pussy clenched, wanting Jace inside her.

Jace growled and sucked up the tequila, licking and running his cheek along her skin, the scratchiness of his beard sending shots of heat down her back and sides. Before she could beg him for more, he moved up and bit into the lime clenched between her teeth. Juice and some of the meat from the lime spilled down her chin, and Jace licked that up as well.

That had been the singularly hottest thing that had ever happened to her.

Considering she'd just had a threesome with Dante and Jace—that was saying something.

Jace pulled her into his arms, and she sat up, wrapping her legs against his waist. He pulled back, breathing hard. "I was going to let you do a shot off me, but I don't think my dick can handle that. I need to taste you."

She swallowed hard and nodded. There would plenty of time for more body shots. He kissed her again, one hand fisted in her hair, crushing her to him, the other on her lower back, pulling her closer.

God, she'd never felt so taken, so wanted.

He wrenched his mouth from her then pulled her down

so she was standing in front of him. His fingers shook as he undid her pants and stripped her down so she was in nothing but skin and so freaking ready for him.

"Gods, baby, you are so fucking hot." He kissed her stomach then gripped her ass cheeks, spreading them, forcing her legs to move apart. He licked her clit with one firm swipe, and her legs gave out.

"Jace!"

He looked up at her, his eyes dark. Without a word, he picked her up and set her on the bar again. She gripped the edge of the wood, needing the support. Jace knelt before her, spread her thighs, and then buried his face in her pussy.

She cried out, his tongue piercing her before he licked up to her clit, twisting his tongue in such a way that she saw stars. When he speared her with two of his fingers, touching that bundle of nerves deep within her, she came against his face, screaming his name as she fought to keep consciousness.

Jace finally moved so he stood between her legs, his forehead pressed against hers with one hand on the back of her neck, keeping her steady. "You okay, baby?"

"I...I..."

She had thoughts and words and everything, yet they didn't seem to be working quite yet.

Jace chuckled softly, sounding entirely too pleased with himself. Well, she'd just have to show him *exactly* what he'd done to her.

She wiggled away from him, dropped to the floor, and

pushed him so his back was to the bar. His eyes widened as she went to her knees and undid his jeans.

"Nadie, what are you doing?"

"If you have to ask, then I guess I just have to make sure I do it properly."

Jace lifted her chin. "I'll let you put your mouth on any part of me. I just don't want to come down that pretty throat before I come in your pussy."

She grinned at his words and peeled his jeans down his legs. He moved one leg then the other, helping her strip him completely. Her bear went commando—something that, for some reason, was freaking hot. His cock jutted out, right in front of her face. It took all within her not to grab on and lick him up like an ice cream cone.

"You can do both, can't you?" she asked, fluttering her eyelashes. "Aren't big bad bears supposed to have an amazing recovery time?"

Jace narrowed his eyes, even as his mouth twitched. He fisted his hand into her hair, pulling her closer. "I see I'm going to have to show you just how fast I can recover. And, darling, never tempt a bear by doubting his prowess."

She grinned up at him then took his cock in her hand, pumping his length twice before licking the crown. Jace's hold tightened in her hair, and she let out a breath.

"I've never done this before, you know."

Jace's thumb traced her cheek. "I know, love. Just do what feels right. You don't have to swallow it all."

She rolled her eyes. "I would choke, Jace," she said dryly.

He grinned again. "I do love it when you compliment me."

Nadie tightened her grip then took the tip of his cock and settled it on her tongue. Jace moaned, his hand in her hair pulling her slightly closer but not pushing. She swallowed him a bit farther then pulled back, rolling her tongue along his length.

From Jace's strangled moan, she figured he enjoyed that. She explored him with her hands and tongue, loving the way she could make him thrust and groan. When she cupped his balls, rolling them in her hands, he pulled back on her hair, and she looked up at him.

"I was busy," she pouted.

"Do you want me to come down your throat or in you, darling?" he asked, his words coming out between pants.

"Can't it be both?" she asked as she squirmed.

He pulled her up so she was standing then gripped her ass. She let out a gasp as he picked her up, crushing his mouth to hers. His cock lay between her legs, pressed against her clit, and she rubbed up against him, wanting to come so bad.

Jace set her back on the bar, and she wrapped her arms around him, needing him inside her. Her bear held one hip while using his other hand to keep a firm grip on the back of her neck. He pressed his forehead against hers and let out a breath before he *moved*.

With a gasp, she arched against him, his cock filling her in one stroke. He pulled out, her body shaking she was so ready. He pumped his hips, and she moved with him, needing him as close as possible. Their gazes never left each other's, their bodies moving in sync as he fucked her on the bar top.

No, not fucked. This was so much more, but she couldn't breathe. He slammed into her once more, and she came with him. They both screamed out the other's names as her succubus took over, pulling in Jace's life force through their bond. She could feel her body warming, growing strong with her bear deep within her.

Jace kissed her then, licking and sucking on her lips as they both came down from their high.

"Again," she whispered.

Jace growled and pushed inside her, once, twice. "As you wish, my Nadie."

Nadie grinned and pulled her bear closer.

Yes. This is what she wanted. *Who* she wanted. For a lifetime.

Jace pulled himself off Nadie as she slept in their big bed for their afternoon nap. He moved to the window, looking out into the distance. He could have sworn he'd heard, or at least *felt,* something waking him from his sleep. It was as if someone was watching them, but who?

It didn't make any sense. No one knew they were there. There wouldn't be a reason to watch them.

Would there?

He turned and looked at the woman who'd stolen his

heart. He'd just have to keep an eye out and watch over her. He already knew this woman would be part of his future, and he'd be damned if he let anything happen to her.

Jace crawled back into bed, pulling her into his arms. He needed Dante to come home safe and sound, and then everything would be all right.

It had to be.

CHAPTER 10

D ante stood outside his home, his hands fisted at his sides as the wind blew around him. It tangled his hair and stung his eyes. The storm on the horizon would be a vicious one.

If only that were his only problem.

He knew Jace and Nadie were inside, warm, worried, but utterly content in a way that Dante knew they had made love. He could feel them through the bond and had a feeling Jace could sense him outside but was letting him come inside when he wanted to. Or at least that's what Dante hoped. Nadie wouldn't be able to use those senses quite yet.

That would be something Dante and Jace would have to teach her. It wouldn't be safe for her to go unaware while the world shifted around her. He ran a hand over his face, frustrated as all hell at the utter feeling of helplessness surrounding him.

He'd promised Nadie he would tell her everything and not keep secrets, yet he wasn't sure how he was going to tell them that everything might slip through their fingers. Death or being torn away for five hundred years seemed to be the only two options on the table right then, and Dante didn't have a particular need for either of those.

No, the other two he needed were inside his house, waiting for him.

He licked his lips and took a deep breath. He'd kept them waiting long enough. As it was, he'd kept them waiting *too* long in the grand scheme of things. There wasn't a moment to waste, and standing outside and feeling sorry for himself wasn't helping anything.

He was a ten-thousand-year-old dragon—give or take a few years—not some teenage kid who needed to croon about his angst and put on guyliner. He already had the long hair and piercings, but he would go only so far into the whole look.

Now he was officially putting off the inevitable.

"Dante?"

He looked up at the woman with the sweet, sweet voice who held half his heart and tried to smile but failed.

"I'm home."

She frowned only for a moment before running to him. He caught her in his arms when she jumped, the utter faith in him at the action leaving him breathless. She nuzzled into him, squeezing him hard, and he pressed his nose to her neck, inhaling her honey and fire scent. He ran his hand down her back, cupping her ass, bringing her even closer.

His dragon preened, satisfied with the attention that was its due.

Nadie pulled back then punched him in the arm.

Hard.

He winced but didn't let her go. "What was that for? Kind of a strange welcome."

"You left without saying goodbye," Nadie answered, the hurt in her tone making him feel lower than low. "We're going to have a talk about that."

"You're lucky that punch is all she does," Jace said from the house. The bear crossed his arms over his chest and leaned against the doorway. "Get inside before the storm hits. Looks like it's going to be a bad one."

Dante looked into Nadie's narrowed eyes and let out a sigh.

"That's not the only storm we'll be having, Dante Bell," she warned, and Dante held back a smile. It wouldn't be smart to kiss her then, but she was so damn beautiful.

Sobering at the thought of what he could lose if he didn't find a way out, he kissed her anyway. She melted beneath his lips, the little sigh escaping her going straight to his cock. He squeezed her ass, and she rocked against him, the sensation making his dragon rumble with need.

He pulled away as the first drop of rain splashed against his cheek. Nadie looked up at him with dark eyes and swollen lips then brushed the wetness away from his skin.

"Let's go inside, and I'll explain everything," Dante said then started walking, not letting go of the woman and mate in his arms. She felt good there, *right*.

She sighed and leaned on his shoulder. His dragon let out a small tendril of smoke through Dante's nostrils, wrapping it around Nadie, claiming her in its own way. Jace moved out of the way when they got to him, his gaze never leaving Dante's.

"You're okay?" Jace whispered, the worry clear and heart-wrenching.

Dante nodded, knowing it wasn't quite the truth. The bear would have noticed that as well, but let it be. They would talk about it shortly, and then Dante's world would fall apart if he wasn't careful.

And Dante *always* tried to be careful.

He let Nadie down so she stood by him. Before she could move away, he took her hand, needing the connection. She blinked up at him, and he knew she had a feeling something was wrong but couldn't quite voice her thoughts.

Her inner succubus must be trying to scent and feel out all the undercurrents, yet Nadie hadn't firmed the connection with her paranormal yet. That would come with time, but right then, Dante had more pressing matters.

Namely, the Conclave and the big pile of shit they were all in.

He sank onto the couch, pulling Nadie into his side. Jace paced in front of them before sitting on the coffee table. Their knees touched, and the man looked as though his bear was ready to break out of his skin.

Dante leaned forward and brushed his lips against the man, needing the connection as much as Jace clearly did. Jace's shoulders eased slightly as Dante pulled back.

"I needed that," Jace said, licking his lips.

"You might need more soon." He said it as a sensual promise, but the darkness that threatened them outweighed the light. Jace narrowed his eyes, the need still there, but masked with the same fear Dante held.

"Tell us, Dante," Jace ordered. "Sitting on whatever you have isn't helping anything."

"And tell us why you left without a goodbye," Nadie added.

Dante kissed her temple and took a deep breath. "I didn't say goodbye because you were sleeping, and I thought you needed more sleep." He cursed and shook his head. "No, that was only part of it. I was fucking scared about what I was doing and didn't want to scare you. I know I promised to tell you everything, but apparently not keeping all my secrets close is going to take a little while to get used to."

Nadie cupped his cheek, and he turned his head so he could nuzzle her palm. "I forgive you, my dragon. The fear, I think that's what I scent, coming off you tells me that my petty insecurities need to be washed away right now. Tell us what's frightened you."

He leaned down and kissed her softly, needing the connection once more. "Never think your worries are less than mine."

She rolled her eyes. "Right now, I think your worries are *our* worries, so get to it. Stop procrastinating and tell us."

"The Conclave has asked me to join its ranks."

Silence.

Jace quietly stood, his whole body shaking. The other man's eyes glowed gold, the bear close to the surface. Shit.

"You're going to take it, aren't you?" Jace said, his voice straining for control.

Dante blinked. "What the fuck? Why would you think I would take it?"

"You're a dragon, Dante. This is the ultimate in positions in your realm. In *all* realms. Why wouldn't you say yes?"

Dante stood slowly, not believing the words coming out of Jace's mouth. "You're serious. You actually think I'd take the appointment?"

"Wouldn't you? Even if it isn't to be in charge, as a member of the Conclave, you could be real help to the realms. You could do what you've been quietly trying to do for eons—make our realms work in peace."

Dante's dragon clawed at him, wanting to go at the bear for thinking so much less of him, of their newly bound relationship.

"You think so little of me?" he asked, his voice a growl.

Jace curled a lip, his hands fisting. Dante raised his chin, ready to fight the man he loved because there was no one else to fight.

Nadie stood quickly between them, her small hands on each of their chests. "Stop it. Both of you. You're fighting over nothing. Just words and careless thoughts that aren't worth the tension and heartache. Jace, let Dante explain what he means. It's hard enough as it is, and I don't even know all of the logistics and details I need to. Dante, don't harp on Jace for being scared out of his mind. You both are lashing out because you're afraid of what you *think* is coming rather than actually saying what is going on around us. Explain, baby, please."

Dante immediately calmed at her words, his Nadie quickly growing into her inner succubus and standing up to a bear and dragon without a second thought. He could feel some of the tension leaving Jace's body as well, and the two men sat down finally. Nadie stayed standing between them and put her hands on their shoulders.

"Now, Dante, what does it mean that the Conclave wants you to join their ranks?"

He could taste the fear on her words and cupped her hip, soothing.

"Two members from each realm form the Conclave."

Nadie waved her hand. "I know all of that, at least the basics. Jace explained it to me while you were gone." She blushed. "We, uh, talked about a lot of things."

Dante grinned, despite the rising tension in the room. "I bet you...talked...quite well."

Jace snorted. "Don't think talking about sex is going to get you out of this, Dante."

Nadie blushed even harder then moved to sit on Jace's lap. She faced Dante, same as the bear, and they both looked at him, pleading in their gazes.

"Alexander, a very old dragon, and that is something considering my age, wants to, for lack of a better word, retire. He's chosen me as a replacement. While other places would give you an option of saying no, the Conclave doesn't work like that. What the Conclave says, goes. Meaning I don't have a choice."

Nadie sucked in a breath. "What would be so wrong in joining the Conclave?" she asked then held up her hand. "Jace and you both know something I don't when it comes to this, I get that, just explain it carefully for me. It's a lot to take in."

Dante gripped her knee while Jace kissed her temple. He met the other man's gaze, knowing what he said next would hurt. "The Conclave would force me into their care for 'training' for five hundred years." Nadie gasped while Jace growled. "I wouldn't be able to see either one of you for that time. I'd be forced away from my mates, my life, and everything I've built to do what the Conclave says."

"And if you say no?" Nadie asked, her voice a whisper.

"Then they kill me." It hadn't been said in the Conclave chambers, but it had been heavily implied. "They gave me time to make my decision, but we all know it was just a smoke screen. I'm going to use this time to figure out what the hell we're going to do because there is no way I'm leaving either of you. You've got to understand that. I just found you. I'm not losing you."

Nadie threw her arms around his neck, pulling him closer to her and Jace. "We'll find a way. We figured out how to save Lily, Jamie, and Becca, as well as their mates. We can do this."

Dante smiled at her earnestness. If only it were as easy as a djinn, angelic, demonic, or wolf war.

"Yes, we will, Nadie. I'm not giving up." His dragon refused to even think it.

"Why would they even bother to give you time?" Jace asked, his voice carefully neutral. Too careful.

Dante met Jace's gaze. The three of them would have to talk soon. "I think it was because of two of the newest members of the Conclave. A fae and a wizard. They are both extremely young, each less than a thousand."

"A thousand years is young?" Nadie asked.

Dante leaned forward and kissed her soundly. "I'm ten thousand years old, my sprite. That doesn't mean I think you are young, far from it. I was only saying, in terms of what I know about the Conclave, they are young. I wouldn't think anyone younger than five thousand would be part of the decision making."

"Things are changing then," Jace said, his voice ominous.

"Yes, but I don't know what direction this will take them. This is all something to think about and discuss, but first, we need to find a way to get me out of this commitment. I'm not leaving you two, despite what you thought."

"Dante," Nadie admonished.

Jace grinned. "We're alpha, Nadie darling. We're going to fight and butt heads."

Nadie growled, the sound so cute his dragon wanted to eat her up—not that Dante would tell her either of those things. He wanted to live after all.

"I might not be alpha, but I'll fight for what I want too," she said.

"Honey, you're not beta if that's what you're thinking,"

Jace said, laughter in his voice. The sound made Dante relax. "If you're not alpha now, you will be soon. That succubus inside you damn well knows what she wants." His eyes darkened, and the two of them shared a look telling Dante they had explored some of her powers.

Good for them.

His cock ached, and he shifted on the couch. A twinge of jealousy knotted in his belly before it dissipated. He would have both of his mates soon—together, separately, and everywhere in between. He just had to be patient.

Dante could do patient.

He was a dragon after all.

A cell phone rang, and Nadie stood up. "Crap, that's mine. I'll go put it on silent."

Dante shook his head. "Answer it. There's not much we can discuss right now until we have time to form a plan."

She nodded then went off to the other room, cell phone in hand.

Jace came and sat next to him on the couch. "You have any idea what we're going to do?"

Dante leaned into Jace, and the other man put his arm around his shoulders. His dragon, though not usually so submissive in letting others take care of it, calmed. He also liked the word 'we' coming from Jace's lips. After so long without the other man's touch, the achingly hollow place in side of him slowly started to fill. The bond had done some of that, but it was the actual presence of the other man that would complete him—same as it would with Nadie.

"Other than fighting the Conclave?" Dante shook his head into Jace's shoulder. "I don't know, love."

Jace growled softly and squeezed him tight. "The Goodwins will stand behind you, and you know countless others will do the same. If the ones you've helped over time won't stand beside you without prompting, you can call in favors. We will find a way."

Dante closed his eyes, needing to rest after such a stressful day. "I know we will."

He scented Nadie come back in the room before he heard her.

"That was Amara," Nadie explained. "She needs help at the inn, some staffing emergency. Normally, she wouldn't have even asked, but she either couldn't get ahold of anyone else or the ones she did were too busy. I told her I'd call her back because I don't know what I'm doing." She gave a small smile. "That seems to be my phrase of the day, or maybe even the month."

Dante untangled himself from Jace and went to Nadie, pulling her into his arms. "Take one of my cars and go to your friend. She needs help. There's not much more we can do tonight."

"Do you know how long she'll need you?" Jace asked as he stood on the other side of Nadie, blocking her in between the two of them.

"For a couple hours at most." She looked over her shoulder at the rain, which at the moment was just a sprinkle. "It isn't supposed to start really pouring until much later, so I will be back before then."

Dante nodded, happy that she wasn't going to be in danger out on the roads in the middle of a storm. "Be safe and help your friend. We aren't going anywhere."

He and Jace kissed her goodbye and watched her drive off. He could still scent her sweet honey and fire wrapped around him, even as it mixed with the fear seeping from each of them.

Jace came up from behind him and wrapped his arms around Dante's waist. Dante sank into the other man's hold, his ass against Jace's rigid cock.

"Tomorrow we can talk about our plans and what it means for us," Jace said, his warm breath against Dante's neck. "Right now, though, I need you. You scared me so damn much, Dante. Fuck me and let me hold you."

Dante turned in the man's hold so he faced him. "Anything, my bear. Anything."

CHAPTER 11

Dante crushed his mouth to Jace's, craving the man in his arms just as much as the woman who would be joining them later. Jace ran his hands through Dante's hair, and his dragon practically purred. He loved having his scalp massaged and fingers playing with his hair, and Jace knew that.

Damn, the man remembered.

Though he and Jace had never completed the mating bond while they were waiting for Nadie, they'd learned each other in other ways. Other ways that seemed to be coming back to him full force.

Jace growled against him, and Dante put the past in the past and focused on the man in his arms—the man who currently pressed his cock against Dante's through their jeans. Fuck, he loved the fact that they were practically the same height. It would make for some interesting—and fucking amazing—positions.

Dante lowered his hand and cupped Jace's ass, rocking into the other man.

Jace kissed down Dante's jaw then pulled away to cup his face. "What you do to me."

Dante nipped at the other man's lip then went to his knees.

Jace let out a little snort then ran his hand through Dante's hair again. "On your knees? For me?"

Dante grinned then undid Jace's pants, pulling the other man's cock out with a quick efficiency. He pumped along Jace's length before squeezing tightly, forcing a strangled moan from the other man.

"God," Jace groaned.

"No, I'm Dante, but thank you for noticing."

Jace chuckled. "I can't believe you pulled that line out."

Dante licked the crown of Jace's cock, the salty precum settling on his tongue. "I'm fucking old, Jace. I *invented* those lines."

He looked up as Jace rolled his eyes. "Okay, oh-experienced-one. Why don't you suck my cock and show me how godlike you are?"

"Take off your shirt," Dante ordered then swallowed Jace whole.

Jace grunted and flexed his hips into Dante's mouth. Dante gripped his mate's hips, keeping him steady. The other man might think he was in charge, but Dante knew who was more alpha.

He looked up to see Jace had taken his shirt off, the tanned lines of his body sexy as hell. Dante let his jaw relax and took Jace down his throat so his face pressed up against Jace's groin. He felt the other man's body shake as Dante swallowed, his throat squeezing around Jace's cock.

He pulled back and let go of Jace's dick, taking a deep breath before swallowing him whole again. Jace fisted his hand in Dante's hair and held him steady. Dante grunted around his bear's erection and let his jaw relax again as Jace fucked his mouth.

Dante pulled away, licking his lips before pulling Jace's jeans down his legs fully. Soon, Jace was naked, and Dante's mouth was on him again. He sucked, licked, and rubbed his mate down, loving his taste. While his mouth was busy, he gripped Jace's ass in both hands, spreading his cheeks. While Jace groaned, pushing deeper into Dante's mouth, Dante pressed one finger against his lover's hole.

The action broke Jace's rhythm, but Dante didn't care. He passed through the tight ring of muscle—knowing he wouldn't go that much farther without lube—and rubbed along Jace's prostate. Jace bucked once, twice, before shouting and holding Dante's head closer to his body. Dante swallowed every drop of Jace's cum, his face pressed once again against Jace's groin.

Finally, Dante pulled back and stood up. He quickly stripped out of his clothes and licked his lips. "Go get the lube," he ordered Jace.

Jace raised a brow but did as he was told, walking naked, sweaty, and way too fucking sexy to the bedroom as Dante took his own cock in his fist, waiting for the other man to come back. Jace returned to the room quickly, his cock hard again and slapping his belly as he walked.

Dante growled at the sight and caught the lube when Jace threw it at him. "Bend over the table," he ordered.

Jace licked his lips but didn't move.

"Did I stutter?"

His bear snorted. "I love it when you're all growly. Just remember, I get to fuck that ass of yours soon. Got me?"

Dante squeezed his dick so he wouldn't come at the thought of Jace deep inside him. Yes, they would do that. Soon.

"Table. Now."

Jace turned on his heel and moved to the table, bending over for him and even going as far as spreading his ass cheeks.

Fuck. Yeah.

Dante prowled to his mate and ran a hand down his back. Jace arched for him, the utter trust he'd placed in Dante's hands overwhelming. Dante slowly prepared his mate, making sure he wouldn't hurt him once he entered him. As much as he knew Jace would take it, he wanted their first time together when it was the two of them to be...theirs.

Once he was sure Jace would be ready to take all of him, he leaned over his mate and kissed his neck. Jace looked over his shoulder, his back moving as he panted in need. Dante kissed his bear softly, taking in every movement, every taste as if it would be their last.

He kissed down Jace's back before moving so he could grip the other man's hips.

"Ready?" he asked, his voice strained.

"Always," Jace moaned.

Dante nodded then pumped his hips. Hard. He entered Jace in one stroke, and they both yelled out. Jace's ass gripped Dante's dick like a vise, and they both stilled, accommodating themselves to the sensations. He couldn't take it anymore, though, and pulled out a fraction before thrusting back in. He pistoned into his lover, bending over him so his chest pressed against Jace's back. They both panted, sweat pouring down their bodies as Dante slammed into his lover, his dick ready to explode.

Dante pulled back, moving Jace so the other man could grasp his own cock in his hand. "Get yourself off, Jace. Fuck your hand while I fuck your ass so we can come together."

Jace merely grunted, his arm working in tandem with Dante's thrusts. Dante's balls tightened, and he picked up his pace until he yelled Jace's name, coming hard, filling up his mate's ass. Jace's voice cracked as he came as well.

Dante pulled out, pulled his lover to his feet, and flipped Jace over so they faced each other. He cupped his mate's cheeks and kissed him, their breaths coming in pants as they came down from their peak.

"Gods, that was better than I thought it could be," Jace said.

"It's only the beginning," Dante replied. "Only the beginning."

A FEW HOURS LATER, DANTE PUT HIS HANDS ON HIS HIPS, staring out into the window as Jace came up behind him after they'd repeated their lovemaking. "She'll be home soon," he whispered, more to himself than the bear behind him.

Jace kissed his neck, and Dante leaned back. "The rain is coming down early." The worry in his mate's tone matched the worry in Dante's heart.

Dante nodded, a prickly feeling sending an odd sensation over him. The wind howled around them, the rain coming down in sheets, but it seemed to be centered on his land. "I don't think this is a normal storm, Jace."

Jace let out a breath even as Dante felt the bear within the man rise to the surface, ready to fight for what was theirs. "I was afraid of that. Let's get our pants on and go out and find our mate. I don't want her alone out in this."

Dante nodded, knowing the bear was right. Something was off, and he'd be damned if he let Nadie get hurt because of it....because of him.

THE WINDSHIELD WIPERS WERE USELESS AGAINST THE onslaught of rain hitting her car. Nadie thought about pulling over to the side of the road, but she knew she was coming up on Dante's home. It wouldn't do any good to pull over and get stuck in a place she didn't know as well as she should. After all, she had less than a mile to go. She could do that.

Hopefully.

She'd been gone an hour longer than she'd planned, and as it was, the storm had come early. It had been a stupid idea to drive in this weather, but Amara had desperately needed her. The inn where her friend managed had run low on staff and high on occupants.

Now, though, going home wasn't looking like a feasible option. Amara had offered to let Nadie stay at the inn, sleeping on the pull-out couch Amara had in her manager's apartment, but Nadie had refused. She'd wanted to go home to her men, her mates.

With the rain pounding into her car and flooding the streets, she had a feeling she'd made the wrong decision.

Only half a mile to go.

As soon as she thought that, a flash of light bounced off the front of her car, temporarily blinding her. She screamed and held onto the wheel, pumping the brakes, not slamming down like her instincts told her to do at first.

It didn't matter though.

Her tires squealed as she hit...something...and her car fishtailed before turning around and sliding into the other lane. She screamed, trying to gain control, but she knew it was no use. She just prayed the airbags would work.

When the car spun again, she could have sworn she saw a man in the shadows, the rain pelting him as he stared at her...but she wasn't sure. As soon as she tried to focus on him, the car spun again, out of control.

The car sped toward a tree, and she screamed, trying to

find a way to stop the damn thing before she crashed into it. But it would be no use, she knew that.

The large roar in the distance seemed to grow louder by the second. At first she thought it was the sound of her car, but no, no, she knew, she *prayed* she knew what that was.

Who that was.

Nadie slammed on the brakes, trying to stop the car as two men came out of the shadows, their bodies ramming into the car as they tried to stop the car. At least that's what she thought they were doing. She cried out. No, they were in human form, their weaker one. Tears streamed down her face, not for her, but for the two men who must be hurt because of her.

Finally, her car stopped before it rammed into the tree. Her body shook as she tried to undo her seatbelt. Before she could finish that though, Dante ripped the door off the hinges. Blood and bruises covered the side of his body that had hit the car, but he didn't seem to mind. Jace stood behind him, blood also covering his face, but both men looked okay.

Alive.

As was she.

She finally got her seatbelt off and threw her arms around Dante's neck. He might have been hurt, but he didn't wince or groan at her hold. No, he pulled her out of the car, holding her close to him as Jace came around them and sandwiched her between them.

"Thank God you're here," she cried into Dante's neck.

And Nadie had a feeling that had not been a little car accident.

"We will always be here," Dante promised. "Where are you hurt?"

"Let us take you home," Jace added.

"I'm fine," she answered. "But what about you two? You just got hit by a car. My car." She blinked. "No, Dante's car. Crap. I'm sorry about your car."

Dante grinned and seemed surprised he could do so just then. "Don't worry about my fucking car. Come on. We're taking you home. We'll deal with the damage here when it's not raining. Luckily you made it as far to my property since you were on my long driveway, so we won't have to deal with any authorities."

She wrapped her body around him as tight as she could, needing to make sure he was real. She'd never forget the sound of screeching metal or the roar of a dragon.

Soon she found herself naked on the bed and wrapped in blankets and her men. Neither man had spoken much, only enough to make sure she was okay as well as care for each other. She burrowed closer to Jace, her body unable to get warm.

"Your body is in shock, darling," Jace said, squeezing her tight.

"There was someone in the road," Nadie said at last.

"Someone?" Dante asked, his voice like the edge of a blade.

"I think so. I don't know. Maybe I was imagining it, but it didn't feel right."

Dante snuggled up to her back and ran his hand over her hip. "I don't think you're imagining it. The storm didn't feel right. I don't know who it was. What it was. But we will find out."

Jace kissed her brow and sighed. "We can speculate all we want, but right now, we're going to keep vigilant and refuse to let anyone hurt us or our bond."

Nadie nodded, knowing her men were trying to help, but she didn't believe they could right then.

Something had tried to kill her tonight, but she knew it hadn't been about her.

No, whatever had been out there had been out to hurt the ones she cared for. She'd just have been collateral damage. A pawn.

That angered her more than the idea that someone had tried to hurt her. Attacking her outright would scare her, but she'd cope. Attacking her so they could harm those she cared for?

No, that would not be tolerated.

Nadie might have been weak right then, but it wouldn't last for long. She would learn to protect not only herself, but those of her bond. She had a purpose now. Those who had tried to kill her had made a mistake tonight.

A deadly one.

CHAPTER 12

"Isn't it too soon?"

Jace closed his eyes at Nadie's repeated comment, but as he wasn't facing her, she couldn't tell. It wasn't that he was annoyed she'd asked the same question more than once. It was that she felt the need to ask it at all. If she'd been born into the world she lived now, things would have been different, but she hadn't been, and now, things were complicated. He could barely breathe with how much he cared for her, and after the accident, he'd done his best to hide the depths of his fears and feelings from Nadie.

He hadn't wanted to scare her.

His momma would love her though. However, telling Nadie that only made the woman freak out all the more. Apparently meeting the parents—whether bear or human— was a big deal for her.

Good to know.

"No, it's not too soon. We're going to my den, not just because I want you to meet my parents, but because we need to for Dante."

Nadie's arms wrapped around his waist from behind and he ran his hand over her skin. So soft. His bear stretched, awakened by her sweet scent. He smiled at the furry beast. His bear could kill in seconds, but when it came to Nadie, it seemed he was a teddy bear.

His bear growled, and Jace held back a chuckle.

Okay, maybe not a teddy bear, but soft with Nadie nonetheless.

Nadie nuzzled into his back, and he stood still, soaking in the moment, not wanting to let it go. He'd waited so long for this, and now, the big, tough Mediator was falling for the little sprite, his succubus.

Who would have thought?

"I've never been to another realm before."

He turned and lifted her up so she was sitting on the counter. As both he and Dante were well over a foot taller than her, they were going to have to find ways to make talking easier on her neck. Looking up all day took its toll.

Or so he'd heard. After all, he'd been over six feet since he was thirteen.

They grew them big in the dens.

He tucked a strand of hair behind her ear, and she raised a brow. "Stop pawing me, Jace. Remember when we said we were going to try and see what happens when we *don't* touch each other like that? I need to drain my energy to

discover my limits powerwise in case I hurt myself later."
She blushed as she said it, and Jace had to hold back a groan.

Yes, he remembered the conversation from that morning. It didn't mean he had to like it. The three of them knew that even *if* Dante was able to stay with them—gods willing —they wouldn't be at each other's sides every hour of every day. As a succubus, Nadie needed to not only pull life energy through their mating bond, but through sex as well. Just being near one another wouldn't cut it.

They'd have to get sweaty.

Not that Jace minded.

At. All.

"Hey, I can see that heat in your eyes, Jace Goodwin." Nadie pressed her hand on his chest and pushed him back a bit.

She could only do that because he let her, but it didn't matter.

"I'm just thinking," he said.

"About sex. I might be new to the whole thing, but I've been around long enough to know when a man is thinking about sex. So, like I was saying, I've never been to another realm before. What do we have to do?"

He grinned down at her but didn't move to touch her. They were refraining for a day, if he could last, to see if they could actually make it. With the world going to shit around them and the idea that Dante could be gone from their grasps forever, not touching felt like a painful process. The eternity they would have to live if their dragon had to become part of the Conclave was not something he wanted to think about.

His hands fisted as he thought about it. Taking a deep breath, he let his bear bring his control back. As a Mediator, he had more control than most—and not just with the man. If the man within got to be too much, the bear would breathe in the control needed. It was a symbiotic relationship that few held—let alone understood.

"The bear realm isn't as secret as some of the others. My family lives in a den within the realm itself. That's why I just call it my den, rather than realm most days. With realms like the angelic one, you have to practically give a blood oath to enter. The demonic realm is even worse. With the bear one, though, you only have to be a bear or be welcomed by bears."

Nadie shook her head. "Doesn't that make it hard to protect the realm if anyone welcomed can enter?"

Jace grinned, but it wasn't a nice one. "While I said it wasn't a secret, I didn't mean it wasn't difficult. To be welcomed by the bears, you must pass their tests, promise their oaths, be their mates, or tie yourselves to the bears' lives. A bear doesn't allow entry easily. Also, one does not mess with a bear and live."

Nadie nodded. "You got really creepy and alpha just then, but I kind of liked it."

He snorted, surprised at her response.

"He *is* creepy and alpha," Dante said as he walked into the kitchen.

Though he smiled as he said it, Jace could see the darkness in the other man's gaze. The shadows were upon them, and Jace could smell the fight for their lives coming. He just didn't know how much longer they had.

"I'm not creepy. Alpha, I'll take, but not creepy."

Nadie smiled, though she too held a sadness she couldn't hide worth a damn.

"He just pretends to be this sweet, cuddly bear, but inside, he's that grizzly," Dante said as he came to stand beside the counter.

Nadie shifted so her knee was touching his side. The movement was so subtle that Jace wasn't sure she'd done it consciously. It boded well for their bond, but he knew the human in her still had reservations. He didn't blame her. The mating bond was only the first step. They still had to ensure she actually *liked* them beyond what fate had decreed.

Blindly following fate only led to heartache.

Though the main reason they were going to his parents' home was to discuss the Dante and Conclave situation, he would have taken Nadie there anyway. The world was crashing down around them, but he needed to show Nadie what their future could be like. Scrambling and praying did nothing. They would move on as though they had no worries on one plane but find out how to get Dante out of the commitment he didn't want to make on the other.

It was the only way Jace could figure out how to not go bear and kill someone.

Jace shook his head, clearing his thoughts. "Let's get going. We only need to use the clearing to gain access to the realm since it runs parallel to ours. Once we're there, we can open the gate and get through easily."

"You know I have no idea what you're talking about, right?" Nadie asked with a smile. "We're just winging it here, but I'll take it. Just show me what to do so I don't end up with a lost body part or something."

Jace laughed, thankful he could even do that with the tension riding him.

"You won't lose an arm or anything, my sprite," Dante said, laughter in his voice.

"You don't know that," Nadie said, her voice very matter-of-fact. "Just because it hasn't happened before— that you know of—doesn't mean I won't be the person who loses a toe or something."

"A toe?" Jace asked. "Really? A toe?"

Nadie rolled her eyes. "I didn't want to think of losing something I needed to live. A toe I could probably live without. Maybe. And now I'm becoming the creepy one." She jumped off the counter before Dante and Jace could help her. She raised a brow at both of their outstretched hands. "Okay, this is another thing. While I love the fact that you both try to care for me in every way possible, you need to learn that it's okay if I take care of myself. Even though I was a little quieter than the other women in the circle, I've never been completely helpless."

"You were human," Jace put in and knew he'd said the wrong thing.

Dante winced, and Nadie narrowed her eyes.

"Prejudiced much?" she said, her hands fisted on her hips.

"No, no. That's not what I meant. It's only that humans are much weaker than paranormals." He looked to Dante for help, but from the expression on the dragon's face, Jace was on his own with this one.

"That is true, *physically*," Nadie said, her tone not boding well for the rest of the sentence. "But I'm not talking about that. Yes, I know I will need to learn how to use my offensive powers, if I even have them. That's why we're going to the succubus realm as soon as they get back to Dante."

Jace nodded. Dante had put in a formal request to the secretive realm so Nadie could meet the people who might one day be hers, but they hadn't heard anything back from them yet.

"However," Nadie continued, "you two are treating me like fine china who can't even walk on my own. I might not be as strong as you, but I am stronger than you're giving me credit for. Please don't forget that."

Jace frowned, his bear huffing and growling, wanting to pull Nadie into its arms and never let go. He was a predator and alpha. He *couldn't* stand back and not help those he cared for...but maybe he was edging along the ways of pushiness.

Dante cupped her face and nodded. "I'll do my best, Nadie. I've never thought you any less than the person you are—strong, beautiful, and *mine*. But I will do my best to make sure you know that I value you."

Jace let out a breath. If the damn dragon could act like a reasonable mate, then so could he.

"I'll do my best too."

Nadie looked between them and smiled. "We're a bit crazy right now with the bond and Dante's...*thing*...so it's okay that we're on edge. Let's not stay there. And we should go now so we're not late. It wouldn't be good to be late the first time I'm meeting your folks." She bit her lip. "I've never met anyone's parents before. Well, I've met parents before, but...damn, you know what I mean."

Jace grinned at how flustered she was acting. "You'll be fine. My mom is one big momma bear, and Dad will love you. My brothers and sisters will be there too since they not only want to meet you, they want to see Dante too. They haven't seen him—or me for that matter—in a while."

"I love the fact that the two of you have a history together," she said as they made their way to the clearing behind Dante's house.

Jace gripped her hand while Dante took the other. "As I like that you and Dante have one. You and I are the only real newbies here."

"We're making up for lost time."

He held back a growl, thinking of the ways they were exploring one another—including the tequila and tastes. He didn't need a hard-on going into the bear realm.

"Ready?" Dante asked, and Jace nodded, Nadie doing the same.

Jace closed his eyes and pictured his realm, the warmth

and earth of the land around him, the scents of home, bear, and family. Nadie gasped beside him, and he opened his eyes, smiling down at her. The realm opened up like a small wormhole, encompassing them in light, freedom, and warmth.

They finally stepped through the portal, the wormhole closing behind them quickly. He felt the awe in Nadie by his side and the slight relief in Dante.

The latter made sense to Jace because of the utter acceptance that the Goodwins gave when it came to the black and blue dragon.

After spending thousands upon thousands of years floating from one realm to the next, a royal dragon nomad, Dante had found a home with Jace's family—even before Jace had been born.

Jace's grandmother lived today because of the man who was now his mate. It was because of that moment in time that Dante was family through and through. Now Jace was bringing the dragon home as his bonded mate. Jace couldn't wait to see the look on his mother's face, the look when she gazed upon the bonded dragon...the look when she would meet Nadie for the first time.

While they did have to discuss their plan of attack with the Conclave, coming home where he could re-collect himself was what he needed. He hadn't realized just how much he'd missed home and needed his family until he scented the pine and oak of home.

Nor had he until he scented a certain family of bears who didn't understand the concept of personal space.

"Brace yourself," Jace murmured. Dante chuckled, and Nadie looked up at him, her brow scrunched.

"Huh?" she asked.

Before Jace would warn her further, she was in the arms of a very large man who just happened to shift into a bear every time he felt like it. The other man squeezed Nadie to his chest and twisted her around like a cherished ragdoll. Nadie's feet had to be at least a foot or more off the ground.

"Torrent, put Nadie down," Jace ordered, laughter in his tone. "She's smaller than you and not a toy. Don't break her."

His baby brother had Nadie in a very comfy looking bear hug, that constant smile on his face never wavering.

"But she's so fluffy!" Torrent said with a laugh. He set Nadie down, and she stared up at him, blinking. The half-dazed, half-amused expression on her face made Jace smile.

No one could be angry at Torrent. It just didn't happen. Confused by him, yes, but never angry. Torrent was the epitome of a teddy bear—one who could fight with knives like no other.

"Nadie, this is baby brother, Torrent."

Nadie raised a brow at him then looked up—way up—at the man in front of her. "Baby?"

Torrent grinned, that piece of hair their mom still tucked away when she saw him falling over his forehead. "I'm the youngest boy in a family of overprotective grizzly bears. Of course I'm the baby. It's good to finally meet you, Nadie. Our brother has been talking about you for sixty years. Well, not *you*, but who you could be. It's nice to see the woman who can wrangle not only a bear but a dragon too is as strong as you are."

Nadie grinned, her face brightening, then looked at Jace and Dante. "I think I'm going to like your brother, Jace."

Jace growled. "As long as you like me more."

Nadie rolled her eyes. "Alpha much?"

"You bet your ass," Jace said.

Torrent snorted then took two steps toward Dante, his arms wide open. Dante held out his own arm, blocking the bear, but the twitch of the dragon's lips told Jace his mate was enjoying himself.

"You can hug me but don't lift me," Dante warned, a small tendril of smoke escaping his nostril.

Very intimidating.

"You're family, you deserve a bear hug," Torrent explained.

Dante lifted a lip and bared fang.

"But since you're our Dante, I'll restrain myself," Torrent said solemnly, and then he grinned. "Maybe."

By the time Torrent finished his bear hugs and let them start walking the short distance to their folks' place, Jace's sides hurt with laughter. If he hadn't loved his brother before, he would have right then because, with Torrent's gentle and not-so-gentle care, the tension had all dissipated. Nadie and Dante actually looked ready to see the rest of the Goodwins—rather than nervous or worried about the other things on their agenda.

Those things would come, of course, but the fact that

they could smile made Jace want to bring Torrent into a bear hug of his own.

Jace's family home came into view, and his bear relaxed, at peace. The three-story log cabin-like home had to be big enough for all eight of the Goodwin grizzlies and any friends who stopped along the way. Plus both sets of grandparents often stayed for long visits.

The bear realm did not consist of perfect royal houses. Rather they ruled by brute force when needed and lived on their own during times of peace. Jace's family was stronger than most and ruled in times of war and great peril. However, during times of peace, each den remained separate, the members free to live as they liked. If a bear crossed borders and went out of control, the other families dealt justice.

It was the way of the bears, and it worked for them.

Nadie froze beside him and looked up at him wide-eyed.

"Feel like Goldilocks, baby?" he teased.

She snorted, and Dante punched his shoulder.

"Really?" Dante asked. "A three bears joke? I expected better from you."

"What? It's not like I made a knight and windmill joke when I met you."

Dante and Nadie chuckled. "Actually, you did, but I let that pass," Dante said with a smile.

"Well, don't just stand out there. Come in and let me meet the girl. Oh, and, Dante, you better move those buns to greet me proper. It's been too damn long."

Jace smiled at the blonde woman who stood at a petite

six feet. "Nadie, I would like you to meet my mother, Sydney."

His mother smiled, pure delight in her eyes. While generally any stranger would have been offered cool eyes and a stare down until they were measured, Nadie was his mate and, therefore, family.

"Hello, Mrs. Goodwin," Nadie said politely.

His mom wrinkled her nose. "Nadie darling, you call me Sydney, Sid, Mom, Momma, or Ma. Mrs. Goodwin is my mother-in-law. Now come in so I can dote on you properly."

Soon they were surrounded by bears and warmth. They towered over Nadie, but his little mate took it in stride. He introduced her to his father, Gordon, his sisters, Sasha and Lorena, and his other two brothers, Ivan and Red.

"Red, you're the mechanic," Nadie said, smiling when she was introduced.

Red, the quietest of their group, nodded. "That's me. Your car should be fixed soon."

Nadie's eyes widened. "Oh! Thank you. Just let me know about the bill. I'm so happy you had time to take care of it."

Red's eyes narrowed. "You're family. You don't pay."

Nadie blushed. "But then how do you make any money? You seem to have a lot of family."

The room broke out into laughter and Jace pulled her to his side. She fit just right against him, tiny in a field of giants.

"Red makes money from others outside the family," his father said once they all quieted down. "With family, we barter our services. So you can pay Red back with some-thing he needs and you can provide easily."

Jace growled, low, deep.

His father scowled. "Get your mind out of the gutter, boy. You said Nadie was a teacher? Maybe she could help teach something, huh? You're lucky I don't beat you sense-less for that."

Jace ducked his head, heat crawling up his neck. He felt Dante's hand on his shoulder and Nadie's arm on his waist.

"We're all a little stressed right now, and Jace just wasn't thinking," Nadie explained.

"Hmph," his father said. "Let's eat the food your momma's spent all morning cooking and talk about how stressed you seem to be."

Jace relaxed and led his mates to the dining room where a feast containing every one of Jace's and Dante's favorite foods was served. Damn, he loved his mom. Seriously, there had to be at least eight honey dishes—come on, he was a bear—and seven roasted meats. His dragon loved the stuff—though back in the day Dante would have preferred to do his own roasting.

Times changed, but dragons didn't change as quickly.

"I didn't know what Nadie liked, so there's a bit of everything," his mom explained. "I'll know better for next time so she gets exactly what she wants."

Nadie put her hand on his mom's arm and smiled. "Everything looks amazing, Sydney. I don't see a single thing I wouldn't eat. Plus, these two guys here make sure I never go wanting, so I'm taken care of. Thank you so much for doing all of this."

If Nadie did nothing else to show her worth and love in his mother's eyes, she'd be golden for the rest of her life. Right then he knew his mother had fallen in love with his mate like a caring mother would. As soon as she found Nadie was also planning to learn to use her new powers to protect herself, Nadie could do no wrong. After all, in a maternal bear's eyes, someone who cared for others and knew how to fight back and protect her cubs was the perfect mate.

Nadie—and Dante as well—were perfect for not only him, but for his family as well.

Fate, it seemed, had gotten something right.

If only they could keep it.

At that dark thought, everyone sat down and began eating. He served Nadie and then himself, with Dante doing the same on the other side. She just rolled her eyes as they took care of her. She'd get them back later and force them to sit down and relax, but right then, he just wanted to pamper her.

Based on the smile on his mother's face, she hadn't missed the action.

He gorged himself on honey chicken, honey pies, and honey ribs while everyone talked about lighter things around him.

"Honey?" Nadie whispered.

"Yes, dear?"

Nadie rolled her eyes.

"Bears, Nadie. Bears."

"I guess I shouldn't make any getting stuck-in-the-honey-tree jokes, then," she said, her eyes filled with laugher.

"Oh my God, let me tell you the story about the time Torrent and Jace got stuck in a tree!" Lorena said, her smile bright.

From that moment, each sibling and his parents deemed it necessary to explain to Nadie each and every embarrassing event from his childhood. He had a feeling if he wasn't careful his mom would bring out the photos.

Dante, the traitor, even told a few stories of his own, but those had been when they'd first met and had been adults. He still loved hearing them, and by the smile on Nadie's face, she did too.

Once people started to slow down, the conversation turned from stories of the past to what the Conclave had told his dragon. His family sat in silence once Dante finished speaking, the tension and worry in the air palpable.

His father spoke first. "We know of the Conclave through Jace. As god-touched, he was allowed to explain his role as Mediator and where his duties originated. I always thought of them as a council with too much power. Now I see that a few of them—if not the whole of them—are bullies as well."

Dangerous words if they had not been said within the confines of his home. Jace had shielded his house from prying ears, much like Dante had done to his own. Only private dwellings under those protections were safe.

At least as safe as Jace could make it.

One never knew who was listening.

"Not all agreed with Alexander," Dante put in.

His father nodded. "Then they are potential allies. I see your path unfolding only in certain ways. One, you agree with the Conclave and serve out your five hundred years of training and then any time they need after that."

Jace and Dante both growled while Nadie, sitting between them, patted their arms.

"Stop it, both of you," Nadie admonished. "He's laying it all out, not telling Dante he should leave us." Jace settled somewhat at her words but was still on edge.

Jace's father nodded at Nadie before continuing. "The other options are trickier. Find another dragon to take Dante's place. If you find one who would not only have the power but isn't cruel, all the better."

"There is a dragon who works for Alexander," Dante said slowly. "I believe his name is Rock. I don't know him well."

"Check him out," his father ordered.

"We will have to go to the dragon realm," Dante said.

Nadie clutched Jace's hand. "We?"

Dante leaned over and brushed a kiss on her lips, letting Jace relax. "I need to introduce you and Jace as my mates. It's required of my house and will allow you to fall under my protection."

Jace held back a scowl at that. He did not like the dragon realm, but to complete all aspects of their mating, he would journey there.

"You said options," Nadie said. "What's the other one?"

His father raised his head, his lips thinning to a firm line. "We fight."

Jace held back a sigh.

He'd known that was the only other feasible option, as finding a suitable replacement was beyond farfetched. But it still hurt to hear it.

The Conclave had untold powers. If they were to fight, Jace was not sure who would win.

"The bears would stand behind you."

Jace frowned at his father's words even as they warmed him.

"And if you die fighting?" Jace asked. He had to.

Nadie flinched beside him, and he took her hand, running his thumb along her wrist.

"Then we die beside family fighting for what is right," his mother put in. "Absolute power will only corrupt. If my son and his mates cannot live in peace because of the selfishness and cruelty of a Conclave of others we've never met, then we must fight."

Dante squeezed his shoulder, and Jace gave in. A fight for a future that would be dictated by them and not a power they didn't understand was on the horizon.

They would fight if necessary.

They would die for one another.

He looked around at the power of his blood and of his heart.

But what of the cost?

CHAPTER 13

O ver a month later, Nadie still couldn't get a grasp on how much things had changed. The woman in the bathroom mirror was not the same woman who had decided to walk out of Dante's Circle and never return. She hadn't changed physically except for the spread of dark ink splashed with blood-red roses.

Nadie loved the ink, though she had never thought she was a tattoo person. The image of long lines of ink down a certain dragon's arms filled her mind, and she clutched the sink, a wave of deep, unending need shocking her system.

Jace had joked with her about how long she would last until she needed one of them again, and she had laughed. Oh she knew how weak her human half was compared to her other one. She was a starving succubus, desire running through her veins more potent than blood. She couldn't last long without release, without the life force of one of her men. The dependency chided, but Dante said she would find her equilibrium soon.

He also said that both he and Jace craved her just as much, if not more. Their own dependency was masked by the dominance of their beasts.

So far, with their testing, she had been able to last only twelve hours at most until, as Dante had once put it, she would need to *feed* again.

She felt like a leech.

A leech who got to be with two of the most sensual and dangerous men she had ever met.

Nadie ran a hand over her face, frustrated as hell she couldn't just get over it and learn to be this new person. It wasn't that she hated this new feeling, no, far from it. She'd never been the prudish and proper little girl her parents wanted her to be—had tried to force her to be. The frustration came from the fact that she didn't know how to control it. She hated feeling helpless. She'd felt helpless for two years every time she was near Dante but couldn't do anything about it. Two years when her body would grow weak, her limbs heavy, her mind ready to break.

Now it seemed she was back to square one.

She shook her head. No, that wasn't right. She was just being melodramatic. It wasn't like before where she felt undeniably at odds with everything in her life and could only cling to the thread of what she thought she could feel with Dante.

Now she had two men in her life who truly cared for her,

and she thought they soon would love her. She wasn't delusional in the fact that love was an option, but not a fact yet. That would come. She might have loved the dream of Dante when she was younger, but now she was falling in love with the man and dragon he was. Jace, too, had entered her heart in all the best possible ways. She wasn't ashamed of what she had, and she'd hurt anyone who said she should be.

Another reason she wouldn't be introducing her two men to her family. She didn't want the heartbreak and the tension. She'd begun cutting ties years ago, and as with Becca and her mother, she'd sever them completely.

Strong hands clutched her hips, and she closed her eyes, inhaling that spicy scent mixed with dark chocolate and danger. She leaned back, her dragon's chest hard and perfect for her.

"You're thinking too hard," he mumbled, his hands gliding over her hips, her stomach, between her breasts in a soothing exploration.

She moaned into him, that inner power stretching after waking up from a nap, reaching out to the man who held her with such care. She moaned, rocking her body back. His erection pressed against her back, and she let her head fall to the side, baring her neck for him. Dante licked along the line of her neck then bit down.

Hard.

She gasped, the fire of his bite shocking her, her body shaking. He held on, his teeth scraping against her before he licked around the bite, soothing.

When her knees finally stopped shaking, she swallowed hard, clearing her head. "What…what was that for?"

Dante's gaze caught hers in the mirror. "We're going to the succubus realm in a few moments. While the mating bond is potent and others should be able to sense it, I wanted to make a claim." He grinned, slow, sensual. "Plus I like having you come apart in my arms."

Nadie blinked then smiled, liking how alpha her man was. "What about me? Do I get to make a claim?"

Her mate's eyes darkened, and he turned her quickly in his arms before lifting by her hips to sit her on the sink. He brushed his hair to the side, and she glimpsed the long lines of his neck, but not before she saw a mark on the other side.

She licked her lips. "I take it you and Jace have already marked each other."

He smiled at her again, his eyes twinkling. "You took a long time in the shower. We had to find *something* to occupy our time."

She couldn't help the laugh that escaped her mouth before she pulled at his shirt so he moved closer. "I'm going to make sure none of those women—and the men too—make a move on you. You and Jace are all mine."

He grinned, showing very white teeth. "Of that we have no doubt. Now sink those pretty teeth into my flesh. You don't have sharp canines like Jace or me, so a dark bruise will work just the same. Then we'll find our bear, and you two can mark each other before we go."

She squirmed on the counter, this talk of claiming and marking filling her with need.

Dante seemed to know exactly what she was thinking about, but he didn't move to help her with her ache.

"When we get home, we'll enjoy all the tastes and sensations, my sprite. For now, this will have to do."

She scowled but moved him closer, craving his taste. He growled underneath her hold, and she licked him, his salty taste settling on her tongue. As he groaned, she bit down, not hard enough to draw blood, but to mark him as hers. He rocked against her, his fists on either side of her as if he was holding back his desire to crush her to him.

Her dragon, so strong yet so gentle.

Nadie sucked and licked until she was happy with her mark on his skin. It definitely looked like a primal claim.

Perfect.

"I see we're all getting ready to go then," Jace said from the doorway.

Dante grinned at her, that tongue ring of his glinting as he licked his lips. "She's all yours," he whispered over his shoulder before turning back to her. "At least for now. Once we get home though...well, I think we'll share quite nicely."

Nadie rolled her eyes. It seemed she wasn't the only one pounding with need when it came to the triad.

"I'm going to be all hot and bothered when we go to the other realm, you know," she said, unsure if she actually cared or not that everyone would know.

Jace moved Dante out of the way and leaned down to capture her lips in a sweet kiss. She moaned beneath him, his tongue darting into her mouth before pulling back.

"We're going to a realm that thrives on sex and sensuality," Jace explained. "The fact that we'll all walk in there with prominent marks, need radiating off each of us, and a bond that they can't challenge will only help."

"I'm so glad you guys are here to help with this, even though it's so weird that I'm not a human anymore."

Jace fisted her hair behind her head and forced her gaze to his. "You're Nadie. You're *our* Nadie. That's all that matters."

She knew that he believed that, or he tried to. He didn't say that, without that hope, fighting for what they wanted, finding a way to keep their Dante would be fruitless. Right then, though, looking into those light green eyes, she didn't want to think about that anymore. She deserved to think about herself and what she wanted…if only for the moment.

"Now…about that mark," he whispered before tugging her head to the side and sinking his fangs into her flesh.

She cried out, not in pain, but from the scorching heat shooting down her spine. She clung to Jace, wrapping her legs around his waist. He growled against her, rocking his erection against her core.

He pulled away too soon, leaving them both in such need she wasn't sure she could walk.

"My turn," he growled then moved his head to the side, baring the unmarked side of his neck. She went at him as she had Dante, wanting to crawl all over both her men, never letting them go.

Soon, she thought to herself. *Soon.*

THE WIND DANCED THROUGH HER HAIR, AND SHE TOOK A DEEP breath. The three of them stood in the clearing, waiting for the portal to open to let them through to the succubus realm. Dante held the invitation that had been sent by messenger just the week before. It had taken longer than she'd thought for the succubi to get back to them about meeting, but the men said it wasn't unusual.

According to Dante, the entire paranormal world and its realms knew the seven lightning-struck existed. Some were excited about new life, others much more violent in their reactions. Nadie was the only succubus of the group of women so far, and now she was about to meet the people that could be her own.

She only hoped they accepted her—at least to the point that she'd understand her powers.

"Ready?" Dante asked, his hand firmly holding hers.

"Ready," Nadie answered, breathless.

He blew a small tendril of fire, and she smiled, loving the small sparks of his dragon. She'd yet to see his other form— nor had she seen Jace's. They were all getting to know their human halves, and hopefully soon, she'd get to know their other ones as well.

The portal opened in front of them. Unlike the bear one, which had been a splash of color and smelled of home, this one was...sensual. Dark smoke spiraled and curled around the opening, a deceptive laziness she was sure was meant to entice the summoner and summoned as one. Dark red spirals of smoke mixed in with the black before fading away, purples and pinks taking their place before the red made another appearance.

Dante pulled her forward, and soon the three of them were surrounded by warmth…but not of home and hearth. No, this was velvet and silk against her skin, dark chocolate and strawberries on her tongue, firm hands on her hips and in her hair, a sin so inviting she almost moaned in response.

Once they made their way through and the portal closed behind them, she sucked in a breath, her body cooling as they stood in a large room.

Dante tugged her closer, his hand a proprietary grip on her hip. Jace stood on the other side of her, his arm draped around her shoulder in a move no one could dismiss as casual. No, the fact that the marks on all three were blatant and in view of all others due to their hair being pulled back hadn't been enough.

Not by far.

Couples, triads, and more were scattered around the large room, their bodies writhing as they lay with one another. Some were clothed, the bare hint of skin and seduction more heady than the full-on nudity of others. While none of them were actually having full-on sex— Nadie had a feeling that would come soon—they all were so sensual and inviting that her inner succubus stretched, wanting a piece of it all.

The dragon to her left and the bear to her right, however, blocked her in, reminding her succubus that she was theirs.

Her succubus reached through her body, wrapping its

power around her, filling her with an inner need and peace she hadn't known she'd possessed.

"Welcome, Nadie Morgan, to the realm that may one day call you their own," a woman said in front of them, her voice like a whip on bare skin, shocking yet intoxicating.

Nadie raised her head and met the gaze of the woman who'd called her name, barely holding back from sucking in a breath at her beauty.

The woman's long black hair fell in soft curls around her breasts, bringing attention to the drop-dead gorgeous curves that seemed to scream sex and desire. Red-painted lips were a sharp contrast to porcelain skin and dark eyes. She had the look of a cinema siren rather than a succubus… or maybe it was both.

She wore a cream silk dress that covered her body from neck to toe, a very different look from the others in the room who showed more skin. However, when the woman stepped closer, Nadie saw why the woman oozed evocative-ness and seduction. The slits up the sides of her dress reached the tops of her hips—the fact that she wasn't wearing anything under plain and clear. But only when the woman moved a certain way could anyone see skin.

The tease was more of a tantalization than the blatant exoticness clothes of others.

Bravo.

The woman looked between the two men at Nadie's sides and smiled a smile filled with such dark promise that no one could have mistaken it for anything else. Nadie's hackles rose, and she bared her teeth.

Dante and Jace were *hers*.

The woman raised a brow then smiled for real this time. "Nadie, I am Corena, Queen of the Succubi." She raised an arm, directing Nadie's attention to a man by her side that Nadie hadn't noticed.

Her mind had been so focused on her own men and the woman in front of her that she'd missed one of the most beautiful men she'd ever seen. Full lips, a careless grace upon his face, dark eyes, and silky chestnut hair.

Oh yes, this man was sex on a stick but paled in comparison to the mates at her sides. She pushed warmth through the mating bond—something both had taught her to do—and her men growled softly at her side, accepting it.

"This is Dresden, King of the Incubi," Corena explained.

Ah, yes, Dante had explained this. The realm was rumored to be matriarchal. However, the queen had a king who acted more of a Consort than king. Their relationship was rumored to be open to many partners—both casual and with meaning—but the king and queen had ruled for hundreds of years, side by side.

It was a love story Nadie wanted to know more of, but right then, all she wanted to do was take her men back to their home and have their way with them. The heat and carnal energy in the room was intoxicating.

Dresden nodded, and Nadie had to hold back the sudden urge to rub herself all over her men, marking her territory.

Corena grinned. "You'll learn to hide your urges better in the future, young one." Nadie blushed but didn't respond. "Dante, Jace, it is good to finally meet you. We've heard of both of you, as you know. To have you mated to one who might one day be our own will only honor us."

"One day?" Nadie asked then cursed herself.

Corena nodded. "We do not know you or how you've come to be, Nadie. We are not like those in other realms who will cast you out with no reason, but we are also... leery. I will protect my people no matter the cost, and once we find out how we blend and who we are as a people with you as one of us, then we can become something less...informal."

For some reason, the honesty allowed Nadie to relax. She didn't misunderstand and think these people would welcome her with open arms. While it might have been that way with Lily and the brownies, Becca and Jamie had to fight all out hostility. The cautious approach of the succubi made sense, and Nadie wouldn't waste her chance.

"Thank you for the welcome," Dante said, his voice low. Nadie couldn't tell what he was feeling, but she was glad he was there.

"Yes, thank you," Jace added in.

"Now, Nadie, take a seat with your men, and let's discuss why you are here today."

Nadie gripped her men's hands then followed Corena to a table, which was low to the ground; pillows surrounded it in a decadent array of comfort. Nadie sat between her men, not quite relaxed but feeling better than she had before.

"I'd like to know more about what I can do, who I am," Nadie said after the attendants filled their wine glasses. Dante brought hers to his nose then to her lips.

Corena laughed softly as Dante tilted the glass so Nadie could take a drink. "We aren't going to poison your mate, dragon. You know we don't like confrontation."

Dante winked at Nadie then set the glass down. "I trust no one at first glance. I'm a dragon."

Dresden snorted, Jace joining in.

Corena shook her head, her lips twitching. "Now, Nadie, we will be able to tell you more about who you are and what you can do once you tell us what mark you bear."

Nadie frowned. "You mean the ink?"

Corena nodded. "Yes, your ink. Each succubus holds a mark on their skin that reflects their house. As you grow into your power, your ink will change and evolve to add your own personality, but the initial mark will always be your history. As yours comes from dormant DNA, I'm interested to see what house lost your line so many years ago."

"You're saying that each house has a different power?" she asked, though Dante had explained it as such before. It didn't hurt to hear it from the queen as well.

"Yes. Some have more defensive skills than those with offensive ones, while others can heal or read minds." Corena waved her hand, and an attendant came forward, a large book in his hands. "You can have a look at our history and such in this. Normally, I wouldn't hand it off to one I do not know, but it's merely a copy, and you're mated to a Royal dragon and bear. That makes things different."

Jace accepted the volume and placed it near him. They'd look at it later when they were alone.

She looked at both her men, who nodded. With a strained smile, she stood between them. They each placed a hand on one of her legs, and she centered herself before turning to bare her side. She pulled up her shirt and pulled her slacks down slightly so they could see her hip. She wasn't as open showing her body to strangers as some in the room, and with her two mates at her side, she didn't want to incite a confrontation.

Corena gasped then murmured to Dresden before standing. Nadie tilted her head as she righted her clothes.

"What's wrong? What did I do?"

Corena shook her head, tears filling her eyes. "You did nothing, child," she said before baring her hip.

Though parts of the design were different—showing Corena's own path rather than her line's history—the resemblance was striking.

Black leaves with crimson-red roses.

"You are of my line, Nadie Morgan. You are royalty."

Nadie blinked and sat down, needing to be near her men.

"What…what does that mean?"

Corena smiled again then sat down, gripping Dresden's hand. "It means that, though our bond is diluted, we are family." She looked at Nadie's two men before gazing at Nadie once more. "Our line isn't as large as the others because of who we are, but to find another can only bring joy and acceptance. You are one of us, Nadie. There will be no questions, no waiting."

Dante squeezed her side, and Jace did the same. "Does

this mean you will fight for her if there comes a time she is in danger?" Dante asked.

Nadie started then looked at her dragon.

Corena tilted her head, interest on her face. "If we must, we will. We do not fight wars like the others in our worlds, but if one of our own is in danger, then we will fight. Now tell us about this possible danger and what you see in your future."

Dante told the succubus and incubus everything, surprising Nadie at the amount of trust involved. It seemed that Dante was gathering forces and not hindered by the fact that he wasn't supposed to talk of the Conclave. With a potential battle on the horizon, the need for secrecy from a group of paranormals that thought they ruled the world went out the window.

By the end, Corena's scowl made Nadie want to back away from the woman. "We must discuss this further. I will do what I can to show Nadie how to fight for herself as well." She met Nadie's gaze. "Your dragon can help. Nadie, our line has an offensive power. We use the life force we gain through sex and sensual contact to make a form of splintered lightning. You will be able to use this to injure and, one day, kill your attackers. It is not easy, but it can be managed."

Nadie swallowed hard at the facts she laid out. "I want to learn it all. I don't want to be their weakness."

Both men growled beside her as what Nadie thought was pride filled Corena's eyes. "We won't let that happen. Now, I have to talk with my own council about this," she told them all. "We cannot let a ruling body force us to abide by their dictates without our own voices." She stood with a feline grace, and the rest followed. "I will be in contact with you soon." She moved then, gripping Nadie's hands. "It is good to meet you, Nadie Morgan."

"You as well."

Corena grinned then waved them off, Dresden at her side. Nadie followed Dante and Jace through the portal as soon as they made their way through the room with the writhing bodies—only this time they stared at her with awed wonder rather than mere curiosity. That would be something to think about later.

Right then she needed her men.

As soon as they hit the clearing, Jace's phone rang, and Nadie frowned.

"Shit, I missed four calls," Jace mumbled as he listened to whoever was on the other line.

Nadie felt Dante tense beside her, and she wrapped her arms around his waist, wanting to soothe but not knowing why he was reacting this way.

When Jace hung up, Dante scowled.

"You know I have to do this," Jace said.

"Do what?" Nadie asked.

Jace cupped her face and kissed her softly. "I need to meet with another Meditator. I will have an assignment soon, and I have to keep up my training."

In all that had happened since she'd met him, she'd almost forgotten he had a duty as Mediator. He'd been on break since he'd met her, and for some reason, she'd thought they'd have more time before he would be gone for long stretches of time...leaving her alone with a dragon who might not be beside her once the dust settled and the Conclave had their way.

She fought back panic and raised her chin, determined to be stronger than her fears.

"It's just training? You'll be back soon?" she asked.

"Yes. I'm going to do all in my power to take time for us. I had told them this after my last assignment." The one that had separated him from them all for so long. "I will find a way to make this work."

It seemed they were all saying that to each other more often than not.

She didn't know how she felt about that.

He kissed her again then did the same to Dante, who hadn't spoken. Jace gave them both a sad smile then turned to run to where his bike was parked on the other side of the house. He would take his bike to another clearing and open a portal. Sometimes he would be able to do it from Dante's clearing, but right then, she had a feeling he needed to be alone. Or at least away from Dante. She leaned into Dante, wanting to take his mind off the pain of watching Jace going away—even if it was just for the short term.

Dante looked down at her and sighed. "I'm sorry I'm acting like an ass."

She grinned at him. "You know how you can make it up to me, don't you?"

His eyes darkened, and he licked his lips. "I have a few ideas."

CHAPTER 14

Nadie wiggled away. "You'll have to catch me first."
She darted away, running as fast as she could,
reaching the house and clamoring to open the door.

Dante roared a laugh behind her, loving the way his
mate knew him. "I'm a dragon, my darling. You should
know better than to give chase."

She tossed a look over her shoulder then turned to run
through the house. Before she could take another step, he
pounced on her, clutching her to his chest.

"I wanted you to catch me," she said, breathless.

Dante growled, biting down on her lower lip. "Next time
I'll let you run longer. Right now I need to be inside you as I
suck on those pretty tits."

She pushed against him, rubbing along his body like a
cat in heat.

"Inside me. Now."

He quickly stripped her down to her skin and pulled his clothes off as well. Her breasts fell heavy into his hands, and he sucked one nipple into his mouth, biting down with the tip of a fang. She moaned against him as he plumped her other breast with his free hand. Gods, he loved the taste of her skin.

Dante licked and kissed up her body until he towered over her.

"Dante," she gasped.

He grinned, his dragon ready to take her, possess her.

"Nadie."

He kissed her then, hard, fast, demanding. Her arms went to his back, her fingernails clawing his skin. He pulled away slightly, holding back the roar that would show her that he fucking loved it.

When he went back to his knees, she blinked down at him, licking her lips.

"Face the wall," he ordered.

Her eyes widened, but she did as she was told.

He kissed her lower back then gripped her ass, spreading her cheeks and lowering his face. She gasped at his movement, pressing her body closer to him. He tongued her hole, licking and sucking before burying his face in her pussy. She rocked against him, rolling her hips in time with his penetrations. Since she was facing away from him, her hands braced against the wall, he was able to let his hands roam so he could cup her breasts.

"That feels so good," she moaned.

He growled, knowing the vibrations would be a shock

against her clit. When he rolled both nipples between his fingers, he heard her cry out and felt her come on his tongue. He didn't stop licking her up but moved his hands down so he could fuck her with his fingers. He changed positions slightly, allowing one hand better access to her pussy while he used her juices to play with her ass with his other hand.

She rolled her hips, and he grinned before sucking on her clit.

"Dante, please, fuck me."

"I love the way you beg, my sprite. I'm going to make you come on my face one more time, and then I'll fuck you hard. Make it good for me, darling."

She moved her hips faster, and he grinned before gently letting his thumb breach her ass. His mate froze for a moment, and Dante stopped, thinking he'd gone too far, but when she arched her back, taking his thumb deeper, he growled. She danced her hips in circles on his face, and he fucked her pussy with one hand and her ass with his thumb.

"Give it to me," he whispered, his voice full of need and sin.

"Yes!" she screamed as she came again.

Before she finished her orgasm, Dante pulled back and stood, gripping her hips. He entered her in one thrust, both of them crying out.

"Move, please," she begged, pressing her ass closer to his groin.

"You're so fucking tight."

"Then make it good."

He grinned then pumped into her, gripping her hips so hard he was sure he would leave bruises. His Nadie could take it though, and from the way she moved with him, she would wear those bruises with pride.

Fuck he loved his mate.

Nadie looked over his shoulder, and he leaned down to capture her lips, his body never losing rhythm as he made love to his mate.

"Come in me, please, my dragon, come in me. With me."

How could he deny that request?

He slammed into her once more and roared as he came within her. Nadie called out with him, her pussy clenching his cock as she milked him.

When they finally stopped shaking, he fell to the floor, pulling Nadie into his lap and holding her close. They both were drenched in sweat, yet he didn't want to move. He just wanted his Nadie.

His mate nuzzled into him, and he ran his hands down her body.

"Best. Ever."

Dante grinned at her words. "Better than the first time?"

She pulled back and looked at him, tilting her head. "Um, I don't want to choose. Let's just call them all the best ever."

He chuckled and kissed her forehead. "Deal. And, yes, it *was* the best ever."

And his dragon couldn't wait to do it again.

They stood in the clearing again, only this time while Dante changed into a dragon, he would be doing it with Jace and Nadie there. Jace had seen his form many years ago, but Nadie had not. His dragon preened at the idea of their mate seeing its form. Dante was surprised the damn thing didn't want to primp and shine up its scales before the big reveal.

Jace had come back quickly from his meeting, his decision made it seemed. They were not going to follow the Conclave's demands until all was calm. His lover seemed to be okay with the decision, but Dante wasn't sure. The time would come when they would all have to figure out Jace's line of work and duty, but not right then.

He'd put off going to the dragon realm for far too long, and now, two weeks after their journey to the succubus realm, they were heading into the den of fire. While Nadie might have looked excited to see his dragon, none of them were looking forward to spending any amount of time with the rest of the dragons.

This wasn't going to be pretty.

He not only needed to introduce Nadie and Jace to his family, but to his House as well. His family was filled with sadistic, murdering bastards who wanted power, wealth, and sex without having to do any work. The House, though, was filled with females.

Black-and-blue-scaled females that had been hounding him for centuries to mate with him. He *really* didn't want to deal with them *and* Nadie's and Jace's reactions.

When had his life turned into a soap opera?

He used to be the nomadic hermit dragon with friends from other realms and no worries other than keeping others at bay. Now he had a potential war, two mates who he loved and didn't want to leave, and now...this.

Dragon shit.

"Ready?" Jace asked from his side, his hand resting on the small of Dante's back.

Dante relaxed for a moment, leaning into the other man. He closed his eyes, needing to regroup before they left. It wouldn't do anyone any good for him to be a stressed-out basket case. He'd either end up throwing his mates in his hoard and hiding them from the outside or start growling and spitting fire at random dragons that dared enter his line of sight.

Nadie nuzzled into his side, and he grinned, wrapping one arm around her so he could press her as close to him as possible.

"I'm ready now," he said after a few moments of blissed silence. He pulled away from them so he could have the space to shift without crushing anyone. "Stand back."

Jace took Nadie's hand, and they took a few steps backward, curiosity on both their faces. Even though Jace had seen his dragon form, it had been many years.

He sucked in a breath and drew on his dragon's essence. He knew what his mates saw—white smoky eyes and an almost glowing presence—as well as what they felt—a manic energy and the sudden drop of temperature.

He pulled harder on his dragon, and it shimmered into existence.

"You're…you're beautiful," Nadie whispered.

Dante ducked his head, his snout touching the ground so he could be closer to Nadie without hurting her. The dragon wanted to reach out with its claw and hold her close, never letting her go, but the man didn't want to scare her. After all, he was one fucking huge dragon.

Nadie raised her arm as if to touch him then froze.

Dante moved closer, butting her hand with his snout, wanting her touch.

She sighed as her palm brushed against his scales, and if he'd been a cat, he'd have purred. As it was, his fire rumbled, content and ready to move closer.

"You're warm," she said in awe, and Jace chuckled beside her. She looked over at their mate and frowned. "What?"

Jace shrugged then put his hand next to her. Dante sighed at the contact of his two mates. "I think I said the exact same things you have when I first saw Dante's dragon. He's one beautiful beast."

His dragon wanted to bow and preen, as was his due.

Dante relished their touch for a few more moments, but if they didn't leave soon, they never would. He pulled away and smiled at the put-out faces.

"Come on, you'll be riding me into the realm," Dante said. His voice was lower, more of a growl in this form than his human one.

Jace snorted. "We can talk about a different kind of riding later."

"You can talk." Nadie blinked up at him, and Dante

snorted a laugh, a small tendril of smoke escaping his nostril.

Jace picked up Nadie by the waist and set her on Dante's arm. "Climb up, I'll be right behind you."

Nadie did as ordered, her movements careful. As if Dante or Jace would ever let her fall.

"You can talk," she repeated.

"Yes, I can. Not all paranormals can. In fact only a few who shift into fully new creatures can. Dragons spend most of their days in their dragon form, so it's only natural they would be able to talk in this form."

"That is really, really wicked," she said, a smile in her voice.

"I can't talk in my bear form, so I'm kind of jealous," Jace put in.

Dante felt the two of them settling on his upper back, their thighs squeezing him tight. He didn't have a harness for them up there, so Jace would have to hold on tight— something they'd done in the past. Now, though, if Dante ever wanted to take Nadie on a ride of her own, he'd have to make a saddle of some sort. Demeaning in some respects, but for his mates, he'd do anything.

Nadie patted his scales, and he moved back into her touch. "We're going to have to have a talk about this whole dragon thing. Watching old movies with sexy men in kilts really didn't prepare me for this."

Dante growled, Jace joining in. "Kilts? You want me to wear a kilt? Because if you're talking about some other man you think is sexy, I will have to kill him."

Nadie sighed dramatically. "That's all you got out of that? Okay, fine, no other man in the world is sexy. They ceased to exist for me."

"Good," Dante said.

"I was joking, Dante."

"I really don't think you were," Jace added in.

"Fine, you two are alpha idiots, but I adore you. Now as for the kilt thing...please?" She bounced on Dante's back, and he grinned. "Please wear a kilt for me. You don't have to wear anything else."

Jace coughed a laugh, and Dante looked over his shoulder, his long neck curving. Jace grinned. "I'll wear a kilt if Dante does."

Dante nodded. He'd worn them before when he'd been living in Scotland during the time of Highlanders and Lowlanders and times of war. "Done. Now hold on tight and let's go."

He pulled open a portal and lifted off the ground. Nadie squealed—not with fright, but with pure delight. He moved his wings, and he flew through the portal. Fire and star-bursts surrounded them but didn't touch them, the fire real, but not harmful to those who entered invited.

Soon they found themselves on the rocky cliffs of the dragon realm, the portal closing behind them. Nadie and Jace didn't speak, but they looked around, Dante doing the same. The jagged cliffs and peaks dotted the landscape. The vast sea crashed into the cliffs, the foamy waves violent but still soothing to Dante's ears.

There were castles off in the distance, each belonging to a

different dragon in the same House. They were on Azure Royal land, Dante's land. His own castle was the closest to them, but he wouldn't be taking his mates there. No, he would be going to the head palace where he could get this over with.

"Almost there," he whispered, aware they weren't alone. Dante was never alone.

He knew dragons had spotted their entry and were waiting for Dante's next move. If he'd brought in outsiders, then it had to be for only a few reasons. Either they were to be used for fucking or for a meal. After all, paranormals weren't human. No, they might have human form, but they weren't what their diluted prodigy were.

It was a rare concept indeed that these would be his mates.

Hence the reason they were there.

Protection came in many forms, and knowledge was one of them.

Caves dotted the cliffs, a dragon's hoard a secret and cosseted possession. Most of the visual caves were decoys and booby-trapped for those who dared enter their territory. The traps usually didn't kill, as a dragon wanted to experience that particular enjoyment themselves.

He landed on the edge of the Royal House and lowered his head so Nadie and Jace could slide off his back safely. Jace put Nadie between him and Dante, and the dragon approved. Nadie didn't have a handle on her powers yet and needed the help. One day she would be a fighting force, but until then, they all had to be careful.

Five female dragons stalked into the room, their blue scales mixed with the colors of their various other lines. Two were of the Scarlet House, another from the Chartreuse House, while two more held Alabaster scales.

"Dante!" the Chartreuse dragon purred. "You're home!"

"Finally," one of the Scarlets said. "We've been waiting forever."

"What can we do for you?" an Alabaster said. She smiled with lots of teeth. "We'll do *anything* for you."

Dante closed his eyes and prayed for patience. Or a really sharp stick.

Nadie cleared her throat beside him, and Dante lifted a lip, baring a fang.

The five female dragons blinked and looked down at Nadie, confusion on their faces. He saw their eyes light up, and for a moment, Dante was afraid he was going to have to kill those of his House.

"You're mated!" one of the Scarlets said. It could have been the one that had spoken before, but Dante couldn't tell. He didn't care who they were or their names. They weren't Nadie, so they didn't matter.

All five shimmered, and suddenly they were five dragons in human form. Each of them wore clothing, and while some would have found their curves and long, wavy hair sexy, Dante couldn't be bothered.

"Yes, he is," Nadie said, that inner succubus of hers shining through. Dante grinned. He liked this Nadie.

One of the Alabasters came up and brought Nadie in a

hug. Dante growled, as did Jace right behind Nadie, both ready to fight.

"We're so happy for all of you," that same Alabaster said. "I'm Vivian, this is Moira, Bree, Donna, and Lauren." She pointed to each of them, but for the life of him, Dante couldn't figure out who was who.

"It's about time Dante's found his mates," Moira or Bree said. "Oh! And you're a bear."

Jace nodded, his eyes wide. This hadn't been the welcome either of them had expected.

All five dragons were talking a mile a minute, and he felt Nadie becoming overwhelmed through their bond. He wouldn't be having that.

He opened his mouth and roared.

Everyone stopped moving and turned to him, their eyes wide.

"Thanks," Nadie said after she blinked.

Dante lowered his head so she could pet him. "These are my mates, Nadie and Jace. We are here to introduce them to the House and show they are under my protection." They were also there to see his family and do the same, as well as find out if Rock was the dragon he needed to take over the Conclave's position, but he didn't mention that. Yet.

"We're so happy you mated," Lauren said. Or at least he thought it was Lauren. Dear gods, these women confused him. They always had.

"Seriously," another dragon put in. "While Dante is beyond sexy, as you well know,"—she winked—"he wasn't the true half for any of us so it wouldn't have worked. But now that he has mates, we need to celebrate."

Nadie started laughing and shook her head. "You guys are crazy."

One of them raised their brow. "Duh. We're mateless dragons. It happens."

"Now tell us everything. How you met, how you mated. Everything."

Dante closed his eyes at Vivian's demands but didn't say anything. Nadie seemed to have entered into yet another group of women. He shimmered his body and became human again, wanting to be able to at least be in the same form as the people around him. They talked with the females for over an hour, and by the time they were through, Dante was laughing so hard he was crying.

It seemed, without the need to hide or fight off women, being in the Royal House wasn't that taxing.

He probably shouldn't have thought that last thought considering, as soon as he did, Obsidian dragons landed beside him.

His family.

He growled but didn't shift to his dragon form, not wanting to give them the luxury and pride of that. He and Jace stood in front of Nadie while, surprisingly, the five female dragons moved so they surrounded the triad, ready to fight.

"I see you've mated," his father, Udell, drawled.

Dante raised his head. "They are under my protection. You've been warned."

His mother, Stacia, glared and chomped her teeth once at Nadie. His beautiful mate rolled her eyes. Dangerous in most cases, but he wouldn't let his mother hurt her. As it was, he had to hold back a laugh at the move.

"Your bitch disrespects me," Stacia snapped.

"Shut up, Mother," his sister Fadia said, bored as ever. "We're here, they're here. They're mated. Let's go. I need to go see Number Four." Fadia had at least six husbands scattered around the realm at last check and numbered them rather than remembering their names. Considering she couldn't keep track, Dante couldn't really care either.

"Dante left us long ago, and I want to go home. I want that roasted boar I saw on the table before we left." Dante had to hold back a snarl at his brother Meurig's tone. Dear gods, the man ate constantly and couldn't even be bothered to deal with family business.

"Fine," Stacia growled. "He'll get what's coming to him. I hear there are plans for our Dante." Stacia grinned then, and Dante had to hold back the bile in his throat. Her face really wasn't a pretty picture.

And just what did his mother know about the Conclave? Or was she referencing another threat to his life?

With that, they flew off through the large open arches, leaving a bewildered Dante in their wake. Something was up their sleeves—at least his mother's. They'd been trying to kill him since he was a baby though, so he shouldn't have been surprised.

"Are you okay?" Nadie asked as she placed her palms on his stomach.

He pulled her into his arms as Jace wrapped his own around Dante. "I will be fine. You both are now claimed on a public level. That should help." Or at least it would put the law on their side.

"Now, are we going to find that other dragon?" Jace asked.

"What other dragon?" Vivian asked, the other woman surrounding her.

While Dante didn't trust them fully, the fact that they'd been prepared to fight to protect his mates helped make his decision. "I'm looking for a dragon named Rock."

Donna scrunched up her nose. "Why would you be looking for him? He's a right bastard."

The ladies nodded.

"Plus I hear..." Bree's eyes widened, and she shut her mouth.

"What do you hear?" Nadie asked.

"That he's sleeping with your mom," Lauren answered, a frown on her face. "Sorry, Dante. I know it's gross to hear that your mom's a whore."

Dante grunted. He knew his parents slept around. He hated his family, and now that his mates had met them, he wanted to go jump in a lake and clean them all from the taint that was his family.

"Rock is not a nice dragon," Moira put in. "Whatever reasons you have for talking with him, I'd reconsider. He'd gut you and blame someone else. He's one of *those* dragons."

Dante's hopes fell, but he nodded and thanked them for the information. Soon Jace and Nadie were on his back again, and they returned to the human realm. He shifted back to human form, and his mates were holding him.

"I'm sorry," Nadie said.

"Fuck, Dante, we'll find another way," Jace put in.

Dante shook his head but didn't say anything, merely pulled his mates closer. It didn't matter, not anymore. It looked like a fight was inevitable. Based on what he'd heard, he couldn't trust Rock in a position of power, and he couldn't find another way out of the Conclave's order.

He would have to fight for his right to live as he desired.

The bears, succubi, and even some of the dragons would be on his side...but would it be enough?

He held back a roar and closed his eyes.

There was only so much a dragon could do, and roasting his enemies on a spit wouldn't solve his problems. Between his new mating, Nadie's powers, Jace's job as a Mediator, and the battle on the horizon, his dragon wanted to hide everyone in his hoard and never come out.

The fight was coming. There was no way around it.

Dante wouldn't fail.

He couldn't.

ROCK SCREAMED AND THREW A VASE AGAINST THE WALL. IT wasn't his vase, so he didn't give a shit as it broke into a dozen pieces and littered the floor. He roared, the anger running through his veins ready to burst. If he'd been in dragon form, he'd have spewed fire, but as it was, he'd turned human to fuck the woman on the bed beside him.

He wasn't in the mood, but he'd do anything to get ahead.

Even Stacia.

He'd been watching Dante's little triad of bliss and fucking happiness when Rock wasn't hiding the fact he was watching them from the Conclave. The Conclave kept a watch on Dante as well, ruining every plan Rock could come up with. Between the dragon's natural wards and the fact that the fucking dragon was never alone, he couldn't get close enough to kill the bastard.

He'd almost been able to get at the dragon, but then the Conclave had created a storm and almost killed one of Dante's mates. The woman, Nadie. The Conclave wanted her dead so Dante wouldn't care about her anymore. He wouldn't have cared about her death, but ever since that moment, Dante had increased his power and wards, halting all of Rock's plans.

"Come fuck me, Leonard," Stacia whined behind him. "Get over the stress and put that dick in me. I've had a fucking long day with Udell and my beastly children and need to get sweaty."

Rock whirled around growled. "Don't call me Leonard." He couldn't believe his mother would name him something that sounded so pathetically weak. That's why he went by Rock. That name was tough. Just like his scales.

Stacia held up her hands, legs spread, ready for him. "Sorry, lover. Now get that penis in me."

Rock sighed and walked close so he stood between her legs. He lifted her thighs and pumped into her, annoyed that he'd gotten so angry over that little prick.

Stacia made the appropriate sounds, and he leaned down, sucking a nipple into his mouth. She seemed to like that, pressing him closer to her breast. He pulled away and turned her over. He slammed her face into the bed and fucked her from behind, thrusting as hard as he could, enjoying the way she mewed.

"Enjoying yourself?" he asked.

"Yes, yes, keep going," she said, her words muffled from the sheet in her mouth.

He gripped her hips and stopped for a moment. "I'll keep going, but I need to think about how to kill your son."

She waved her arm around, kind of difficult to do at her current angle but whatever. "Fine, fine, kill my son, just keep going."

Rock shrugged then thrust again, his mind on how to kill the son of the woman he was fucking. What an odd world he lived in, but if he was careful, he'd one day rule it.

Not a bad way to end the day.

CHAPTER 15

The block of wood flying at his head should have been the worst part of his day, but Jace had a feeling it was only the beginning. He ducked out of the way and kept prowling toward his mates.

"Oh my God!" Nadie ran to him, her hair wild around her face. "I'm so sorry, honey. Did I hurt you?"

The sight of this tiny woman worried that she'd hurt a bear as big as himself made him smile, despite the fact that inside he wanted to scream and rage over what wasn't in his control. He tucked a strand of hair behind her ear and smiled.

"You didn't hit me. Don't worry about it. At least you didn't hit the house."

Her eyes widened, and she stepped to the side so she could see around him. "Crap. This whole lightning thing is hard." She looked down at her open palms and wiggled her fingers. "I don't think I'll ever get the hang of it."

Dante walked up behind her, the hair that had escaped his braid flying around his head in the wind. Jace tried to smile at his dragon, but Dante seemed to see beneath the surface and knew something was wrong.

Damn intuitive dragon.

Dante wrapped his arms around Nadie's hips and brought her to his chest. Jace fisted his hands, wanting to join in, craving their touch, but he couldn't. Not yet. Not until he told them what he'd found out and dealt with their reactions.

Jace swallowed hard and put his thoughts to the side for the moment. "What were you practicing?"

Nadie tilted her head and frowned. "You're not telling us something."

Jace sighed and ran a hand through his hair. "Let's talk about it in a bit, okay? I'd rather hear how your powers are progressing and relax before we deal with yet another thing on the outside looking in."

Nadie bit her lip then nodded. "You get a pass for now, but don't think I'll be forgetting any time soon."

Jace smiled softly then pulled her into his arms, unable to hold back any longer. "Thank you, darling." He lowered his head, his lips brushing hers, and she melted against him.

When he pulled back, it was to find Dante even closer, the man's hand behind Jace's head. Jace closed his eyes as his dragon pressed his mouth to Jace's in a rough caress.

"We won't be forgetting," Dante whispered. "Come, you'll want to see how much better Nadie is getting."

Their mate snorted before walking over to the area of trees where they must have been practicing. "Sure, dragon, whatever you say. So far I've burned a hole in the grass and almost knocked Jace out with a piece of wood. So much better."

Jace grinned at her frustration. She was doing much better than she thought, and he and Dante would just have to prove it to her.

"So, what have you been doing?" he asked.

Nadie held out her hands and sighed. "Blowing up things?"

Dante cupped her cheek, and Jace smiled at the possessive dragon. "You've been doing a whole hell of a lot more than that, my sprite, so stop bashing yourself. How did you make that burn mark? Hmm? How about the fact that you had to have done *something* in order to break off a piece of the tree so it could go hurling in Jace's direction? Hmm? Just because you can't control it fully yet doesn't mean you haven't been making progress. Don't sell yourself short."

Nadie sighed, her shoulders low.

Jace couldn't take it anymore and pulled her into his arms again, slapping her ass so she squealed.

"Jace!"

"What? I wanted you to smile. Now, show me what you've been doing."

"Fine. Dante is teaching me to center myself so I can focus on my inner power. It's really weird since I thought my inner power would be all about heat and sex, you know? But it's not. It's about life."

Jace smiled full-on and patted her ass again.

She narrowed her eyes. "Hands off my butt, bear. I need to focus."

He squeezed then let her go. Nadie rolled her eyes then turned away from him, facing the tree that had a huge chunk taken out of it. Ah, this must be her practice tree, and from the size of the hole in the side, Jace was mighty glad he'd ducked out of the way when he had.

"How do you pull on your inner power?" he asked.

"Dante said it was sort of like how he pulls on his dragon or like how you find your bear to shift." She scrunched up her face. "It's weird, like a tug on a bond I didn't know I had. It's not like the mating bond. That's something warm and fragile in some respects but growing strong as we continue to find out how we fit together. The bond I have with my succubus, if you can call it a bond, though, feels warm but sort of like a ball of energy that could get out of control if I don't know how to approach it."

His bear didn't like the thought that she could be hurt with what was inside her, but he knew Dante was teaching her control. After all, the dragon held the fire of a volcano practically inside his chest and knew how to control it. He'd be able to help Nadie. Jace was a little different. While all three held their other paranormal creatures inside, he didn't have any special powers or weapons other than his claws and teeth. The fact that he was a Mediator was something else entirely that had nothing to do with the fact he was a bear.

"Can you show me?"

Nadie smiled. "I can try. You might want to step back though. Flying debris and all."

He took a step back so she would feel more comfortable. Dante stepped closer to Jace so they were hip to hip. Without conscious thought, Jace leaned into his mate, needing the other man's strength, if just for the moment.

Dante wrapped his arm around Jace's hip, and they stood there watching their third hold out her arms and take in the power that made her stronger than any other person he knew, stronger than she thought she was.

Her hands glowed white as her power radiated from her center and shot out from her palms. He heard her suck in a breath as she seemed to push the power out in an arc of lighting so beautiful Jace couldn't form the words to describe it.

It wasn't that the lightning was deadly—because it was—it was because it had come from deep within Nadie, the idea that the life force she'd taken from *them* had turned into something that could protect her.

That in itself made Jace want to fall to his knees and bow to her greatness.

She pulled back after hitting the tree dead center, and she wavered on her feet. Jace ran to her, holding her to his chest as she blinked up at him.

"What's wrong?" he asked, his voice tense.

She smiled dreamily up at him. "That was fun. I don't

think I've hit dead center before. I think you're my good luck charm."

He kissed her forehead, not wanting to let her go. Dante came up to them and cupped her face, turning her to him while Jace still held her in his arms.

"Did you use too much power, my sprite?" their dragon asked.

She shook her head. "Not too much, but just enough. I'm about tapped out I think."

Jace cupped her ass, bringing her closer. "I guess we'll have to replenish your source," he teased.

Nadie threw her head back and laughed. "Oh God, that has to be the worst pickup line I've ever heard."

Dante chuckled beside them, his hands on each of their backs, keeping them close. "You obliviously hadn't heard the lines our angel friends have used."

Nadie raised a brow. "I'm going to have to ask Lily and Jamie it seems." She'd talked to her friends about what had been going on, but with everyone's lives so busy, getting together to talk about more than a few things at a time seemed almost impossible. The others knew a fight was coming and would be on their side, but she still missed them.

Jace nuzzled her side. "I wasn't kidding about the replenishing thing, but I'll be more romantic about it."

She turned her head and bit her lip. "I like the sound of that, but first, we're going to go inside, and you're going to tell us why you were so worried and drawn when you came out here. And don't think you can get out of it, mister."

He sighed but gripped her hand, leading them into the house. Dante walked behind them, a quiet storm that Jace feared would rage once the other man found out what was on Jace's mind. He didn't have a choice though. Jace never had a choice.

And that was the problem.

Jace led them to the living room and pulled away, tucking his hands in his pockets.

"Tell us," Dante said, his voice low.

Jace raised his chin. "I've been given another assignment. I'm supposed to leave for the pixie realm in three days. I don't know how long I'll be gone. I don't know what it entails as they haven't given me the information. I'm sorry."

Nadie frowned at him, and Jace wanted to pull her into his arms, tell her he was sorry he was going to have to leave her so soon. Dante didn't move, didn't blink, didn't do anything.

That was scarier than any reaction Jace could have imagined.

A dragon who masked his emotions was a dangerous dragon.

"You can't get out of it? You'll have to leave again?" Nadie walked toward him but didn't make any move to touch him.

His bear raged at the loss, but he stood there, ready to take their wrath at leaving them so soon. He shook his head, sadness enveloping him.

"I'm sorry, I don't have any control over what they tell

me to do. I go where I'm needed and come back home when I can."

"Bullshit," Dante snapped.

Jace met the fire in his dragon's eyes and growled. "I don't have control. I do what I'm told."

"You're a fucking idiot, that's what you are. What the fuck are we doing here if you're just going to leave with no contact for what could be years? I'm pulling in forces to battle the fucking Conclave and you're just leaving to deal with their orders. Think about it, Jace. Who gives you orders? The Conclave. They're trying to separate us. And you're letting them."

His bear raged, and he fisted his hands. "I'm not a fucking puppet, and I *know* it's the Conclave, but unlike your summons, the pixies actually need my help."

"And the pixies are more important than us?" Dante lashed out. "No, they aren't. There are a hundred other Mediators that can do this. Mediators without mates and wars on the horizon. Why didn't the Conclave ask them? Because they want you away from us. Well, fuck that. Tell them no. You're allowed to, but you've always done what you've been told because there hasn't been a reason not to. Now you have a damned good reason to refuse."

Jace growled, his head lowered, ready to ram into the bastard. Did the other man not think Jace would do anything to be with his mates? How the hell was he supposed to give up his duties, the duties that would protect an entire realm?

"I can't be selfish, dragon."

Nadie stood between them both in an instant, and Jace froze. "Stop it. Both of you. How is fighting going to help right now? You're not being selfish by wanting to go against the Conclave, Jace. It's fishy timing, and we all know it. If Dante is right, and there are other Meditators out there to help the pixies, why can't one of them take it? Have you ever taken a break?"

Jace snarled.

"You don't scare me, grizzly," Nadie shot back. "Don't snarl at me."

"No, he's never taken a break," Dante spat. "We lost years because he was stuck in that fucking realm and now look at us. We're fighting again. We could have lost everything because of your job and Nadie would've been hurt because of it."

Jace staggered back at the words. "You still blame me?" he asked, and the anger leached out of him. Gods, he didn't deserve the two in front of him, and now the others knew it.

"Dante!" Nadie yelled before stepping on the coffee table so she could cup Jace's face. "Don't listen to him. You know I don't blame you. I don't even blame Dante for keeping everything from me for all those years." She glared over her shoulder at the dragon who looked as if he'd break at any moment.

"Shit, Jace, I didn't mean that. I..."

Jace pulled away from Nadie. "What the fuck are we

doing? We're fighting over things we can't control and lashing out like we don't even know each other. Maybe that's the problem though. We *don't* know each other."

Nadie slapped him. Hard. "Get control of yourself, ass." She pulled her hand to her chest, the sting surprising her. "Jesus. Now I'm hitting people. We need to take a step back and calm down."

Jace blinked at her then cupped her face. "That was a very dominant thing to do, love. You can hit me any time you think I'm acting like an idiot."

"She'll be hitting you often then," Dante mumbled.

She looked over her shoulder and held her arm out. "Get over here, you big brute. Now the three of us are going to calmly talk about this because lashing out with accusations and slapping people won't help." She blushed and kissed Jace's cheek. "I'm sorry."

He turned his face, kissing her palm. "Don't be. I was so surprised you actually did it that it brought me out of my funk."

Dante gripped Nadie by the hips and brought her to his chest. "I'm sorry, sprite." He kissed her neck and wrapped her arms around him.

"It's okay, my dragon. Now let's sit down and talk like we should have done in the beginning."

"Jace, you can get out of that duty, you and I both know it," Dante said as he settled onto the couch, Nadie in his lap. She picked her legs up and settled them on Jace, wanting the connection.

Jace closed his eyes and took a deep breath. "Yeah, I can.

Maybe. It will be a huge slap in the Conclave's face. I'm not that old, and honestly, it's usually the older ones who get out of doing things like this."

"But do the younger ones have true halves?" Nadie asked.

Jace shook his head. "It's rare to find one, let alone two."

Nadie nodded. "We need to stop fighting over things we can't control and figure out how to live with what we *can*. You can take time off. You're allowed to, and we all know it. Dante is doing his damned best to find a way to keep from leaving us for five hundred years, and I'm learning to protect myself in case all goes to hell."

She let out a breath and sagged against Dante's chest, utterly spent.

Jace rubbed her feet, and she moaned. "I'm sorry," she whispered. "I know I keep saying that, but I am. I have a short fuse, and I lost it."

Dante played with her hip and squeezed. "I had a shorter fuse it seemed."

Her eyes closed she snuggled closer. "I had the shortest considering I hit Jace." She blushed, mortified. "That was an idiotic thing to do."

Jace pressed his thumb against the arch of her foot, and she moaned again.

"No, that was what you needed to do," Jace said. "You're also spent and in need of energy, so I'll let that pass."

She felt Dante's cock push against her ass, and she wiggled before he squeezed her hip harder.

"Sprite..."

"What?" she asked innocently.

"Be careful or you're going to be punished for teasing," her dragon warned.

Jace moved his hand up her calf. "Speaking of punishing...I think our Nadie needs to learn what happens when she loses her temper."

She moaned again. "I take it we're done talking?"

Dante slid his hand up her stomach to cup her breast. "About things we can't control where we already have plans in place? Yes. Dirty talk and your screams as I eat that pretty pussy and the gorgeous tits? Not yet."

She arched her back.

"Bring it," she tempted.

And oh yeah, she loved how her mates took that command and made it their own. They totally brought it.

CHAPTER 16

T he bottle of tequila on the bar called her name, and when Nadie risked a glance at Jace, it took all her power not to blush or rub up along her mate and purr. Jace wrapped an arm around her waist, pulling her close.

"What could you possibly be thinking, Nadie Morgan?" he whispered in her ear, the deep vibrations sending shivers down her body.

She wiggled her ass slightly against his rock-hard cock and leaned back. "I'm thinking that we're in the middle of Dante's bar and my friends are right behind us probably watching every move we make. I don't think I should be thinking about finding a way to get you on top of the bar so I can lick tequila off your naked body."

Jace barked out a laugh and turned her in his arms so they were facing each other. "We'll do that when we get home."

Home.

Yes. Home. She and Jace had officially moved into Dante's house. Nadie's lease had run out the week before, and it didn't make any sense to keep the place open since she hadn't slept there in months anyway. Jace kept a place—separate from his parents—in the den, but he'd said they'd use it when the three of them stayed there as well. While at first Nadie could have blamed the quickly moving relationship on the fact that there *was* a danger out there, now she knew she'd just been deluding herself.

She'd been Dante's, as he'd been hers, from the first moment they'd seen each other. They just hadn't done anything about it for far too long. She wasn't human anymore and had to live her life to the fullest as part of a world where falling for another and moving quickly when it came to a true mating bond was just par for the course.

Jace cupped her face. "Hey, where'd you go?"

Nadie shook her head, bringing her thoughts to the present rather than worrying about what she couldn't fix, what she didn't *want* to fix.

"Nowhere. Let's go to the table and sit with the girls."

Jace frowned but took her hand and led her to the circular table in the corner that she and her friends had claimed years ago. There were a few other patrons in the bar, but she figured they'd be leaving soon as the bar was closing early. Dante wanted to get home before it got too late so he could keep them behind wards.

Soon the fact she always had an eye on her would start feeling constricting, but right then, her men needed to feel as though they were doing something to keep each other safe, so she would go with the flow.

For now.

"God, you look so freaking happy it's sickening," Faith sneered, though she was smiling so Nadie knew the other woman wasn't totally serious. Just somewhat.

Her friends hadn't blinked an eye when she'd shown up with two men. Yeah, they had heard about it and had questions for Jace at first to make sure he was treating her right, but they'd been happy for her. Faith had even grilled Dante to make sure he had apologized correctly. Groveling had apparently been required and Nadie thought he'd done well with that. Since Jamie already broke the ice with the triad thing within their group, Nadie having two men had only led to penis jokes.

After all, size mattered.

At least in their humor.

"It can't be helped," Dante said as he sat down next to Nadie, leaving her sandwiched between her two men—a common occurrence.

Faith rolled her eyes and leaned into Eliana. Amara sat on the other side of Faith, her head in her books. She was, trying to finish her master's degree. The other lightning-struck were with their mates and children, leaving the single women and Nadie at the bar. Not that Nadie would ever call Faith, Amara, and Eliana the "single women" out loud. Nadie liked her face the way it was, thanks.

They talked for another twenty minutes or so about nothing important, the simplicity of the conversation letting Nadie relax. She'd been on edge since she'd first heard about the Conclave and then she'd had the accident. She knew something was coming, they all knew, but she didn't know what or when. It was as though they were sitting on the edge of a blade ready to find out if they'd cut themselves or be thrown off, never to recover.

Neither of those outcomes sounded pleasant to her.

The other patrons had gone home now, leaving her friends and mates alone in the bar so they could talk freely about the things in their lives that might not seem so normal to others.

Dante stood in the middle of Eliana's question about different kind of shifters, and everyone went silent. Jace rose with him, and an icy sensation slid down her spine.

Something was coming.

Dante looked across the table at Faith and the others and growled. "Get to the back room. Now. Nadie, go with them. Use your powers to protect them as best you can."

The faith he put in her powers might have made her feel warm all over on any other day. Right then, though, she wanted to know what the heck was going on.

Faith, it seemed, agreed. "What the fuck is going on?"

Jace pulled Nadie behind him, and she started toward the back, Eliana and Amara on her heels, dragging Faith behind them.

"If a dragon and a bear tell you to hide or make a break for it, you do it!" Eliana screamed.

Faith huffed but stopped fighting and went. Her friends were human, weaker than whatever was coming. Nadie might be a succubus, but she wasn't fully ready to fight either. She hadn't practiced on anything other than trees at this point, and though she didn't feel prepared, she would not let her friends get hurt. She risked a look over her shoulder at her mates.

She would not let her mates get hurt either.

The sound of a train, tornado...something so loud she could barely hear her own thoughts filled the room, and she threw herself over Faith and Amara, pulling Eliana down with her. They hit the floor as a stream of fire shot overhead.

They screamed and curled into balls before trying to crawl out of the way. But there was nowhere to go. She heard a fight begin behind her but couldn't move her head to look for fear of catching on fire.

Dear God, there had to be another dragon in the room. She knew the feel of Dante's magic, of the fire in his veins, and this was not it.

"Come on!" Faith yelled over the roar of flames and the dragon.

Nadie nodded and pulled Amara to her side. The four of them huddled in the corner, blocked from reaching an exit on all sides.

"Can you block the flames?" Amara asked.

Nadie shook her head. "I don't think so, but I can try." She held up her arms and let her power flow through her. She had no idea if this would work since she'd been told her powers could only act like lightning, but maybe she could divert the flames...or at least harm whoever was on the other side of the wall of fire, the one who had the audacity to come into her mate's bar and attack them.

Lightning power shot from her palms, sending a shock of white light through the fire. The girls gasped behind her, and sweat poured down her face from the intense heat and concentration. She didn't know if she could help, but she would not go down acting worthless.

Her friends touched her, bringing her focus to what was in front of her.

"Oh my God, it's working," she panted. The fire couldn't come closer, not with the shield her succubus seemed to be providing. She couldn't let it fall. She couldn't let the fire touch them.

But what of her mates?

DANTE ROARED BUT COULDN'T SHIFT TO HIS DRAGON FORM, not when they were inside the building. He'd break through the roof, endangering everyone in his care. He could, however, beat the fuck out of the little shit who dared come to his land and threaten his mates.

Jace growled beside him, stripping off his clothes and shifting to a six-hundred-pound grizzly. His mate pawed at the ground, ready to pounce at the dragon in human form in front of them.

Rock.

How wrong Dante had been to even consider this piece of crap dragon to take his place. That would be something he could beat himself over later. Right now, he needed to teach this fucker a lesson.

Rock spewed more fire, but Dante held out his hands, letting the fire in his heart, in his veins break free. Instead of attacking Rock, the fire attacked the enemy flames. He felt Nadie through the bond and saw her powers in use as she tried to shield herself and her friends.

But that couldn't last forever.

She was still so new, so young. Her succubus would run out of energy before too long, and then it would be too late. He wouldn't lose her. Couldn't lose her.

The fire died down around them, Rock's power no match for Dante's. Beside him, Jace leapt on the other man, clawing at the other's face and sides. He knew that Jace wouldn't kill the other man, not until they had answers, but his mate would maim him. Just a little.

Dante ran back to Nadie, who stood in front of her friends, her face pale, her arms red and burnt. He roared, fury slamming through him, the steady staccato of anger about to burst free. He reined in his temper, refusing to go dragon and kill all in his path for daring to harm his mate.

Nadie came up to him, tears streaming down his face and cupped his cheek. "I'm fine. It's only on the surface. Go to Jace. I've got this."

Dante didn't touch her, afraid once he did he'd never let her go. He only nodded and gave a cursory glance at her friends to ensure they were unharmed before stalking back toward Jace and his prey.

Rock would pay for harming his mate.

For damaging his bar.

For daring to attack him.

Painfully.

Dante crouched down, staring into the eyes of the dragon he didn't know but had apparently caused so much hatred that Rock had attacked. "Tell me why you've done this."

The other man didn't answer through his bloody lips. Jace pressed down on Rock's neck with his paw until the other man choked, gasping for breath. Dante patted Jace's forearm until his bear pulled back slightly, letting Rock breathe enough so he could answer the question.

"You should have died long ago," Rock sneered.

Dante snorted softly, a small tendril of smoke escaping his nostril. This dragon was truly an idiot. Dante nodded at Jace, who growled before pressing down on Rock's throat.

He could feel Nadie and the others behind him, but thankfully they were far enough away that he could protect them in case Rock got a crazy idea in his head, like escaping. Nadie, he knew now, could protect herself as well. That alone calmed his dragon from raging beyond redemption.

Jace let up after a few minutes, and Rock gasped for breath.

"Tell me," Dante ordered. "Tell me why you are here. Why you tried to hurt my mates." The sight of burns on Nadie's arms would haunt him forever. He knew her succubus would heal her slowly, but once they got home, he'd do what he could to help it along.

"I couldn't get to your home the day that bitch ran off the road, so I came here. You must die so I can rule."

Dante growled and stood slowly. "Did you run my mate off the road?"

Rock shook his head—or at least tried to. It was hard since Jace had his claw on the bastard's jugular.

"It wasn't me. It was happenstance. I was there to break through your wards. Someone else tried to kill the bitch."

"Call my friend a bitch one more time, and I'll let the dragon fry you to a crisp," Faith yelled.

Dante smirked. "I could always let the human at you, Rock. I'm sure she could torture you just as well as I could."

"Damn straight," Faith agreed.

How Dante loved his friends.

"You'll never get me," Rock sneered. "You know nothing, Dante Bell."

Jace growled, and Dante tilted his head. He was missing something. Something important. The dragon sounded too confident considering he was about to die.

The scent of burnt sage and jasmine filled his nostrils, and Dante cursed, throwing out a ring of protective fire around Nadie and the girls. Jace jumped back, and Rock screamed before going up in flames.

Jace shifted back to human, standing naked next to Dante. "What the fuck just happened?"

"Why is Jace naked?" Faith asked.

"Not the time, Faith!" Eliana screamed.

"There is always a time to ask why someone that hung is naked!" Faith yelled back.

Dante could tell the girls were freaked out of their minds, so he let them yell at each other while he looked at the charred circle on his floor.

Nadie came to his side, and he held out his arm. "What happened?"

Jace growled, and Dante knew the other man had spotted her burns. As it was, he himself was on the verge of changing to his dragon, letting out a stream of fire so long he'd burn the entire city to the ground because someone had hurt his mate. But he was controlling himself for her.

For now.

"That was Rock," Dante explained.

"Why did he want you dead?" Nadie asked.

"I think he wanted the Conclave's position," Jace growled.

"That would seem so," Dante agreed.

"At least he's dead now," Faith added in from his side.

Dante shook his head. "No, I'm afraid he still lives."

Everyone grew silent.

"Dante, baby, he went up in flames," Nadie said. "How could he still be alive?"

Dante sighed. "Because he's a dragon and because he had help. Someone with powers to call other dragons who have shared blood...or other things...to their side."

Jace cursed. "Your mother? Your mother fucking took him back to her side?"

The girls gasped beside him, and Dante ground his teeth. "It would seem my mother and Rock have joined forces to kill me and take over the dragon realm."

"Well shit. That doesn't sound like the best family reunion," Faith muttered.

Dante nodded. No, he'd missed something. Something far greater than he could have imagined. The end was coming, and he needed to look at the pieces and figure out how he could save his mates.

They were running out of time with the Conclave, and his mother had thrown a new player into the fold. Nadie gripped his hand, and he knew it was time to get everyone home so he could try to heal her. He pulled her closer and closed his eyes.

He'd fought off a dragon for his mates, and now it would seem he'd have to kill his mother. It was never ending, and he'd be damned if he'd lose. He had too much to live for.

FAITH TOSSED HER BAG ON THE TABLE AND THREW HERSELF ON her couch. It had been one hell of a night, and frankly, Faith was tired of nights like these. It seemed that every time someone in their group found their mate or mates, the world went crazy and people had to fight for their lives.

She'd watched each of her friends who'd bonded almost die, and then when they were healed, they lost a part of themselves. Oh, they told Faith they were happy with all the changes and *loved* being part of a mating bond where it seemed they would readily sacrifice themselves for their loved ones.

Hell no.

It didn't seem worth it.

Not one bit.

It didn't help that she was the weak one in every situation—not something she was used to. She might be able to fight with knives, but that meant nothing against a fucking dragon or wolf with claws and fangs. Everyone was moving on, and Faith was left behind.

She needed to find a way to protect herself and her friends because she'd be damned if she had to hide behind little Nadie again. Not that she wasn't grateful that the little succubus could protect them and herself, but Faith didn't want to have to rely on anyone.

And she damn sure didn't want to rely on a mate.

Men lied, cheated, and treated her like trash.

No thank you.

It seemed the only way to find a way to grow stronger and become the paranormal the lightning had triggered was to bond with her true half. That was something Faith wasn't prepared to do. Not now. Maybe not ever.

She'd just have to find another way.

Because there was no way Faith would allow herself to be weak, helpless, and she'd never rely on the kindness of others.

There was no way she'd give up her freedom...her heart...for a man she would never be able to trust.

She'd just have to find another way.

Somehow.

CHAPTER 17

L evi ran a hand through his hair and promised himself that if he made it through this Conclave meeting without killing someone, he'd get himself a present. Like a beer. Or a willing woman.

Anything to entice him to stay somewhat sane and not...dead.

Because if he started murdering, or at least maiming, those of the Conclave who were so out of touch with the rest of the universe, he'd surely be killed by one of their cronies. Gods, it sounded as though he worked with part of the human mafia, not a group of powerful supernaturals who were supposed to be the rule makers, the *protectors* of their realms.

And now he was sitting in a room as the others plotted to kill when they didn't get what they wanted.

Levi didn't know what to do, but he knew he *had* to do something.

"What's your plan?" Tristan, his fellow member and friend, whispered to him. While Levi was a wizard, Tristan was fae. The two of them in some respects would have different ways of helping their own realm, but right then, they had the same goal.

To keep the Conclave from falling to the hells it was on the fast track to.

"I would try reason, but I think we're long past that."

Tristan snorted. "They're going to war. You know this."

Levi nodded. "You'll have to stay here. There are those who will stay behind with you, trying to take over the Conclave or use its powers to harm even more."

Tristan's expression darkened, but he nodded. "And you'll go with the Conclave. Protect the innocent."

Levi nodded. That was why he had joined the Conclave with Tristan at such a young age. He'd sacrificed so much to do what he thought was right, and now it seemed he might have made a mistake. Levi closed his eyes, taking a deep breath, before standing, his chin held high.

He'd follow the Conclave to Dante's and do his best to find a way to protect them all. He'd been too late with the accident on the road, too late with the lightning in the first place. He just prayed he wasn't too late for this.

Jace leaned against the wall, watching his two mates

practice hand-to-hand combat in their gym. While Nadie's powers were growing day by day, as was her ability to control those powers, he and Dante wanted her to learn to use every weapon she had.

"It annoys me that we need to teach her these things," Faith said as she walked up to him and leaned on the wall as well. "It annoys me that *I* need to learn these things."

Faith had come to their place so she could learn along with Nadie. Though, at least in Jace's mind, Faith's skill was well beyond Nadie's in hand-to-hand and blade combat.

"It annoys me as well that any of you have to learn this. The seven of you should have been able to live your lives the way you wanted to. Now, as each of you learn your new powers and realms, it seems we're always on the brink of war."

Faith snorted. "I'll stand by all of my friends and wish them luck in every area of love and all that crap they want, but that won't be me. I won't start a war for any man. I'm learning so I'm not the weak one in any fight—human or not."

Jace thought Faith's words would come back to bite her in the ass later, but he didn't comment on that. "I don't think anyone would ever mistake you for weak."

"Such flattery," Faith mumbled. "I'm still not prepared to go against a dragon."

Jace shook his head. "I'm not either. I could only take down Rock in my bear form because Dante's fire was there. Without it? I would have lost easily. Only a dragon can take down a dragon."

"Sounds shitty to me."

"Agreed. You do know that we won't let you actually fight against the Conclave when they come, right?" And they would come.

Faith turned so she was facing him, her hands on her hips. "Really? You're not going to *let* me?"

"Stop bullying my mate," Nadie said as she walked up to his side.

Jace held out an arm, and she sank into him as if without thought. "She's not bullying me, or at least she's not succeeding."

Faith rolled her eyes, but she grinned anyway.

"You're doing better, my sprite," Dante said as he prowled toward them. Honestly, the man never walked. He always looked as though he was ready to fight or take someone to bed when he moved—something Jace appreciated.

"I'm not fully there yet, but I'm getting better."

Jace kissed the crown of Nadie's head. Her skills improved by leaps and bounds every day, and he was beyond proud concerning how well she was doing. Dante was patient with her and taught her to use her own strengths while fighting. As each moment passed, the three of them were learning facets about each other that he never thought he'd know. These two were the center of his life, and his role as Mediator could be damned. He'd already shunned his responsibilities, as well as a Conclave that had tried to pull him away from the ones he loved. The pixies were being cared for by another.

Now, it was Jace's time.

Jace had straightened, ready to take his mates and Faith back to the kitchen to get something to eat when the house shook. Nadie dug her fists into his shirt, and he gripped her hip, trying to decide if it was a normal earthquake or something far worse.

He met Dante's gaze and knew the time had come.

"The Conclave is here," Dante growled and let his hand fall from Faith's shoulder.

"Where are they?" Jace asked.

Dante tilted his head as if sensing something. "They're in the clearing, and there are more than a few of them."

Dread settled in Jace's stomach, but he buried it. "What are our options?"

"Running and hiding won't work. They've put their own wards *around* my wards. No one can get out, but others can come in." Dante raised a brow. "They did that for their own reinforcements, but I'm bringing in my own." He turned to Faith. "I would tell you to hide in the basement with my mate until this is over." He held up his hand to silence both women. "But I know that wouldn't work. Even if I thought I could keep either of you away from this, being by our sides will be safer."

Jace pulled Nadie in front of him. "I'm going to go call my parents and have them come here. I want you by my side or Dante's the entire time until I tell you to go somewhere else."

Nadie nodded, worry in her gaze. "I will. I can use the

powers I have to protect myself and Faith. I won't do something stupid. I promise."

Jace cupped her face and kissed her. Hard. "I'm not going to lose you." He pulled away and kissed Dante the same, repeating the phrase until he started to believe it himself.

Dante growled. "Go call your family and tell them to come here quickly. Faith, call Shade and the others. I will call my House. We have only thirty minutes at most I believe until the Conclave is gathered before they come at us. They need to fully get through our wards first. They're taunting us right now, and we're going to use the time to prepare."

Jace fisted his hands but didn't let the others know anything was amiss other than the fact that they were about to go into battle.

The time had come, and he'd be damned if he'd lose. He was a grizzly and would fight by tooth and claw until the end.

JACE GROWLED ONCE THEY MADE IT OUTSIDE. THE PHONE calls had been made, messages sent, and the Conclave was on the other side of the trees. Waiting.

"Ready?" Dante asked, his hair undone so the wind blew it behind him.

"As I'll ever be," Jace answered.

Nadie moved to his other side. He felt the tension wafting off her, but she didn't look scared. No, she looked determined, a far cry from the woman he'd met in the bar those months ago with the broken-down car.

"It's time."

At Dante's words, Jace moved off to the side and shifted. The warm feeling of home and an inner rage spread over his body, and soon he stood on four legs as a six-hundred-pound grizzly. It didn't hurt to shift. It felt as if he was in his second skin.

He'd be able to fight as a bear easier than as a human, able to cause more damage with his claws than hands. The ground shifted beneath his paws as Dante shifted to his dragon form. Soon he and Jace dwarfed the two women between them, ready to fight for all they loved, all they needed.

Dante led them, prowling toward the clearing, his head high. The path to the area where the Conclave stood wasn't hindered by trees, so Dante could move without destroying anything, but the trail wove around so it wasn't a straight line.

Nadie and Faith walked side by side. Faith had strapped knives to her body, ready to fight that way if needed, and Jace was so fucking happy Nadie had friends like hers. The other women in their group either had not learned their powers yet or were mothers to very young children. Jace had a feeling their mates would not let them come to this fight.

There was only so much loss one could take before it became too much to bear and all hope diminished into a nothingness that left them alone, fragmented, and ready for death.

"Have you made your decision, Dante Bell?" the dragon who looked so old he had to be Alexander asked.

Dante stood in front of their entourage, Nadie and Faith not quite hidden but standing as off to the side as possible. Jace stood behind them all, his eyes moving over the crowd of Conclave members that had come for Dante's death.

There had to be at least forty paranormals in front of him and only a couple pairs of paranormals from the same realm. The diversity of realms made Jace want to scream at the injustice of it all. So many wanted his mate dead. Wanted the power in the hands of the few rather than the people they governed in secret.

Jace's family and the rest of their people would come soon, but by the looks on the members of the Conclave's faces, they wouldn't be fast enough.

Jace risked a glance at Nadie, who had come to his side, her hand in his fur, petting him. He couldn't speak to her in this form, but he leaned into her touch, letting her know he was there—would *always* be there for her as long as he still breathed.

"Your silence doesn't bode well," a male pixie said from beside the dragon, and his eyes narrowed.

"You come to my land and dare threaten me?" Dante asked. "I asked for time, not to contemplate my decision of whether to join your ranks but how to live with the decision I have made. I will not be put in a corner and forced to fight like a dragon with no honor. I choose to live with my mates."

The crowd rumbled, and Jace kept his attention on the masses, his senses going out to find the greatest threat but not ignoring even the weakest of ones.

"Don't act surprised at my words. You knew from the start I didn't want this. I want to choose my own life, but no, you've decided for me. I will not let that stand."

"You're *just* a dragon," a witch sneered.

"Just?" Dante bellowed. "*Just?* You've forgotten your place. All of you. You were supposed to protect your people, not rule them from afar and treat them like ants."

"Enough!" Alexander shouted, and Jace's hackles rose. He pawed at the dirt, ready to fight. Words were useless now, and they all knew it.

"You don't say no to the Conclave," the witch yelled.

"I bow to no one," Dante growled.

"So be it," Alexander rumbled. "We tried to give you time to come to your senses. We even tried to take the woman you think you care for from you so you would have an easier path to take to us. Instead, she lived and you won't come to us like you should. It is an *honor* to be part of the Conclave, and yet you deny it. You are worthless and not the dragon we thought you were."

Jace stood on two legs, towering over Nadie and Faith, throwing his head back, letting out a roar that would be heard for miles.

They'd thought they could attack Nadie when she was

on her own? He'd never been as scared as he'd been when he'd thought he'd lost her.

He wouldn't be that scared again.

Dante roared with him then calmed—at least it looked that way to others. Smoke escaped from his nostrils. "You go too far."

Alexander snorted, smoke surrounding his face as he blew small fires—a dragon in waiting. "We clearly haven't gone far enough with you, blue dragon. We are the Conclave. We are gods. We changed fate because we could. We alone have the power to do all in our grasp. We are the ones who brought the lightning to Dante's Circle. We are the ones who turned these women into who they are today. And what are they? Failures. They are nothing but abominations that must be destroyed. We wanted to see how they would fit in with their realms, how the lighting would change their DNA. We know now that the women were weak. *Are* weak. They are worthless. Much like you."

At his side, Nadie and Faith gasped, and Jace lifted a lip, baring a fang. These fucking crazy lunatics had played with the lives of seven women just to see what would happen? Dear gods, the Conclave was crazy. It wasn't just that they wanted Dante for themselves, but they'd forced the lightning-struck to learn about a new world that was far more dangerous than anything they'd ever lived before.

Nadie could have *died* because of the selfishness and curiosity of a group of people Jace couldn't even respect or care for.

He's spent his entire life acting as Mediator on orders

from the Conclave. He'd thought he'd been doing something worth living for, something *needed*. But what if all of that had been a lie? What if he'd only acted because the Conclave had a vendetta?

His bear growled, ready for blood, for redemption.

If they lived through this, things would change.

They had to.

Dante let out another roar, and Jace's attention fell on the two newcomers to the area.

Well, fuck, talking about shitty timing.

Stacia and Rock stood beside the Conclave, menacing grins on their faces.

"Rock? What the hell are you doing here?" Alexander asked, clueless idiot that he was.

"What you should have done long before this," Rock answered.

"Yes, it's time to kill the dragon and his little mates," Stacia sneered.

Dante opened his mouth, a stream of fire encircling Jace and the girls, holding anger so potent that Jace could taste it on his tongue.

The fight was on, and Jace would not back down.

It was time for them to see what an angry bear could do.

CHAPTER 18

Dante stood on his back legs, rearing up as he spewed fire at the centaur who'd dared try to pierce his scales with a long blade. He knocked the bastard with his claw, sending the other man across the clearing, knocked out in a jumble of limbs.

He lowered his body, stalking toward his prey.

Rock stood on the other end of the clearing, the usual smirk on his face as he waited for Dante to come to him.

Others fought around him as he moved, the battle in full force. As soon as Stacia and Rock had shown up, so had Dante's cavalry. Jace's parents and siblings had come first, all in bear form. They were off to the side, fighting against Conclave members. Some were using magic, others fangs and claws.

At the moment, it looked to be an even match.

Torrent, alone, however, stayed in human form. He

stood by Faith and Nadie, fighting with knives. It eased the worry in Dante's heart to know that Torrent would fight by Nadie's side. The other man was a master in blade work and at his side, Faith was doing well. Nadie was not only using her powers to shock others with lightning before Faith attacked them with her knives, but his mate was also using her succubus powers to create a small shield around Faith and herself. It wouldn't last forever, but she was doing her best, and Dante was damned proud of her and how far she'd come.

Balin also fought at Faith's side. The demon was a master with the sword and, with his immense strength, would ensure that the human woman would be as safe as possible.

Ambrose and Shade were high above them, fighting with the other winged Conclave members. As warrior angels, they were stonger than most, but their enemy was stronger.

Something that Dante couldn't think about. No, his prey was waiting.

Hunter was in wolf form fighting the wolf member of the Conclave. Dante didn't think that the wolf was part of Hunter's Nocturne Pack, but it didn't matter. Hunter was one strong Alpha and had come when called.

They all had.

Even the succubi.

The usually distant realm had come when Nadie called them for help. Corena and Dresden were in the front of the masses, using their own lightning and other powers to fight off the horde of members.

The dragons had also come to his side. The five warrior women with royal blood fought against five members at a time, their strength unfettered, though Dante knew this would not be the end.

No, the Conclave's powers were unmatched, and they all knew it. Dante just prayed that his family and those he called friends had the strength to overcome their own weaknesses. Though they did not have the power their enemy had, they had the perseverance and inability to give up behind them.

It had to be enough.

The Conclave could not go on in this manner, and the other realms would know it. Even if Dante lost this day, the Conclave would not win in the end. They could not go against all the realms in their universe.

And their enemy knew it.

Out of the corner of his eye, he saw the wizard Conclave member fight *against* his own people. The act shocked Dante, though it shouldn't have. It seemed the wizard had chosen a side that might lose this day, but if they won, Dante would want this man in a position of power. It seemed that the tides were turning.

It was about damn time.

"The seat is mine," Rock shouted.

"Fuck you and just die already, you little shit," Dante yelled back then opened his mouth, fire from deep within his belly shooting out toward the other man.

Rock spewed fire at the same time, their streams hitting halfway between the distance that separated them. Dante put his full force behind it, knocking the other man back. He rose up into the air, Rock following, and they slammed into each other, attacking one another with their claws and teeth as they fought in the air.

For every shot Dante managed, Rock would counter. He slammed the other man into the ground, using his own weight to hurt him as much as possible. Rock threw him off, shaking with rage before nipping at Dante's neck, trying to sever an artery.

They kicked, bit, and clawed at each other. Soon Dante's blood splattered the ground, mixing with Rock's, but neither was through yet. In the corner of his mind, he knew his mother was around as well, but he couldn't see her.

That alone scared him, but he needed to focus on Rock and keeping alive.

He slammed Rock into the ground again, this time near where Jace's family fought. They were covered in blood, but were tearing large gashes into their opponents.

Dante flicked a merman in human form away with his tail as it tried to pounce on Jace's mother's back, before flying into the sky again, dragging Rock with him. He passed Shade and Ambrose in the air who were fighting the others, blood dripping from deep wounds, but still alive.

As Rock slashed his side, Dante roared, looking down at the female dragons who had backed up against the succubi and incubi, fighting alongside as equals. Hunter pounced on a mountain lion shifter in the center of the dragon circle, tearing into it's neck with bloody fangs.

Dante pummeled Rock again, turning so he could find

Jace in the fray. His mate and lover fought Alexander, the old dragon powerful with age, but Jace had a bone to pick with the bastard. It was not lost on any of them that Jace had been Mediator for too long without knowing the full ramifications of what he'd been forced to do.

That would be something to contemplate later.

Now, the fact that Jace was alive would have to be enough.

Rock slammed into Dante's side, and they plummeted to the ground, dirt and rocks spraying into the air at the force of their hit. Dante rolled to his feet, slashing at Rock as he did so. The fall had put him near where Faith fought alongside Balin, who in turn stood by Torrent and Nadie.

All four seemed unharmed, Nadie's shield doing more work and offering more protection than Dante had ever thought possible. Dante bit into Rock again, the other man's blood filling his mouth. He pulled away and roared, ready to kill the dragon.

He had Rock on the ground, his claw over the man's neck, when Nadie screamed.

He turned his head to watch Nadie push her hands forward, her power dwindling but still useful. A djinn passed through her shield, his arms raised to kill with his magic. Torrent shouted at her to move, but Dante didn't think she'd be fast enough.

Nadie moved her hands again, a shot of lightning arching across her palms and hitting the djinn square in the chest. The djinn looked down at the gaping hole then fell to the ground.

Dante roared in triumph then screamed.

Torrent looked over his shoulder at Nadie, the ever-present smile on his face at Nadie's kill, that lock of hair that always made him seem younger than he looked falling over his forehead. Then, in the next breath, fire surrounded the bear he called brother, friend.

Nadie screamed, tears running down her face as Torrent went up in flames, surprise on his face for a moment before he fell to the ground.

Dead.

Stacia stood behind the body, smoke curling from her mouth, a smirk on her dragon face.

For a moment, Dante couldn't hear anything. It was like the silence of a vacuum, the idea that one of their own no longer lived was not even in the realm of what he could comprehend.

That it was Torrent...the one who never failed to smile, to laugh, to love.

Dante roared, one of his eardrums bursting at the sheer force of the sound.

Jace's bellow echoed his own, his pain so fierce Dante could feel it across the battlefield. In the far corner of his brain, he knew there were others around him, fighting, dying, bleeding.

Right then, though, the only thing that mattered were his mates. His family.

With one last bout of strength, he wrapped his claw around Rock's neck and squeezed. The other dragon's eyes bulged, blood pouring out of his mouth.

"You are nothing," Dante growled. "You were never worth this. Never."

With that, he wrenched his hand, pulling Rock's head from his body. He threw the bastard's head into the clearing, the others around them slowly falling silent as they watched what was happening.

Dante prowled toward Nadie, needing to be by her now more than ever.

Jace growled on the other side of where Nadie stood, blood seeping from a wound in his side, and Dante knew if they didn't win this now, they would never win it. Jace jumped onto the back of Alexander's long neck and bit down. The other dragon gasped in surprise, throwing his head around, trying to knock the bear lose, but Dante knew his mate wouldn't budge.

Alexander had started this.

The triad would finish it.

Jace bit down harder, and Dante watched the light go out of Alexander's eyes.

Jace jumped to the ground before the dragon could even fall to its final resting place. He shifted to human, running toward Nadie. Dante stayed as a dragon, throwing himself in front of them so he could face his mother. He knew Jace raged and grieved behind him with Nadie. The others came toward him, their fights postponed or done after the death of such a high-up leader in all of this mess.

Dante would grieve later. He would deal with the ramifications and everything that surrounded him when he wasn't covered in blood, wasn't facing his mother as she looked too pleased at her kill.

He would deal with this bitch in a moment.

"What have we become?" Dante bellowed. "You kill and kill, demand penance for what? For the sake of being right? You are *not* my Conclave. You are *not* my leaders. You are just petty children with too much power. You might decide to kill us all after you catch your breath, and you can try. But no matter what happens on this field today, know this, others will find out what took place. Others will know who you are and what you've become. Is that what you want your legacy to be? To be the terror in a child's dream? To be the ones that others rise against in the name of freedom? Think of who you are and what you think you represent because, right now, I don't fucking know what that is."

The wizard limped toward him. "It's over, Dante. They will fall back."

"Who are you?" Dante asked.

The wizard raised his head. "I am Levi. The Conclave once served a needed purpose. Now, though, now it's nothing like it was. We will change that. If you do decide to come back as a dragon for us,"—he looked over at Alexander's body—"there's a spot opened. You wouldn't need to leave your mates."

Dante growled, not wanting to think about that with the cold-blooded woman in front of him and his pained mates behind him.

Levi held up his hands. "It's over," he declared, and the

members of the Conclave who were still living nodded in agreement. "I apologize for my brethren."

If Dante had eyebrows, he'd have raised them both. This wizard had fought alongside him and his mates, yet spoke for the others as if he was their leader. Dante's gaze landed on those who still lived and finally understood. The most menacing paranormals had been killed while the weaker realms had lived because they hadn't fought as hard.

It seemed dissention was in the ranks.

Again, Dante would care later.

Now he had a mother to kill.

Dante let out a puff of smoke, and Levi nodded, seeming to know that, though the battle with the Conclave was over, the end was not near. The wizard turned to the side, his gaze settling on something behind him. Levi sucked in a breath, seeming to go pale before shaking it off and moving to face the dragon who had killed one of their own.

Dante would deal with Levi's reaction later.

"It's about time you focus on me, you spoiled little brat," his mother spat.

Before Dante could reach out and strangle the woman who had given him life, his mother went up in flames.

Fuck.

He'd forgotten she could do that trick by expending a lot of energy. He turned on his heel, not knowing where she would show up. In the same way she could use her fire to bring others to her, Stacia could use it to almost teleport herself to another place as long as she could see it.

Anything that had been in her line of vision would be fair game.

As soon as he turned, everything seemed to go in slow motion. Stacia appeared on the other side, her claws reaching out before Dante could blink. Jace pulled at Nadie, bringing her closer at the same time that Faith jumped in front of his mates, the seemingly instinctual response sending a shock of terror through him.

"No!" Nadie screamed as Faith fell to the ground, blood pouring through the gaping wounds in her chest and stomach.

Dante roared, jumping on Stacia's back and flipping her over. She tried to claw at him, but he punched her through the chest, gripping the heart she didn't claim to have, and pulled. His mother gasped then fell to the ground, her heart still beating warm in his claws.

Without giving the woman a second thought, he shifted to his human form and threw her heart to the ground. He ran to Nadie's side and pulled her into his arms. Jace had his hands on Faith's lifeless form, trying to keep her chest together, but Dante knew it was no use.

The human woman wouldn't be able to live through that kind of trauma. Even paranormals wouldn't be able to in most cases. Hunter ran to their side and shifted to his human form. "I can get Becca," he panted. "She can heal."

Tears fell on Dante's cheeks as he shook his head. Jace pulled Faith into his arms, and Nadie cried out.

"Why did she do that?" his mate cried. "Why? She's human! Why did she sacrifice herself for me?"

"Because she's Faith," Dante answered. "She's your protector. She's always been your protector."

"Get out of my way," Levi said as he pushed his way through the dragons, angels, and bears to kneel next to them. His face paled at the sight of Faith in Jace's arms, his body shaking.

"Give her to me. I can help her."

"You can't bring back the dead, wizard," Jace's father whispered, and Nadie sucked in a breath against Dante's chest.

Dante ran a hand down her back, trying to comfort, though there was nothing left inside him to do so. They'd lost so much today, yet what had they gained? Had it been worth it?

"She's my true half," Levi explained, and everyone around them quieted. "I have only a small window, but I can bond with her so she can live. Her life force will be tied to mine, but at least she'll live."

"How can you do that?" Nadie asked, a small kernel of hope in her voice. If this wizard was lying, Dante would kill the man himself for giving Nadie hope where there was none.

"I'm a wizard. I can use my powers and tie her to me in a form of the mating bond." His hands shook as he placed them on Faith's wounds. "It's not a full mating bond. That can only be formed one way."

"Do it, please," Nadie begged.

Dante met Jace's eyes over Faith's body. "She's not going to forgive us for this," he said.

Levi shook his head. "You said her name is Faith?" the man asked of the one he was about to tie himself forever.

"Yes," Nadie answered. "Faith. She's so strong." She hiccupped a cry, and Dante squeezed her tighter. "She'll hate you for this. I know it's selfish, but I don't care. We can fix that later. I promise you, if you heal her, I'll do all in my power to pave the way for you to have the mate you want."

"We'll never forget this," Jace said, his voice hollow. Dante knew they hadn't dealt with the pain of losing Torrent, probably never would, but right then, Faith was someone they might be able to save.

Levi nodded then closed his eyes. Magic filled the air as the wizard chanted. Dante pulled Nadie closer, needing to know she was alive, safe.

An hour passed, and others moved to clear the dead and mend their own wounds, but their circle never broke. Finally, Levi fell to his side, and Ambrose held the other man up.

"It's done," Levi whispered.

They watched Faith's body. Waited.

Finally, she sucked in a breath, and Dante let out one of his own. The wounds had closed up on Faith's body. The wizard's healing had worked, though the man looked drained from it. Nadie cried softly against his skin, and he held her close.

"The bond..." Levi rasped out. "The bond is weak, but it's there. It will grow with time. She will have to sleep for a long time before she's fully recovered." Levi met Dante's gaze. "Keep her somewhere safe. She'll sleep for months, if not more. I don't know. I've never done this before, but I know the magic. She won't need to eat or be cared for other than be kept in a safe place. That's all I can promise you."

"What about you?" Nadie asked.

Levi looked at the woman in his arms, and Dante had no idea what the man could be thinking.

"I don't know her," the man whispered. "We're tied together, but I don't know her. I'm not leaving, but I cannot stay either."

Dante nodded and stood, understanding. He brought Nadie to his chest, refusing to let her stand on her own. His dragon couldn't handle not touching her.

"Thank you," Nadie said. "Thank you so much. I know you don't know my friend, but what you did…it cannot be repaid. I know that. All of us will be here if you need us. Please know that."

The others agreed, and Levi stood, holding Faith to his chest as if he, too was unable to let go of the woman who was his mate. The woman he'd never known before this battle.

"We'll take Faith to Amara's Inn," Ambrose said, breaking through the silence. "She'll be safe there, and we can set up wards. That way you'll be free to come and go, and she won't be in danger from other factions."

It made sense, and the others nodded while Levi handed over the woman he'd just met to the angel they all knew would care for her like his own.

Others left them one by one, Jace's family taking Torrent's body with them. Dante knew he and his mates would follow soon, the battle over, the war won. The costs were almost too much to bear.

Jace threw his arms around them, and the three of them stood in the center of the silent battlefield, tears streaming down their faces, their bodies shaking.

In the end, his dragon would heal, would one day fly again knowing that he'd done all he could to protect his people, his family. They'd lost so much today, yet as he held his two mates, he knew that he'd fight it all again to have them in his arms.

Jace and Nadie were his reasons for breathing, and he'd tear down the fabric of the realms to keep them.

He'd proven it today, and as he held the soft weight of Nadie against him and felt Jace's strong hold along his side, he knew it had been worth it.

They were his mates, his salvation.

His everything.

CHAPTER 19

B y the time they got home, Nadie was ready to be in her mates' arms. She couldn't wait any longer. While she should have been tired, she wanted. No, she wanted her mates, there, now, and everything.

She needed to know they would be there, be in her life and in her arms.

The three of them took a silent shower in the master bathroom. She'd long since given up the idea of calling it Dante's. No, it was the three of theirs.

There was nothing sensual in the movements, just the idea of wiping off the grime and who knows what else made her body feel better.

When they finished, Dante and Jace took turns drying her off then she took the extra towel to do the same to them. She gently patted them dry, checking their bruises and wounds. Luckily they had all started to heal quickly and she had a feeling with what she wanted to do next, they'd heal fully.

There were perks to being a succubus after all.

"Ready for bed?" Dante asked, his voice low, cautious.

She turned naked in his arms and stood on her tip toes. Dante seemed to get the message and lowered his head for her. She cupped his face and kissed him.

"Make love to me. Both of you. I need you both inside me. We'll heal, we'll be together. Please."

Dante's eyebrow rose, the glint from the overhead light on his eyebrow ring looking just as sexy as it had when she'd first seen him.

"Both of us?" he asked, his voice even huskier.

She reached out and slid her arm down Jace's chest. He stood beside her, his breath coming in pants. "Yes. Please. We've waited long enough for this."

"Anything, my sprite, anything," Dante growled and took her mouth.

She gasped into him then tangled her tongue with his. Her other hand drifted down to Jace's cock, squeezing.

Jace let out a grunt then ran his hand down her back, cupping her ass. She moved into his touch, rocking her hips. She could feel him moving behind her, sliding his hands down her legs as he knelt.

Dante kept his mouth on hers, kissing her with all the passion of an age old dragon. His hands played with her nipples, egging her on.

Jace spread her cheeks and she moaned. He massaged the globes of her ass, then licked her pussy from behind. She wiggled in her men's hold, trying to get more of...something. She just wanted them both, the sensations so intense, yet not hard enough.

He licked around her hole, then tonged her ass, preparing her. God, it felt so good, so dirty. She loved it.

Dante fucked her mouth with his tongue while Jace fucked her ass with his. Her inner succubus reveled in it, wanting more. Before she could pull back and ask for more, Dante stood back and Jace did the same. Her two men shared a look before leaning over her and kissing, hard, full of desire.

They pulled back, breathing heavily, before leading her out of the bathroom.

"Jace is going to fuck your pussy while I take your ass," Dante purred. "Does that sound good?"

She nodded, breathless. "Yes, and the other way too. I want it all."

Dante grinned. "We'll try the other way tomorrow. And then maybe put Jace between us again."

"And then our dragon can play the creamy center of our Oreo," Jace added in.

Nadie snorted then pushed her bear onto the bed. He let her and fell on his back. She climbed up on top of him, beyond ready for his cock.

On her way up, she stopped at his dick and took a quick swipe, loving the flavor on her tongue. He groaned and tangled his fingers in her hair.

"I'll come down your throat next, baby. Now jump on so our dragon can get that ass ready."

She did as she was told and hovered above his cock. He grinned at her as she rocked against him, sliding her pussy along his cock, but not letting the head enter her.

"Tease," he grunted.

"You know it," she teased, then rose up so he was at her entrance. He gripped her hips and she held his cock in one hand and his wrist in the other for balance. With their gazes locked, she lowered herself on him, his girth stretching her in all the best ways.

When she was fully seated, they both let out a groan. "I love the way you feel around me, Nadie. All warm, wet, and *mine*."

Jace moved one hand off her hip and fingered her clit. She'd been so ready for him, for everything that came with her mates, that she came with one touch.

A rustling behind her told her that Dante was ready for her, and she bit her lip, bending over Jace so she was ready.

Dante's hand ran down her back, and she shivered. "I'll never get over how beautiful you look with Jace's cock in that pussy, your body all blushed and ready for more. I'm going to prepare you now, my sprite. Get you all nice and ready so you can take my cock."

She nodded, unable to speak.

Jace wrapped his arms around her waist and started to move slowly, his cock gliding in and out of her as Dante spread her ass. He'd warmed up the lube before he touched her so she didn't gasp like she had when they'd played with her ass with their fingers before.

He slowly worked one finger in her tight sheath before

adding a second, then a third. The sweet pain that came from the intrusion didn't feel wrong, no, it made her want more. Made her want the dragon who was so careful behind her.

He and Jace would never hurt her.

She wanted them.

Together.

Forever.

"Ready?" Dante asked when he pulled his fingers away.

She nodded and Jace stilled lifting his hips up so she was in a better position for Dante. The bed dipped as Dante moved behind her.

"Push out when I tell you," her dragon whispered.

"I'm ready," she panted.

The head of his cock breached her entrance and she gasped, not at pain, but at wanting him deeper. He froze and she couldn't wait anymore. With a deep breath, she pushed out, then moved her ass back.

"Sweet goddess, you feel so good," Dante ground out.

She smiled and stilled when Dante gripped her hips hard enough to leave bruises. Bruises she'd wear as a badge of honor, of passion.

By the time Dante was fully seated, sweat covered all three of them. The tension from holding back almost too much to bear.

"I feel so…full…" she whispered.

"You're so beautiful, baby," Jace whispered, then kissed her.

She kissed him back, wishing she could do the same to

Dante, but in this position on their first time, she wasn't sure she could accomplish that.

When they were ready, her men took turns slowly pushing in and out of her. Their cocks rubbed together with that thin layer of tissue between them and from the groans that escaped their mouths, she knew they loved it.

She arched her back trying to take more of them as they sped up. Her succubus, already raring to go from their first orgasm, pulled on the bonds, taking her mates' energies before pushing back.

Dante and Jace increased their tempo and she closed her eyes, trying to memorize every breath, every touch.

Dante's hand moved between her and Jace and fingered her clit. With that one touch she shot off, coming hard. Her pussy and ass clamped down on her men and they shouted, filling her up with their seed.

Panting, they moved with their cocks still deep inside of her so they were laying down on their sides.

"Mine," Jace whispered against her lips.

"Yours," she whispered back.

"Ours," Dante added in and she smiled.

Yes. Ours. Theirs. Forever.

"IS IT ME, OR IS DANTE DANCING BEHIND THE BAR?" BECCA asked as she leaned into Nadie's side, a couple of weeks since the battle.

Nadie's lemon drop almost went down the wrong pipe,

and she swallowed hard, setting her glass down to look at her very sexy, tattooed mate, who was indeed shaking his ass behind the bar.

She licked her lips and leaned back, enjoying the view of that jean-clad butt grooving it to the music coming out of the speakers on the wall. In the months they'd been together, her dragon had loosened up somewhat.

Dante had been quieter in the days since the final battle. He'd lost friends, family, and had to kill his own mother. The others had been quiet, not knowing how to deal with such a brutal battle and its tattered remains. Tonight they were supposed to learn to smile again. To show everyone that, despite their losses, there was something worth fighting for. She didn't know how to comfort him other than be there for him. Be there for Jace. What else could she do?

"Stop staring at my ass, Becca Brooks," Dante said, his back to them as he kept his focus on whatever he was doing behind the bar. "You have your own mate and wolf right by your side, woman."

Nadie snorted as Hunter, Becca's mate, growled softly beside her. She could tell, though, that he didn't mean anything by it—it was just a normal *I'm-a-dude-and-this-is-my-woman* growl.

"It's a scrawny ass anyway," Becca shot back, and Nadie did her own growling.

"Hey, my mate's ass is firm and amazing. Don't talk crap about his glorious behind."

Jace, who had been quietly chuckling beside her the entire time, threw his head back and laughed.

She turned to him and tried to keep from smiling. "What? You don't agree about our mate's fine ass?"

Jace cupped her face and kissed her softly. "I think you're at your limit on those lemon drops, love. But, yes, Dante does have one fine ass."

"Can we please stop saying ass?" Amara asked from the other side of the table, her eyes practically rolling to the back of her head. She'd been unsure she could join them that night. She'd been spending her days at her closed inn— the owners having closed it for finacial reasons—caring for Faith and watching the other woman sleep. Nadie knew it had to be hard and visited daily, but the burden rested on Amara's shoulders. Tonight, though, Levi had said he would watch over Faith so she could leave and smile. Nadie knew the wizard had to be reeling from what he'd discovered on the battlefield, but he was closed off. She also knew Faith would wake up and never forgive them.

But Faith would live to be angry.

That's all that mattered.

"Unlike *some* of us," Amara continued, "I don't need to hear about your mates and their butts. Considering I have a feeling you guys are all gonna go home and show off how much you love those butts, I think we can stop the conversation here."

Nadie met Jace's gaze then started giggling like a lunatic.

"You are *really* obsessed with butts, aren't you, Amara?" Eliana asked, batting her eyelashes as she leaned into Jamie.

"Is it because you aren't getting to see any butts of your own?"

"Shut it, Eliana."

"That was too close to home," Becca added in and then squealed, as Hunter must have done something under the table that Nadie wasn't sure she wanted to know about.

It had been almost entirely too long since most of them had been back to Dante's Circle to drink—those who weren't breastfeeding that was—and hang out with their mates. It wasn't the same without Faith, and it never would be. She wasn't ready to give up hope on her friend, and Levi had told them that once Faith's body was ready to wake up she would.

It didn't make it any easier to move on. Faith was one of her best friends and, frankly, one of the closest among the other women in the room. When Faith had moved in front of her...

Nadie shook her head, swallowing hard.

Faith would heal. Levi had made sure of that.

Though Nadie didn't want to think about how Faith would feel once she woke up and found out just *exactly* how she'd been saved.

There might not be any coming back from that.

For any of them.

Nadie looked around the bar at the friends who were still with her, sighing that they weren't all together, but at least they were trying to be strong for a woman they all loved. Even the women with babies and new lives had come that night.

All of the new babies were currently in Hunter's den being fawned over by Fawkes and Leslie. Apparently, the new couple wanted to "practice" to see if they were ready to jump head first into demon pups. Or whatever they turned into since Nadie wasn't sure which of the two had the most dominant DNA. In Lily and Shade's case, it had been the angelic DNA of course that held true. Baby Kelly was an adorable little angel that would one day have wings of her own—the same with Ambrose, Balin, and Jamie's little Samantha. Hunter and Becca's daughter, Hazel, was a little wolf pup and already had the Pack wrapped around her little finger.

Nadie sighed and looked up at Jace.

"What is it?" he asked, pulling her closer.

"Just thinking about babies and how cute little dragons and bears are gonna be rolling around our house."

Oh crap. Maybe she *was* a little drunk.

After all, she hadn't even told the men she loved them, and now she was talking about babies. Sure, they were mated, living together, working together, and had fought for their right to be together, but she might have been moving too fast.

"Dear gods, can you imagine little Dantes crawling around and learning to use their fire?" Jace's eyes went wide, but he didn't look panicked. No, he looked as though he couldn't wait for it.

"We'll teach them how to use that, just like you'll teach them how to use their claws," Dante said as he came up and sat beside them, his dancing jig apparently over.

Nadie sat back and stared at her two men. They never spoke about how they felt. Sure, they cared for her, taught her how to fight for herself, and discussed the future—come on, five hundred years was a freaking long time. But, at some point, the words and promises for someone who had been human her whole life would be nice.

"I love you," she said. "Both of you."

She blinked again as both of her men smiled widely at her. She looked over her shoulder, aware that she probably shouldn't have said that for the first time in the middle of a bar in front of the people who were her family, but not her mates.

However, no one seemed to be paying attention, their focus on their own mates or friends.

She looked back, and Jace and Dante were still smiling.

"I love you both, too," Jace said. "Though I think I've said it before."

"You both know I love you, but it's still nice to hear," Dante put in.

Nadie slapped their arms. "Come on! This was supposed to be romantic and cherished for our memories for all time!"

Dante kissed her. Hard. "I've looked into your face and known your heart since the moment you knew what I was, what I could turn into. I've loved you from the start, Nadie Morgan. I might not say it, but it will shown in all of my actions, my thoughts, and my hopes."

Well then.

"Okay, so maybe I'm an idiot," Nadie mumbled.

Jace kissed her temple. "But you're our idiot."

"Hey!"

"Aww, I love watching you three," Lily said from her perch on Shade's lap. "You guys are so adorable."

Nadie waved off her friend and sighed into her mates.

She'd never forget the bear that had given his life for her, never forget the smile on Torrent's face as he fought with pride.

The bears hadn't blamed her for his death as the blame lay on Stacia. Now, Nadie spent her days in the bear realm, teaching cubs and watching the future Torrents and Jaces learn to growl and claw with the best of them. She did it in his honor and knew that Jace loved her all the more for it.

Things had changed so much since the night she'd decided to give it all up. Instead of walking away alone, she'd given up the fear of the unknown and had fallen head over heels in love with a dragon and a bear. She'd found the power within and learned that not only could she fight for her life and the ones she loved but she was fucking good at it.

The innocence she'd fought to hold for so long had tangled into something beautiful, something seductive, powerful, and loved.

She was Nadie Morgan.

Succubus.

Mate.

Fighter.

Lighting-struck.

There was no going back, only going forward. And as

she leaned into the dragon, then the bear she called her own, she knew she'd be okay.

After all, she had everything to fight for.

The End

Next up in the Dante's Circle Series:
Faith finds her path in FIERCE ENCHANTMENT

A NOTE FROM CARRIE ANN

Thank you so much for reading Tangled Innocence I do hope if you liked this story, that you would please leave a review! Reviews help authors and readers.

Thank you so much for going on this journey with me and I do hope you enjoyed my Dante's Circle series. Without you readers, I wouldn't be where I am today.

If you want to make sure you know what's coming next from me, you can sign up for my newsletter at www.CarrieAnnRyan.com; follow me on twitter at @CarrieAnnRyan, or like my Facebook page. I also have a Facebook Fan Club where we have trivia, chats, and other goodies. You guys are the reason I get to do what I do and I thank you.

Make sure you're signed up for my MAILING LIST so you can know when the next releases are available as well as find giveaways and FREE READS.

Happy Reading!
Carrie Ann

Dante's Circle Series:
Book 1: Dust of My Wings
Book 2: Her Warriors' Three Wishes
Book 3: An Unlucky Moon
The Dante's Circle Box Set (Contains Books 1-3)
Book 3.5: His Choice
Book 4: Tangled Innocence
Book 5: Fierce Enchantment
Book 6: An Immortal's Song
Book 7: Prowled Darkness
The Complete Dante's Circle Series (Contains Books 1-7)

ABOUT THE AUTHOR

Carrie Ann Ryan is the New York Times and USA Today bestselling author of contemporary and paranormal romance. Her works include the Montgomery Ink, Redwood Pack, Talon Pack, and Gallagher Brothers series, which have sold over 2.0 million books worldwide. She started writing while in graduate school for her advanced degree in chemistry and hasn't stopped since. Carrie Ann has written over fifty novels and novellas with more in the works. When she's not writing about bearded tattooed men or alpha wolves that need to find their mates, she's reading as much as she can and exploring the world of baking and gourmet cooking.

www.CarrieAnnRyan.com

MORE FROM CARRIE ANN RYAN

Montgomery Ink:

Book 7.5: Executive Ink
Book 8: Inked Memories
Book 8.5: Inked Nights
Book 8.7: Second Chance Ink

Montgomery Ink: Colorado Springs
Book 1: Fallen Ink
Book 2: Restless Ink
Book 3: Jagged Ink

The Gallagher Brothers Series:
A Montgomery Ink Spin Off Series
Book 1: Love Restored
Book 2: Passion Restored
Book 3: Hope Restored

The Whiskey and Lies Series:
A Montgomery Ink Spin Off Series
Book 1: Whiskey Secrets
Book 2: Whiskey Reveals
Book 3: Whiskey Undone

The Fractured Connections Series:
A Montgomery Ink Spin Off Series
Book 1: Breaking Without You

The Talon Pack:
Book 1: Tattered Loyalties

Book 2: An Alpha's Choice
Book 3: Mated in Mist
Book 4: Wolf Betrayed
Book 5: Fractured Silence
Book 6: Destiny Disgraced
Book 7: Eternal Mourning
Book 8: Strength Enduring
Book 9: Forever Broken

Redwood Pack Series:
Book 1: An Alpha's Path
Book 2: A Taste for a Mate
Book 3: Trinity Bound
Redwood Pack Box Set (Contains Books 1-3)
Book 3.5: A Night Away
Book 4: Enforcer's Redemption
Book 4.5: Blurred Expectations
Book 4.7: Forgiveness
Book 5: Shattered Emotions
Book 6: Hidden Destiny
Book 6.5: A Beta's Haven
Book 7: Fighting Fate
Book 7.5: Loving the Omega
Book 7.7: The Hunted Heart
Book 8: Wicked Wolf
The Complete Redwood Pack Box Set (Contains Books 1-7.7)

The Branded Pack Series:
(Written with Alexandra Ivy)
Book 1: Stolen and Forgiven
Book 2: Abandoned and Unseen
Book 3: Buried and Shadowed

Dante's Circle Series:
Book 1: Dust of My Wings
Book 2: Her Warriors' Three Wishes
Book 3: An Unlucky Moon
The Dante's Circle Box Set (Contains Books 1-3)
Book 3.5: His Choice
Book 4: Tangled Innocence
Book 5: Fierce Enchantment
Book 6: An Immortal's Song
Book 7: Prowled Darkness
The Complete Dante's Circle Series (Contains Books 1-7)

Holiday, Montana Series:
Book 1: Charmed Spirits
Book 2: Santa's Executive
Book 3: Finding Abigail
The Holiday, Montana Box Set (Contains Books 1-3)
Book 4: Her Lucky Love
Book 5: Dreams of Ivory
The Complete Holiday, Montana Box Set (Contains Books 1-5)

The Happy Ever After Series:

Flame and Ink

Ink Ever After

Single Title:

Finally Found You

EXCERPT: FIERCE ENCHANTMENT

Next From New York Times Bestselling Author Carrie Ann Ryan's Dante's Circle Series

Death wasn't supposed to be easy. It was supposed to drown the senses until there weren't any senses left. Yet Faith Sanders could feel. She couldn't feel everything, but she could feel...something. What it was, she didn't know, but it was there.

And it wasn't making this being dead thing work for her.

Death was but a memory. A memory of pain, fire, and loss. So odd that Faith would feel the loss of something she never knew she had, but that ache, that longing, was there. Why she'd have that particular feeling, she couldn't figure out, but whatever pulled at her had to be close to her. It was the only thing that burned when the fragment of memory faded away below the murky waters of her mind.

Nothing made sense in this new world of hers. She wasn't quite awake; no, she wasn't sure she'd ever wake up again. That didn't sit well with her, but it wasn't as if she knew what she was doing. However, she also wasn't asleep. She floated in a sort of in-between stage where she pulled at herself, trying not to drown in the myriad of dulled emotions and fading dreams.

Faith wasn't a weak woman. In fact, most people thought she was a bitch.

Or at least she had been.

She honestly didn't know what to think now that she was dead.

And because she was dead, she knew it was okay to be a little afraid. Fear would help her get through whatever the hell was going on because that was an emotion she could taste, bitter as it was. If she had enough of that, then she didn't feel quite as dead.

She didn't want to be dead.

Faith's mind followed this loop over and over, her brain going fuzzy and then clearing up, only to see the bright pain that had been her life before she fell on the battlefield.

The cavernous labyrinth that was her mind tugged at her again, and she fell into another memory of a time she'd rather forget. Whenever she fell into a fragment of who she'd once been, it was as if she was truly there again in the flesh. Things were slightly blurred at the ends, frayed memories that would never truly be hers again. But whenever she was in the dream, it was always the same. She felt every cut, every blade of steel against her palm as she fought. It was as if she was alive again, only she couldn't control the outcome.

Because death always won.

Always.

Instead of being a casual observer of the war and her subsequent death, whatever held control over her thrust her mind into her body, and she fought just as she had on that dark day. She could feel every brush of wind, every cut and scrape when she fell.

She could feel everything—just not the emotions other than the pain and fear that came with knowing she was dead.

Even if it all dulled a bit after awhile, she could at least feel the pain to know something was there. She opened her eyes, knowing what she'd find.

The battle raged on, and a dragon flew over her. From the dark blue and black of his scales, Faith knew he was her friend...Dante. Yes, his name was Dante, and he had mated her best friend Nadie. The two of them had another mate, a bear shifter named Jace. She wanted to feel happy at that, wanted to remember the joy, and even the envy, at her shyest friend finding her future. Yet Faith couldn't feel that —only pain of knowing what would happen next.

A sharp pain lashed her temple, and her dream self clutched at her head. She pushed thoughts of what could have been and what she wanted to feel away. The harder she fought these dreams, the harder it would be when she fell.

Instead, she looked away from the dragon overhead and stood by Nadie. Only the Nadie she knew before wasn't there anymore. This Nadie was in her new, true succubus form, her hair whipping around her head in the wind, her curves sexy and dangerous as hell. Since Nadie was now mated and had these new powers, she wasn't as weak as Faith was.

And there was nothing Faith hated more than being weak.

Nadie lashed out at a demon that came toward them, fangs and knives bared. Her friend's power shocked them like the lightning that had brought Faith and the others to this new world in the first place. The demon in front of them—so unlike her friend Balin who was also a demon—screamed, frozen in place from Nadie's power. That was when it was Faith's turn to do what she did best.

She was her father's daughter after all.

At least she had been.

She shook her aching head, focusing on the scene at hand, not what was going on in her brain. She stepped forward, her blades spinning as she sank them into the demon's flesh. The demon screamed yet again as she took its life, her skill with a blade unlike most on the battlefield—human or not.

It didn't hurt her to take a life. It should have, but when that life was threatening those she loved, she made the only choice she could.

Another creature that Faith couldn't recognize came at them, and she turned, only to be pulled back behind Nadie. It grated that she had to wait for Nadie to protect her because she was only a mere human. It wasn't her fault she hadn't found her true half, her mate in all ways that mattered, so she could unlock the paranormal within her.

Faith was just a human.

Just a friend who shouldn't have been on the battlefield of heaven and hell.

Out of place and on the path to death.

The image shifted, and she found herself fighting alongside Balin, one of Jamie's mates. Her friend Jamie had two mates, just like Nadie, yet Faith had none. An odd kernel of jealousy bloomed, and she pushed it away. It wasn't as though she ever wanted a mate. In fact, she knew she was perfectly fine being on her own for the rest of her life. She couldn't trust a man with her heart, her life, or her soul. While it would be nice to be able to fight alongside her friends and actually feel equal, it wouldn't be worth tying her life to a man she could never trust. She sighed, knowing all that angst was for nothing. She was dead anyway.

Balin, unlike the others, seemed to think she could be of use. She gave him a feral smile over her shoulder as the two of them cut through the enemy. He was stronger by far and more skilled with a sword and small blade than she was. Of course, he'd had many more years of practice than she since he was a demon, but she held her own.

It felt...good.

She threw her head back and laughed, her brain going a little crazy as she fought. Balin rolled on the ground, cutting the ankles of the creature in front of her. She sliced through the enemy warrior and watched him fall, holding her hand out to Balin.

He smiled at her, a glint in his eye that spoke of war and battle.

Then she screamed.

Torrent, a bear shifter on their side, brother to Jace, one of Nadie's mates, went up in flames as a battle dragon scorched the earth.

Balin wrapped his arm around her waist, pulling her back. She didn't realize she'd been trying to run to the flames, as if she could save the bear shifter with the big smile and innocent face who had been a friend.

Tears spilled down her cheeks, mixing with the grime and whatever else she didn't want to think about that covered her face. She quickly wiped them away and pushed at Balin.

"I need to get to Nadie!" she shouted. "She's alone...and I..." Her voice broke. "I need to get to Nadie. Don't fuck with me, Balin. I'm not your mate. Don't baby me."

"Balin!" Ambrose, his mate, called to him, and Balin looked over his shoulder then back at Faith.

"Go. Be safe," the demon growled.

He released her then ran toward his mate who fought four soldiers at once. Ambrose might be a warrior angel, but everyone needed help once in awhile. Not that she'd ever admit that about herself.

She ran toward Nadie, who was sobbing but still fighting. Faith's other friends were slowly coming closer, grieving over their lost brother, son, friend, but still fighting. Her throat grew tight, but she swallowed hard and ignored any pain. She didn't even know Torrent. She shouldn't be reacting like this.

She was stronger than this.

With a growl, she turned around and started fighting a creature that had been trying to sneak up on her. The others kept fighting, knowing they needed to pick it up if they wanted to win.

Out of the corner of her eye, she spotted a man fighting for their side. His chestnut hair was cut short in the back and on the sides but had length on top. His face was covered in soot—probably from a dragon who got too close—and his vivid blue eyes turned to flames of fire as he held his hands out in front of him, a ball of light or magic, or whatever it was flowing out of him as he fought. A blue aura surrounded him as he worked, intent on whoever was in front of him. She had no idea who he was, but for some reason, even in the heat of battle, she wanted to know him.

For fuck's sake, had she hit her head and not realized it?

He met her gaze for a moment, and a shock went through her.

No. Just fuck no. She didn't know what was going on with her, but this wasn't the time to moon over a man. In fact, there was never a time to moon over a man.

She pulled her attention away and continued to fight by Nadie's side. She pushed all thoughts of men and sexy blue eyes out of her mind.

They fought harder, her strength depleting, even as the others around her looked as though they could continue to do this for hours. They weren't human, and she was the only one here who was. She knew she should have stayed away like Dante had told her to, but she couldn't. These were her friends, and this was her battle. She was a part of this, even if she didn't feel like it. Only right then, all she could feel was pain and exhaustion.

Everything went into slow motion after that.

She turned toward Nadie and screamed at the vision in front of her. Her friend's eyes widened and Nadie's mates yelled her name. Dante's mother, a bitch of a dragon, came at them, her claw outstretched, ready to kill the symbol of Dante's love and future.

Faith did the first thing that came to mind…the only thing she could have done in this situation.

She threw herself in front of Nadie, taking the blow herself.

The claw sliced into her chest, the fiery burn taking its sweet time to engulf her in agony. Something snapped inside her, and her heart beat loudly in her ear once.

Then one more time.

Then stopped.

A trickle of something warm slid down her chest and her chin, and she figured that had to be blood.

Her blood.

Oh. So this was how she was going to die.

Her body felt as though it was on fire, and she gasped for breath, only she wasn't breathing, she wasn't moving. Hands were on her body, doing something with her chest, but she couldn't truly feel it.

After all, she was dying.

She tried to close her eyes but found them already closed.

Maybe if she just slipped away, it wouldn't hurt anymore. It wasn't like her to give up, but having her heart clawed out by a dragon pretty much gave her leeway not to have to fight anymore.

"You said her name is Faith?"

That voice. She liked that voice. Who was that, and why could she hear only him?

Yes, her name was Faith. Odd because she'd never had faith in anyone, let alone herself.

Something warm slid into her chest again, and she tried to frown. What was that?

It didn't matter.

She was dead.

And she hadn't even had a chance to say goodbye.

Or ask who that man with the blue eyes was.

Funny how he would be her last thought.

Whatever it was that controlled Faith pulled her out of reliving that nightmare, and she found herself once again floating in the abyss that was her mind. Or was it the afterlife? She didn't know anymore. She didn't know how much time had passed or even if time passed where she was. When she was alive, she hadn't truly thought about the afterlife and what would happen when she died. It was always something that was far off in the distance that she'd told herself to worry about later. She had way too much to deal with in her own life to fret about what would happen when it all ended.

Then, of course, the world had gone to shit, and she found out the things that went bump in the night were real, and she truly had no idea what would happen when she died.

A few years before the battle that took her life, she and six of her best friends had been sitting at their favorite bar when lightning struck inside the building. Each of them had been struck but believed themselves relatively unharmed. Some big bad Conclave of supernaturals had done it, or at least some of them. And they'd wanted to use her and her friends as an experiment or something, but that was out of her control. Each of them would eventually turn into whatever paranormal had the most hold on their DNA. Only they had to have sex with their mate—or mates in some cases—to transform.

Yeah, Faith had decided that she'd have to find another way to unlock her DNA because there was no way she'd want to mate with a man who thought he would have control over her.

Men lied.

Men left.

Men hurt.

Maybe if she'd been something other than human, she wouldn't have died, but as it was, she was dead and lost.

She really hoped this wasn't the end because it hurt to be dead. It shouldn't hurt, but at least she could feel that. At least that's what she told herself.

Her thoughts went on a loop again, over and over, where she'd either be contemplating what was going on in her brain, or she'd relive how she'd gotten there in the first place.

Maybe this was her hell.

But Balin had lived in the demon realm for most of his life, and that was called hell too. Wherever she was, it didn't look or feel like what Balin and his mates had described.

Maybe everything was wrong, and Faith had no idea where she was.

That, sadly, felt like the right answer.

Something tugged on her chest, or at least where she thought her chest was since she was this floating mass of...something.

What was that?

She strained, trying to figure out what was going on and why she felt something tugging on her. Why couldn't everything just leave her alone so she could be dead in peace?

It tugged on her again, and she gasped at the pain.

Holy hell, she felt that. Oh, she might have thought she'd been feeling some things before, but now she truly felt it.

And it hurt.

It tugged at her again, and her mind felt as though someone had slammed her body into a wall. In fact, it was as if something was pulling at her chest and she was hitting the ceiling and unable to move any farther than that. Her mind twitched, the pain excruciating.

She clawed at the ceiling or whatever barrier held her in place. Maybe this was it. Maybe she was on her way to heaven or hell or whatever was next in her afterlife.

Liquid fire swept over her body, and she screamed, trying to dampen the pain, only she couldn't.

She closed her eyes, scratching at her skin and the barrier that kept her encased.

"Faith!"

She knew that voice. She'd heard it once before.

The moment she'd died.

"Faith, you need to wake up. Open your eyes, darling."

Darling? Who the hell would be calling her darling?"

She pried her eyes open and winced at the light. "I'm not your darling," she rasped out, her voice sounding like she'd swallowed rocks.

Someone was holding her against their chest and had a hand on her face. She blinked again, trying to focus on anything but the blinding light.

Vivid blue eyes stared down at her, and she sucked in a breath.

"You," she gasped. "Why are you here? Why am I here?" She spoke quickly and ended up coughing.

The man frowned then lowered her. She sank onto the bed she could now see and glared.

"You need water."

"No shit," she tried to say, but her throat hurt too much to speak. She knew she shouldn't be such a bitch, but she didn't know this man, and for all she knew, she was his prisoner.

Perhaps he was her hell.

He held a glass to her mouth, and she tried to gulp the water down, but choked.

"Slowly, dar—Faith." He winced and shook his head. "Sorry. You need to drink slowly, and then I'll explain."

She ignored him, her attention on the glorious water soothing her throat. It felt as if she'd been stranded in a desert for years, and this was her first chance to quench her thirst.

When she finished the last drop, her stomach ached a bit, but that pain told her she might be alive. At least that's what she hoped.

"I don't know if I should give you more water until you're fully healed."

"Who are you?" she asked, her voice a little smoother. "Where am I? What happened?"

The man with the gorgeous eyes sighed. "I'm Levi. You died on the battlefield, Faith, and I brought you back the only way I knew how."

She blinked. Well, that was blunt, but still it didn't tell her anything. "Why did you do that? And how did you do that?"

He reached for her hand and seemed to think better of it. Good, because she wasn't the touchy-feely type.

"I'm a wizard and…well, I'm your mate."

She tried to sit up but couldn't. "Excuse me?" She couldn't have heard right. And that still, didn't answer her question. The image of the thread filled her mind, and an aching feeling slid through her. What was that thread? She'd felt it earlier when something had pulled her up through her haze, but she wasn't sure what it was. One end connected deep inside her...but where was the other end? "How did you save my life, Levi?"

Levi met her gaze, a mixture of sadness and hope in his eyes. "I created a mating bond between us. That's how I saved your life. You're my mate, Faith. In truth and in bonds."

Oh, hell no.

Hell. No.

There was no way what he was saying was right. This man, this wizard, was not her mate, and she did not have a mating bond.

Something inside her pulsed, and she pushed it away.

She'd refuse it. She'd do something. Because she was Faith Sanders. Human, photographer, independent, and not mated.

She would never rely on a man. Especially a man who had forced a mating bond on her.

She'd rather be dead.

Again.

**Find out more in Fierce Enchantment. Out Now.
To make sure you're up to date on all of Carrie Ann's
releases, sign up for her mailing list HERE.**

Printed in Great Britain
by Amazon

39840457R00180